"YOU GOT A REBELLION ON YOUR HANDS, COMMANDER," SAID J.J. GRIMLY.

"What?" growled Hector.

"These two fat sheep," said J.J., jerking his thumb at Stern and Hemple, "heard a rumor on the ultra-wave that the raiders had been spotted less than twenty-four hours from here. Instead of keeping the news to themselves, they let it out and the whole town has gone wild. Half the citizens are heading for the hills; and the other half are trying to contact the raiders on the ultra-wave and surrender."

"Surrender!" Hector turned on Stern and Hemple, steadying himself with one hand on a corner of the desk. "You damn fools! You don't surrender to the Spindle Ships, any more than you surrender to a tiger!"

—From "The Invaders"

INVADERS!

GORDON R. DICKSON

Edited and with an Introduction by
Sandra Miesel

INVADERS!

This is a work of fiction. All the characters and events portrayed in this book are fictional, and any resemblance to real people or incidents is purely coincidental.

"The Error of Their Ways." *Astounding Science Fiction,* July, 1951. Copyright, Street and Smith Publications, Inc., 1951.

"Itco's Strong Right Arm." *Cosmos SF & Fantasy,* July, 1954. Copyright, Star Publications, Inc., 1954.

"Fellow of the Bees." *Orbit,* July-August, 1954. Copyright, Hanro Corporation, 1954.

"Ricochet on Miza." *Planet Stories,* March, 1952. Copyright, Love Romances Publishing Company, 1951.

"The Law-Twister Shorty." *The Many Worlds of Science Fiction,* ed. Ben Bova, New York, 1971. Copyright, Ben Bova, 1971.

"An Ounce of Emotion." *Worlds of IF,* October, 1965. Copyright, Galaxy Publishing Corporation, 1965.

"Roofs of Silver." *Magazine of Fantasy & Science Fiction,* December, 1962. Copyright, Mercury Press, Inc., 1962.

"The Invaders" *Space Stories,* October, 1952. Copyright, Standard Magazines, Inc., 1952.

A Baen Book

Baen Enterprises
260 Fifth Avenue
New York, N.Y. 10001

First Printing, November 1985
Second Printing, April 1989

ISBN: 0-671-55994-X

Cover art by Bryn Barnard

Printed in the United States of America

Distributed by
SIMON & SCHUSTER
MASS MERCHANDISE SALES COMPANY
1230 Avenue of the Americas
New York, N.Y. 10020

CONTENTS

Introduction

Sandra Miesel

*And ugly Hate that maketh wars
Is exiled from the shore of stars.*

What? No wars in the stars? Neither warrior nor
astronomer was Ancicius Manilius Severinus Boethius,
the 5th-century Roman scholar and public servant
who wrote these lines. It is a poignant sentiment for
a man imprisoned and awaiting execution by order
of his barbarian king. Boethius devoted his life to
harmonizing and transmitting classical learning, but
his wisdom did not survive a collision with power.
Fifteen centuries later, his vision of cosmic order
seems farther from realization than ever.

Spacewar planning has already begun. Today's mis-
siles and spy satellites are the forerunners of a fabu-
lous arsenal. For although our expansion into the
space frontier offers a splendid opportunity for new
beginnings, the seeds of old conflicts travel with us,
ready to grow and mutate in fresh soil. Sadly, we
will continue to fight among ourselves and against
our surroundings, whether or not we ever collide
with alien beings.

Can nothing avert those wars in the stars? Must
collisions lead to combat? Opposition cannot be abol-

ished: the very fabric of the universe is built out of polarities. Attitudes, not phenomena, need changing. Philosophers have said that wisdom's work is to put things in order. If achieved, universal harmony would be dynamic and creative—energy only flows between levels that differ.

Is such a dream possible? Will some evolutionary advance empower us with the wisdom to bring concord out of discord? Or must our reach forever exceed our grasp? In the absence of surety, we can still chose hope. We can still seek that day when perfect Love, not banished Hate, will move our sun and all the other stars.

Self interest heals conflicts that principle fails to resolve.

The Error of Their Ways

Markun the Smith did not like Hardak the Forester. Hardak did not like Markun. And the long wait at the spaceport was making both of their tempers touchy.

I cursed the government dispatch ship, which was overdue. Government dispatch ships are always overdue. I cursed the new governor, a political appointee who would probably be worse, if anything, than the lurid news reports had pictured him. And I cursed the short-sighted practice by which the Federated World Governments got rid of political unwanteds—by assigning them to responsible posts on the outer planets. Worlds like Arlanis needed the best of men to guide them, not the worst; and the new governor, coming in on the dispatch ship, was a money-grubbing pompous old egotist, according to the news reports I'd read.

Then, to calm myself down, I reached for my hip pocket to feel the reassuring crackle of my resignation sheet. At least, *I* would be out of it.

Hardak stirred restlessly at my right side.

"It is wearisome waiting," he boomed, suddenly, with a side glance at the Villager, "particularly with all this stink of smoke around."

The Smith snapped his head around and glared at him. Then he scratched himself ostentatiously with his third arm.

"Pfaugh!" he grunted in his deep voice, "these wood lice are getting all over me."

I stepped between them.

"Hold it, boys," I said, "take it easy."

The two Arlani looked down at me, disgruntled. I am a good size for a human. But these barbarians were double my height and four times my weight. Moreover they were both fighting men. Still, I was authority personified, the Accredited Representative of the Federated Worlds Government, and they hesitated. What might have happened, I don't know, for at that moment we heard the first, far-off, high-pitched whistle that told of the dispatch ship's approach.

The sound silenced the Arlani, as it always does, and they were tractable as lambs while the ship was landing. This sort of thing was visible magic and they held it in healthy awe. The ship dropped prettily on its flaming jets and I looked at it with gratitude, thinking that the next time it came back, I would be getting on it for passage back to the Inner Systems. Then, I had no more time to daydream, for the gangplank was down, the new governor was trotting out, and my Arlani were bristling at the very sight of him.

To begin with, he was a fat little man of better than middle age, with a white, bushy mustache—and the Arlani abhor fat. To them, fat spells cowardice, indecision, treachery, and all the traits unbecoming in a male.

"Now boys—" I began warningly, and then the new governor was upon us. Ignoring the Arlani, he trotted straight to me, hand outstretched.

"Well, well, my boy," he burbled. "Pleased to meet you. You're Smithson, aren't you? Well, well. My name's Fife, Gregory P. Fife."

"Hi!" I said shortly, giving his hand a quick pump

and letting go. "Forget about me and pay some attention to the boys, here, before we have a rebellion on our hands. And speak in Arlani." He had addressed me in English, although I knew he must have been psycho-conditioned into a full knowledge of the native language before he left the Solar System.

"What? What? Oh!" he said, and turned toward my two friends who were now standing side by side, ready to make common cause against this new enemy.

"Greetings!" said Fife. "I am glad to meet you my ... er ... children. I can see that we shall get along well together. Ha! Yes, indeed. I shall do my best to keep you happy and ... er ... contented. I understand that, if anything, you are a little too fond of fighting each other; but we mustn't carry it to extremes now, must we? I—"

The Arlani, who had listened to the first part of his address in shocked puzzlement, now began to stiffen with rage. I leaped hurriedly into the breach.

"The eminent governor," I snapped hastily, "has heard of how Korbay the Forester and his young men burned down the hut of Gezik of the West Village. He is very angry. If such a thing should happen again, he will give the offender mud to eat."

Markun and Hardak looked from me to the governor and back again, in astonishment; and I could read the indecision at the back of their green heads. *Can this*, they were thinking, *be what the little fatball really means? Ayah! Maybe this is some new kind of human!*

I was gambling upon the fact that the Arlani had never yet caught me lying to them—and it worked. They reversed their long spears and extended the butts to Fife in a gesture of submission.

"At your good will, lord," boomed the Smith, and Hardak was not more than half a second slow in echoing him.

"Tell them you'll hold council tomorrow noon," I hissed in Fife's ear.

"Eh? Oh! Council will be held at noon tomorrow," said the governor. "Now go!"

The two gigantic savages retrieved their spears, clashed shields together in token of good faith, and went off in separate directions. I hurried Fife to the governor's bungalow.

"Hah!" he said, when we were comfortably settled on the verandah, drinks in hand. "That was quick thinking on your part, Smithson. Very good, indeed. I'll mention it in my first report. Yes, indeed."

"Don't bother," I said, grimly.

"What?" barked the little man.

I tossed my resignation in his lap.

"Read it and weep!" I said. "I've got you off to as good a start as I could, and now I'm taking off."

His bushy eyebrows rose on his pink forehead. Slowly he unfolded my resignation, looked at it, and as slowly folded it up again. Then he cleared his throat.

"Mr. Smithson," he began, in a new voice, "may I call you Tom? The full name seems unnecessarily formal."

"If you like," I responded dryly.

"Tom," he continued, "I don't intend to pry into your reasons; but I can't help jumping to the conclusion that your resignation may be the result of hearing all that unfortunate fuss which governmental circles made about my past position."

"If you mean," I said, "the business of your milking the natives of Minar II in order to fill your own pockets, yes, I heard about it, and, no, it doesn't make any difference to me. I don't care whether you're an angel in shining armor or Satan himself. Morality standards don't mean so much out here on the edge of the Federation. But frankly, it takes a man with steel guts whether he's good or bad, to hold these barbarians in line. And, just as frankly, I don't think you've got the guts."

There was a moment of silence; and then—

"Tom," said Fife, "I admire your plain speaking, but don't you think I learned how to handle aliens on Minar II?"

"You learned how to handle one kind," I answered bluntly. "You learned how to handle a bunch of weak humanoids who were corrupted by traders half a century before your time and would do anything for a handful of coin."

"Trade," barked Fife, "is the lifeblood of any civilization. Before I came the Minarians were using a primitive barter system. I merely showed them the error of their ways."

"And made yourself a nice little pile in the process," I said. "O.K., we won't argue the point. The thing is, though, that the Arlani, both the Villagers and the Foresters, consider trading as work for females. They hold it in contempt. The only thing that keeps them from cutting each other's throat and ours is a constant show of muscle. Until we came, it was unthinkable that two strange Arlani, meeting each other for the first time, should not immediately fight. How else could they possibly tell which one was to order the other around? And, on top of that, this Villager-Forester feud has been going on since time immemorial."

"The last governor kept it from breaking out," Fife pointed out, shrewdly.

"He did," I said, and my voice thickened a little at the memory, "until one day a Villager lost his temper and stuck a knife into him. Marquand pulled the knife out, handed it back to the Villager and ordered the headman of the Village to give him a beating. Then he walked back to the bungalow here and collapsed. I was away at the time, and he bled to death before I could reach him."

Fife's face paled beneath its habitual pink.

"Did the Arlani know the knife wound had killed him?" he asked.

"They suspected," I said. "But the main thing was that they saw Marquand place law and order above revenge, and it awed them. It's things like that that have kept the Arlani in line until now. Tell me, Fife, could you do what Marquand did?"

He looked at me.

"No," he said. "I don't think so. But I think I can run this planet. And I may need your help." He beamed suddenly, and the normal pinkness returned to his face.

"So, my boy," he burbled, "I think I'll just hold your resignation, without accepting it, until conditions warrant your release. You can, of course, go over my head to Colonial Center. But that will take several months, at least."

I stared at him.

"You louse," I said. He laughed.

"Come, come," he said. "No hard feelings. Exigencies of government. Have another drink, and then suppose you show me around the nearest Village. I'd like to see some examples of native handicraft."

It was late afternoon when we came to the Village where Markun the Smith was headman. There were, actually, nearer Villages, but since Markun was the head of the Village Assocation, his Village would have to be visited first to avoid giving him serious offense. We drove in among the thatched huts in the official tractor, and parked in the square.

Fife looked around him, puzzled, a curious look on his pink face.

"Something the matter?" I asked.

"Gad!" he said. "They pay no more attention to us than if we were a couple of ants."

"Arlani manners," I said shortly. "It would not only be impolite, but dangerous, for anyone to speak to you before the headman did. And, being a visitor, it is your duty to go to the headman, rather than have him come to you. Come along."

We got off the tractor and strode over to the smithy. Markun, surrounded by a couple of young male helpers, was hammering a new point on a plowshare. I mean that literally. Metal was scarce on Arlanis and plowshares were made of fire-hardened wood with a metal point fitted on them. He took no notice of us until I spoke to him.

"Greetings, Markun the Smith," I said. "The new lord would like to look at your Village."

The brawny savage dropped the hammer he had been holding with his third arm. It fell with a clang on the anvil and I felt Fife start slightly, at my side.

"Let him look, then," he growled. "Greetings, lords."

"We would not walk through the Village without you," I said.

"Oh, it's not necessary—" began the new governor and I jolted him with my elbow. This was all according to convention.

"I have work to do," boomed the Smith, feigning reluctance.

I did a good job of pretending to work myself up into a rage.

"Miserable headman!" I roared. "Your lords demand that you accompany them through your Village. Follow or die!"

"I follow," snarled the Smith. He strode forward, thrusting one of his helpers aside so that the youth went reeling almost into the coals of the forge.

We stepped out of the smithy and turned down the street. Markun, in spite of his talk about following, stalked some three meters in front of us.

"Remember this," I hissed in Fife's ear. "His honor demands that he disagrees with everything you say and resist every command you give him. Your honor demands that you insist."

Fife nodded. "Tell him," he said, "that I'd like to see some of the samples of native handiwork."

"Oh no, I won't," I answered. "That's woman's work. He'll start with his fighting men and work on down the line through the male youths in training, the old men who do the cultivation, and finally to the women. *Then* we'll see the handiwork."

"Nonsense," fumed Fife; and, before I could stop him, he had trotted along to Markun's side.

"Stop!" he barked. "Halt!"

The Smith, startled by this sudden change of procedure, came to an abrupt standstill and wheeled on the governor.

"I wish to see those things that your women make," said Fife.

Markun was nonplussed. The new lord was not interested in his men of war. Was this, perhaps, some veiled insult to the effect that his warriors were not as capable as women? He was puzzled, and, being puzzled, reacted in the typical Arlani way, by losing his temper.

"Am I an animal, to be ordered about and insulted in my own Village!" he screamed, waving his three arms above his head. "Am I a woman, to be sent to the women?"

By this time I had come up to Fife, who was standing, white-faced, facing the almost berserk native.

"Make it stick!" I said to him in English. "Make it stick now or we're both goners. You've insulted him; and you've insulted his warriors by implication. He'll have to answer to them for passing them over in favor of the women. You've got to answer him and at the same time give him an answer he can give to his men. I can't speak for you now—he's too far gone for that. Say the best thing you can think of; and whatever you do—don't back down."

Markun continued to bellow at the top of his voice. By this time, the warriors, disregarding custom, had begun to swarm out of their huts and surround us. They listened attentively, Markun's ravings were half-addressed to them in order to show that he was defending their rights.

Fife looked at Markun steadily. Slowly, the pallor left his face and his normal ruddiness returned. He stood still and waited until the native should pause for breath.

Markun eventually did. But by this time he was keyed up to the limit of tension, hair-triggered to attack at the first wrong word. He paused for breath, and waited.

"Markun," said Fife, slowly, "you are a man of war."

The Smith looked at him.

"So also," said Fife, "your fighting men are men of war, but they are not equal to you. Your young males will one day be fighting men, but now they are boys and not equal to your fighting men. Your old men are cultivators and will never fight, so they are not equal to your young men. And your women are not equal to your men, but they are still Arlani.

"But below all these are the beasts of the plow. And among them the greatest are the males, the lesser the young males, the lesser yet the old males, and the least the females. But you, Markun, when you hitch them to the plow, do not consider whether greater or less, but merely that they are beasts, for the least of the Arlani are that far above all beasts.

"So, Smith, I say to you that the least of the *humani* are that far above all Arlani. That to a lord the Arlani are as beasts. They are only Arlani. Smith, take me to the female Arlani!"

I think that it was the sheer audacity of Fife's speech that carried the day. Markun, for all his ragings was not stupid. He wanted an out as badly as Fife did and this throwing down of the gauntlet to all his kind shifted the responsibility from his individual shoulders. Furthermore, the more fantastic an individual's arrogance was, the more the Arlani admired it. At any rate, the Smith suddenly caved in. His arms came down in submission.

"At your good will, lord," he grumbled; and, turning to the assembled Villagers, roared them back into their huts.

So, he led us to the work huts of the women. I must admit it was something to see. Female Arlani are large-boned and thick-fingered, but they have the patience of the eternal hills; and their pottery, their weapon handles, the woven cloth from which they make garments, and their leather goods are finished with a perfection that is difficult to reconcile with their warlike natures. It was the leather goods in particular that drew Fife's attention. There were few of them, but the hides from which they were made had a dark, soft sheen. Fife bent down and lifted one of the skins from the lap of a female Arlani, whose large, powerful hands were squeezing and twisting it into softness after the tanning-process.

"Where do these come from?" he asked me.

"A large forest animal," I said. "The Forester Arlani practically live off them. They eat the meat and sew the leather into clothes. The Villagers only kill the few occasional ones they find raiding the crops."

Fife's eyes glowed.

"I've never seen anything like it," he murmured. "What they wouldn't pay for leather like this in the Inner Systems."

I laughed.

"Getting ideas already, governor?" I said. "If you're thinking about making something out of hides like that, you might as well give up the idea. It's been thought of before."

"And it didn't work?" asked Fife. "Why not?"

"A number of simple reasons," I answered, "but chiefly because never in the memory of Arlani has a Forester co-operated with a Villager. You see, the Foresters have the hides and use them, but they haven't the secret of tanning them that the Villagers have. The Villagers won't go into the forests to hunt for fear of the Foresters, so they can't get any more than the few hides that walk in on them, so to speak."

"Don't they trade back and forth?" asked Fife.

"Nope," I said. "They steal from each other, but they don't trade."

"Hm-m-m," said Fife, regretfully.

"Sorry to spoil your hopes of making money," I said, somewhat nastily, I'm afraid, "but there's nothing here that will help. Come on and look at the warriors now. You can't put that off any longer."

So we went out of the women's huts and into the huts of the fighting men. These were in a sullen mood, in spite of Fife's clever argument, and it was only the new governor's obvious approval of their weapons and bearing that averted further trouble. It was a situation that troubled me; and, on the way back to the bungalow, after looking at the boys and the old men in the fields, each guarded by a small knot of the warriors then on duty, I spoke to Fife.

"Look," I said, "you did a good job back there at the Village, but you've left Markun's men in an ugly mood. They can't take it out on us, and I don't think they'll take it out on each other; which means that the Foresters are liable to be due for a raid. Consequently, I think it'd be a smart idea if I took off right now and made an unofficial visit to Hardak. If the word gets out that I'm visiting the Forester chief, there's less likely to be trouble while I'm there; and tomorrow we can smooth things over at the council."

Fife beamed at me.

"By all means," he chortled. "You know best, of course, Tom. By all means."

"Then I'll drop you off at the bungalow," I said, "and head off for Hardak's camp."

It was full night when I reached the clearing where the tents of the Foresters were pitched. Not that the hour made much difference, for the moon of Arlanis was a particularly brilliant one. But it was not as easy to associate with the Arlani at night as it is in the daytime. A great deal of their hunting and fighting is done in the dark, and they are liable to be jumpy and nervous when you try to hold them in conversation.

I began, however, to feel uneasy by the time I was within half a kilometer of the camp. Male adult Arlani have an odd sense which does not seem to be either sensory or extrasensory, but a curious blend of both; it is the capability to *feel* the presence of other living beings which happen to be within several hundred yards of them. By now, Hardak's scouts and sentinels should have felt my approach and come to meet me. But, so far, there was nothing.

I continued on through the alternate patches of light and dark, feeling decidedly nervous. But still no Foresters came to meet me. It was not until I had almost reached the edge of the clearing that I was challenged.

A young Arlani of about my own size leaped suddenly out of the shadow to stand at the side of my tractor: "I am Jekla."

I pulled the tractor to a halt.

"Greetings, Jekla," I said. "Where are your men of war?"

"With Hardak," replied the youngster. "At your place, lord." He threw out his chest, flattered with the importance of conversing with me."

"At my place?"

"At the Hut of the Lords."

I swore under my breath. Hardak back at the bungalow, and Fife there alone to meet him. Why, I wondered? And then a sudden realization came to me.

"Jekla," I said.

"Yes, lord."

"Do the Foresters know that the two lords paid a visit to the Village of Markun the Smith?"

"Yes, lord."

I wheeled the tractor and headed back the way I had just come, leaving the boy gaping. It was just

like an Arlani to become suspicious on hearing that a
new overlord had been to see his rival, and I could
not blame Hardak. I could only blame myself for
underestimating the strange speed with which news
traveled on this barbaric planet. It was a mistake I
had made more than once before.

However, when I got back to the bungalow, there
was no sign of Hardak and his men. And the light
shining out the bungalow windows seemed peaceful
enough. Still, there are better planets to take chances
on than Arlanis, and I went up the steps and through
the front door with a blaster in my hand.

Fife looked up from the book he was reading, and
clucked his tongue disapprovingly.

"Tom, my boy," he said, "you shouldn't point the
thing at people like that."

I holstered the weapon.

"A gun in *my* hands is the least of your worries," I
said grimly. "Was Hardak here?"

"Oh, yes," answered Fife. "He seemed annoyed that
I'd gone to visit Markun, first. But I calmed him
down."

"How?" I asked suspiciously.

"Well," said Fife, "I thought I'd kill two birds with
one stone. I told him that if he'd bring in some of
those hides for me, I'd get him and his men some
solid missile firearms."

I stared at him.

"You're insane," I said finally, in a weak voice.
"You're stark, staring, raving mad."

"Why?" he asked. "This is a class N planet. The
governor is authorized to issue solid missile firearms
if he believes it will contribute to the natives' wel-
fare. And I can ship the hides to the Inner Systems
for tanning and dressing."

I had an idiotic desire to laugh.

"Why you fool," I said, "don't you know that part
of the secret of that leather is a secretion from the

hands of the female Arlani that gets worked into the leather when they handle it. It can't be duplicated."

Fife looked astonished.

"What?" he said.

"Not to mention the fact," I continued, "that Hardak's promises are worth less than the effort it takes to utter them. The first thing he'll do with those guns is to wipe out us and then all the Villagers."

"Nonsense," said Fife. "He gave me his solemn word that he would use the weapons only for hunting."

"When did you say the guns would be here?" I asked.

"I ordered them over the matter transmitter," said Fife, a trifle sheepishly. "They'll be here tomorrow morning. I said I'd let him have them at council tomorrow afternoon."

This time I did laugh.

"Then you really have nothing to worry about from Hardak," I said. "The Villagers should take care of us very nicely. What do you think Markun will do when he sees us handing guns to his traditional enemies?"

Fife chewed nervously at one end of his mustache.

"Maybe I could give the Villagers something at the same time," he said.

"Sure," I answered, derisively, "sure. Why don't you get on the transmitter and order some nice harmless knives so the Villagers can make bangles out of them for you to sell in the Inner Systems?"

And with that, I flung out of the room. If I'd stayed there, I would have been tempted to blast him down in his chair.

The morning of council dawned bright and clear. I had ignored Fife and breakfast. Today I had no appetite for either, and I was sitting in the office, checking my blasters for the hundredth time when Fife came to call me to my place.

"Say, Tom," he said nervously, sticking his head in the office door. "They're here. Hardak and Markun and about a hundred fighting men with each of them. "Aren't you coming?"

"Get out!" I shouted; but I got up anyway and followed him out.

They were squatting on the open ground before the bungalow, two groups of them. The Villagers were on the left, the Foresters on the right. I took a quick glance at the two leaders. Hardak had a smug look on his face and there was one of vague suspicion on Markun's. I guessed that Hardak had kept the news of the guns pretty much to himself; and that just enough had leaked out to put the Smith on his toes.

We took our seats. The two leaders rose to their feet and extended their spears, butt foremost.

"At your good will, lords," they chorused.

"Greetings," replied Fife. I shot him a quick glance out of the corner of my eye. He did not seem unduly alarmed. Either he was a good actor or else he had not realized the seriousness of the situation. I was betting on the latter.

He rose to his feet.

"Greetings, my children," he continued. "It is . . . er . . . pleasant to see you all together here, sitting like brothers at one feast." There was very little brotherly appearance in either host, but Fife went smoothly on without seeming to notice this.

"The new lord," he said, "loves his children, the Arlani. He admires the strength of their warriors. He is proud of the sharpness of their weapons and the skill of their women—particularly, the skill of their women.

"The new lord has looked with pleasure upon the hides which the Villager women have worked. He desires hides like these; many hides, and his heart is sad that the Villagers do not have many of these hides to give him, so that he may give them many things that they would want."

He stopped. There was a mutter of puzzlement from the warriors of both groups.

"The new lord has looked with approval upon the men of the forest. The Foresters are strong hunters. They kill many of the beasts from which the hides are taken. This pleases the lord. He would like to see them kill more of these beasts and give their hides to their brothers, the Villagers, so that their women may work them into softness to please the lord."

By this time, the Villagers were staring at the Foresters in open-mouthed astonishment, and vice versa. The idea of trading between the two factions was as novel to them as the notion to an Earthman that he share his lunch with a rattlesnake.

"So," continued Fife, reaching into a box at the left of his chair and holding up a single-shot firearm. "The great lord has decided to give them magic weapons to help them kill many beasts."

Astonishment passed from the Villagers' countenances. This was something they could understand—favoritism on the part of the overlord. An ugly murmur ran through their ranks. Fife held up his hands.

"Silence, my children," he said, "the new lord is just. He has decided to give the Foresters magic weapons that spit little pellets. But, at the same time, his heart is saddened. For it has been whispered in his ear that the Foresters may turn these magic weapons on their brothers, the Villagers."

Now, it was the Foresters' turn to be dumbfounded. What else? they seemed to be thinking.

"So, the new lord has decided to give the Villagers a present, too, so that it can be seen that he loves his Arlani brethren equally. He has decided to give his brothers the Villagers the little pellets that the magic weapons spit, in return for the hides that his brothers the Villagers will give him." Fife stopped suddenly and drew in a deep breath.

"The time for the giving of presents is now!" he shouted.

There was a dazed moment of indecision, and then the two rival leaders came forward, bewildered, but retaining enough presence of mind to scowl at each other. They halted in front of the verandah and I noticed something that I should have seen before. Each carried as his present a hide of the type that Fife wanted: only, of course, Hardak's was a stiff, ungainly thing, while Markun's was sleek as silk. Fife paid no attention to the hides. He turned first to Hardak.

"To my brother of the Forest," he said, "I give, without expecting any return, the magic weapon."

Hardak reached out gingerly, took the gun and hefted it cautiously.

"And to my brother of the Village," continued Fife, turning to Markun before the Forester had time to offer his hide, "I give, in return for the beautiful hide which he has brought me, the little magic pellet which goes in the magic weapon." And, with a gracious smile, he handed Markun a shell, taking, in exchange, the hide which the Smith was carrying.

"Thank you, my brothers," he cried, holding up the hide. "I am pleased with this gift, and my heart will be gladdened by all such that are brought to me. Let my brothers of the Village and Forest now give presents to one another."

There was a breathless hush in the clearing. The idea of giving presents to each other was novel enough, let alone the concept of trading. Finally, Hardak's empty third hand inched out cautiously toward the shell in Markun's right hand, the hand that held the untanned hide following close behind it. For a split-second Markun almost drew back. Then his hand that held the shell crept forward cautiously, while the other groped forward for the untanned hide.

The four hands approached each other, and locked. The eyes of Hardak and Markun were fixed on each other. Their great chests rose and fell in tense breaths; and for a second it looked like a deadlock, with neither one willing to release what he held. Then, slowly, Markun's hand uncurled from around the shell, and

Hardak allowed his fingers to relax so that the hide was drawn out of his grasp. Then, both Arlani stepped back a pace, each holding what had been in the other's hand a moment before. History had been made.

For the first time in the history of Arlanis, a Village male and a Forest Male had touched hands in other than mortal combat.

"My children," said Fife, beaming down on them, "go in peace."

"Well," said Fife, afterward, as we sat in the bungalow, he with the hide spread contentedly over his knees, I with a much-needed drink in my hand. "Shall I send in your resignation now, Tom?"

I looked at him.

"Frankly," I said, "no. You've started something new around here. I'd like to stick around just to see what comes of it."

"Then you don't think," answered Fife, "that it's the beginning of a new era of peace and prosperity?"

"I don't," I said. "They'll find some way of getting around your trading system and back to fighting again. Then what will you do?"

"Why," said Fife, with his eyes twinkling, and his pink cheeks glowing, "I'll just have to think up something else to show them the error of their ways."

Whatever differences flare between strangers, the worst enemies are those of one's own kind.

Itco's Strong Right Arm

It was sunset in the city of Cinya, on the planet of Margaret IV. Flying worms tittered peacefully on the rooftops. In the buildings, female Reechi were tying their young into cubicles for the night. At the temple of the great god Rashta, a large crowd of male Reechi were munching supper as they watched Reechi priests disemboweling a slave with suitable ceremony. At the temple of the great god Itco, a rather small crowd was hopefully waiting for the handouts that would follow the harangue of the human priest now officiating at what was hopefully called evening service. Watching this proceeding with a jaundiced eye was the high priest of Itco, one Ron Baron, who, having seen quite enough, removed his attention from the crowd and directed it to a letter he had just taken from his pocket and which he was now rereading for the fifteenth time.

Dear Ron (it began)
I look on the wall of my office and what do I see? I see one word printed there in letters of fire. And that word is "action"—ACTION—ACTION! In that word the whole policy of the Interstellar Trading Company is stated. Action makes the wheels go around. Action stim-

27

ulates the native, brings in an increased flow of materials and pumps lifeblood into the Company. Action is the duty of every man-jack of us.

Of course, some of us are more limited than others. Much as we would like to stimulate action, we are held in a position back here on Earth where we can do nothing but cheer on our more fortunate brother out on the Frontier. But we take our second-hand glory in the action he creates. Every report of action he sends in causes us to rejoice. And every report indicating a lack of action saddens us.

I regret to say that you have saddened us, Ron. During our recent drive for a hundred percent increase of trade at all the trading stations, where were you? Down at the bottom of the list. Yes, you have saddened us. You have saddened J. B. Hering, our genial president. You have saddened Tom Memworthy, our friendly Chief of Stations. And you have saddened me, Ron.

Come on, now, Ron, you can make that increased quota. Give it the old fight, boy. When you get up in the morning, tell yourself—"I will have action today," and when you go to bed at night, ask yourself, "Did I have action today?" You can do it, you know you can. Don't let those Rashta priests seduce worshipers from good old Itco. We're all behind you, back here on Earth: J. B., Tom Memworthy, and myself—every man-jack of us. You have carte blanche. Anything you say goes—we'll back you to the hilt. Get rid of that Rashta opposition, root 'em out, burn 'em out. You are Itco's strong right arm on Margaret IV, Ron, and we're all rooting for you.

> *Yours for more action,*
> *Bug Palet*
> *Assistant Chief of Stations.*

P.S.—I want to caution you, Ron. Don't forget the Conventions. No rough stuff, now, with the natives. Remember, you're not allowed to destroy any native idols, or harm any native's faith in his own natural religion. Itco wants worshipers, but not to the extent of damaging Rashta. Just bear that in mind and go to it. We're all behind you here, even old Kimbers, who is panting for action himself and who has asked for your job. Naturally, we all just gave him the old horse laugh. Heh-heh!

"Heh-heh," said Ron Baron, but without humor. He put the well-creased letter away and looked back at the crowd in the temple.

The service was over, and from his position on a secluded little balcony behind the Itco idol— a horrendous creation having a multitude of arms, horns, weapons and teeth—he looked down and saw a heaving mass of green bodies pressing tightly around the officiating priest to snatch the highly spiced cakes he was handing out. To one side lay the pile of offerings. Not a very large pile, either. The Reechi went on the principle of what a thing was worth to you rather than worth to them. There wasn't one of them that couldn't stroll out, club and skin a dozen *chicas* and be back in time for lunch, in contrast to the most skilled human hunter who would be lucky if he got one in that length of time. But the skinflint worshipers of Itco had barely brought in a skin apiece as offerings.

Of course, Ron reminded himself, the cakes weren't worth anything to the humans, either—or almost nothing. *Their* value lay in the fact that the Reechi were not advanced enough in cookery to duplicate them. It was the one advantage that Galuga, high priest of Rashta, had not been able to steal away from him.

Nevertheless, he found sufficient resentment to curse the ridiculous taboos of the Reechis that had, by pure chance, reserved *chicha* skins for god-offerings, so that a hard-working trading post official couldn't make ordinary above-board exchanges of cakes for skins, but had to go to this mummery of a fake god and what almost amounted to a religious war.

There was another angle to it, too, he reminded himself as he put the letter away and left the balcony by tunnel for his office in back of the temple. The hell of it was, he was growing to like the Reechi, who, except for a certain childlike bloodthirstiness and a bad tendency to shed odorous flakes of hide all over the place, were not a bad type of alien at all. And this had the result of tying his hands in certain directions.

There were certain things a man could do and still remain, officially, within the Conventions, those rules set up by Central Human Headquarters for the protection of intelligent natives on the New Worlds. Ron knew it. The Itco office back on earth knew it, and knew Ron knew it. And, reading between the lines of Bug Palet's letter, Ron saw only too clearly that he was expected to do just that.

He reached the office just as Jer Bessen, his assistant, came bursting in from the door that led to the temple floor, loaded down with the day's gift offering of hides. Jer was a roly-poly little man with a red face made redder by his exertions, and would have looked ridiculous in his elaborate priestly robes if it had not been for a pair of very small, shrewd eyes that had already gained a reputation among the Reechi for being able to see the state of a Reechi soul, be the Reechi body ever so swaddled in clothes.

"What's up?" he said, dropping into the office's one easy chair.

Ron passed him the letter and sank into the less comfortable seat at the desk.

"I was going to hold it back until I could figure out something," he said. "But you might as well know it now."

Jer read the letter and swore.

"That's Kimber's work," he said, handing it back."

"Kimber?" echoed Ron, straightening up.

"Sure," said Jer, looking at him closely. "Don't you get it? This is his chance to get rid of you. You know both of you are in line for Assistant Chief of Stations when Tom retires and Palet goes up a notch, don't you?"

Ron shook his head.

"It was office gossip just before I came out," said Jer. "I didn't mention it, because I figured you knew it."

"No, I didn't," said Ron.

"Well, it's so," said Jer. "So you can see what Kimber's after. By acting like he's after your job here, he puts the pressure on. He can't lose. If you crack, you're out of line for the A.C.S. job. If you break the Conventions to get results, he drops an anonymous word to the authorities, away goes your Earth citizenship rights, and it's the labor draft to the Colony Planets for you, my boy."

Ron's face was grim. Jer looked at him closely for a long minute.

"There's things we could do—" he began.

"Nuh-uh!" Ron shook his head with finality. "The letter of the Conventions may be stupid in certain cases, but the spirit is right, and I'm going to stick with it as long as I can." He changed the subject. "Do we have any materials for fireworks on hand?"

Jer scrubbed a hand thoughtfully on his round jaw.

"We could make some simple stuff," he said. "Rockets, roman candles, fire bombs, auroras. Anything like set pieces would take an awful lot of time."

"Simple stuff is good enough," said Ron. "We'll put on a bit of a show tomorrow night and see if that won't lure a few worshipers from Rashta."

So it happened that at noon the next day the long trumpet of the great god Itco bellowed like a bull and Ron Baron, high priest and human, went forth to speak to the people of Cinya.

And the burden of speech was this: that the great god Itco, mighty in wrath, had been displeased with the Reechi that they did not, more of them, come and worship at his image and give gifts. Therefore, Itco would speak to the heavens, tonight, concerning his displeasure, and let those who were guilty, beware.

And of those that heard him, there were in the crowd some who had earlier worshiped at the Itco temple and now gave all of their devotion to Rashta. Hearing, they were afraid, and ran to Galuga, high priest of Rashta, and pleaded with him to save them.

The high priest of Rashta listened and went away for a while. Then he came back and said:

"Itco may speak. But he will not be heard."

And from mouth to mouth his words ran through the city, even to the temple of Itco, and the high priest Ron Baron.

"Now, what the devil do you think he's got up his sleeve?" demanded Ron, pacing back and forth in the narrow confines of the office.

"I don't know," answered the little man, honestly. "He can't know what we're planning to do. It may be no more than a bluff."

"It's not like him to bluff where he stands to lose prestige," said Ron. The other shrugged.

"Well," he said, "that's all I can think of. Remember, I've only been out here a couple of months. Anyway, we'll know in a few minutes—" he glanced at his chronometer—"it's almost time to start."

"That's right," said Ron. "Where's Jubiki?" He was referring to the one Reechi they trusted with the inner workings of the temple. Ron had fixed an ingrown toenail for him once, and he was eternally grateful—an interesting reaction, Ron always thought, when he stopped to consider other Reechi whose lives he had saved by various medical treatments, and who blithely deserted back to the spiritual embrace of Rashta the minute they were able to walk.

"I sent him up to the roof to clear a space for the rockets," said Jer. "Better ring for him."

Ron stepped over and touched a button connecting with a buzzer on the roof. In a moment there was the rattling slap of outsize Reechi feet on the stairs outside the office, and Jubiki burst into the room.

He was a big Reechi, as tall as Ron and a lot heavier. He stood on one leg with joy at being summoned into the inner sanctum, and his wide mouth split in a sharp-toothed smile with an ingratiating desire to please.

"Good God!" said Ron, suddenly leaping toward him. He ran one palm over a rough green shoulder and Jubiki wriggled with pleasure. "You're wet!"

"Rain," Jubiki informed him, happily. You could see him making a mental note to get rained on again at the earliest possible opportunity.

"What!" yelped Ron, and dived for the stairway. Jer followed him, and Jubiki brought up the rear. They burst onto the rooftop of the temple almost together.

In the west, the last gleam of the sunset lit a dark and lowering sky with a weird yellow light. A few fat drops of rain splashed about them, pocketing the summer dust on the rooftop. Thunder muttered.

"I knew it!" and, "So that's it!" exclaimed Ron and Jer at once. The station chief swung on Jubiki.

"Jubiki!" he said. "Did you or any of your people know this storm was coming?"

Jubiki grinned in the face of the increasing wind. It was *so* nice to be able to tell the high priest things he wanted to know.

"No," said Jubiki.

Ron and the little man looked at each other, heedless of the rain that now was beginning to fall in earnest.

"I think I know what he meant, now," said Ron slowly. "Whatever the talking Itco was planning to do, he knew it couldn't compete with this thunder and rain."

"But how would he know?" objected Jer.

"There's probably ways most of the natives don't know about," answered Ron. "Back on Earth a medi-

cine man used to see a spider rolling up its web,
certain birds taking to cover, or notice that the fish
were biting unusually well. There must be something
like that here."

"Well," said Jer, despondently, "let's get off the
roof before we get blown off."

They made their way against the increasing wind
to the stairhead, and descended again to the office.

"Well," said Ron, "that's that, then."

The two men had been sitting up over coffee in the
office while the storm rolled with a muted thunder
overhead, half-silenced by the thick stone roof. For
six hours they had been discussing ways and means
to meet this latest setback, and now Ron had come
up with one scheme that set the little man's eyes
popping with alarm.

"You're crazy!" Jer said. "What's going to happen
if you lose? The whole populace is liable to turn on
you. Then it's a choice between being torn to pieces
or shooting your way out and fracturing the Conventions in sixteen different places."

Ron made an impatient gesture with his hand. "I
won't lose," he said. "We'll call it a duel and a test
between the two gods, but essentially it'll just be a
competition in parlor magic between Galuga and
myself. And if I can't outdo a savage in that line, I
deserve to be torn to pieces."

The little man shook his head stubbornly.

"The risk isn't worth it," he said. "All that's needed
is one good bloody sacrifice with a Reechi as the
piece de resistance. You know yourself that little things
like that cake and the trumpets would bring them in
as long as we matched Rashta in the other depart-
ments. When we don't have sacrifices we impress
them as not being—well—er—serious. I'm not suggesting we actually cut up one of the poor devils; but
we should be able to fake it up some way."

"No," said Ron, definitely. "A fake might clear us

as far as the written rules of the Conventions were concerned, but it's just the sort of thing the men that wrote them were against. We've got to lift them up to our level, instead of stooping down to theirs."

The other groaned.

"Oh, well," he said. "It's your neck. Want me to issue the challenge?"

"No," answered Ron. "I think it's best that I just wander out in front of the temple and start working miracles. Galuga'll have to compete to save his own face."

"Okay," said the little man, resignedly. "I'll get some equipment together. And you better get some sleep."

It was a refreshed, but somewhat grim-looking Ron Baron who stepped out onto the broad steps of Itco's temple the following morning. The square before the temple was full of the green Reechi, and as he appeared they drifted in to stand clustered around the foot of the steps, their interested, wide-mouthed faces upturned to him. He had been right in telling Jer that it would be better not to announce his intention. The ubiquitous and superhuman tongue of rumor was a better town crier, and the loungers in the square this morning were witness to that fact.

Loftily ignoring the interested gazes of the crowd, Ron pulled a small table from his robes, set it up, and whipped out a cloth to cover it.

Then he went into his act.

In a small room of the temple, Jer sat before the message unit. He had been busy here ever since finishing Ron's magical paraphernalia early this morning; and now the regular mail from the Itco office back on Earth was about due. So he sat deep in the chair, before the unit, his hands folded together over the dumpy stomach and his eyes half closed.

Only someone who knew the little man intimately would have realized that he was fighting a losing

battle against some overpowering anxiety. He had
sat still now for a long time, and occasionally his
fingers twitched in the fashion of a man who wants a
cigarette, but has made up his mind not to light one.
And this was surprising, because as far as most people knew, Jer Bessen did not smoke. It was not until
his fingers had twitched for the sixteenth time and
the buzzer on the message unit had sounded to announce that the advance pulse of a deep-space message had just been received, that his fingers went to
an inside pocket and drew out a little flattened cylin-
der wrapped in heavy metal foil, whose further end
smoldered suddenly alight as his darting fingers un-
wrapped it and put it to his lips.

He inhaled deeply as a cloud of purple, sickly-
sweet smoke filled the tiny room; and his face changed
subtly, the tension and the amiability fading from
his features to leave them hard and subtly altered.
And his eyes gleamed.

There were dope-peddlers on the Outer Planets,
and men of Central Headquarters Intelligence who
would have recognized the drug for what it was. . . .
It went by the code name of S. E. 47 and was an
almost inhumanly powerful mental stimulant. As it
took effect, Jer leaned forward to the message unit,
and, adjusting its tuning, brought in the message.

There was the fading deep hum of the pulse that
served as a tuning guide, and the machine-gun rattle
of dots on the message tape. Then letters began to
click out on the tape, slowly and purposefully:

ITCO Office, Earth,
          to Ron Baron, Margaret IV.
Dear Ron:

Ignore any earlier letters I may have sent. Itco has
just been informed that Central Headquarters is considering raising the official status of Margaret IV
from that of a Class twelve to that of a Class eleven
planet. As this means the appointment of a human

governor and the stationing of government personnel on the planet, Itco is naturally concerned. I am arriving by deep space message boat to take charge of situation. I should be on Margaret IV within ten hours of your reception of this message. Do nothing until I come. Repeat, *do nothing until I come*.

Bug Palet, Asst. Chief
of Stations
ITCO.

Jer tore the letter from the message tape. For a moment he sat there, holding it in his hands, the brain behind his little black eyes spinning at an impossible speed. Then he rolled up the letter and thrust it into the pocket of his tunic.

He went out toward the front steps of the temple.

As he passed through the front door of the temple, onto the stone porch, he stepped into a great hush. The square was packed with staring, silent Reechi, except for a short, respectful path through their ranks leading from the foot of the steps on which Ron stood to the center of the square, where in a similar circle of polite space, a tall and muscular Reechi clad in vermilion robes stood facing him. Jer hesitated, then stopped, waiting.

The Reechi spoke, half-chanting the words after the manner of the Reechi language spoken in the temples.

"There is no truth in Itco. There is no truth in Ron Baron, the priest of Itco. The one is a little god. The other is bleached by the sun and lies. He is a bleached player of false magic. In the temple of Rashta, the one great god, I, Galuga, high priest of Rashta, have heard of the things he does and come here to prove that he lies. Show us the magic eye, false priest!"

And the crowd took up the cry, swelling the noise in the square until it was a tumult of sound.

"Show us the magic eye! Show us the seer-atdistances, again, Ron Baron! Oh, priest of Itco, show us the eye!"

For a moment, Ron stood tall and straight, facing the storm of voices. Then he reached out and whipped a cloth from the table, uncovering an object the size of a small crystal ball that stood there.

"Behold!" he cried.

The voices stilled into one vast gasp of wonder, for in spite of the fact that they had seen it once this morning, the small scanning unit Jer had sunk into ruby plastic was an impressive thing. It burned and sparkled in the sunlight like some gigantic jewel.

"Let us see it work, Ron Baron," said Galuga. "Tell us what is happening on the steps of the temple of Rashta."

Ron peered into the red depths of the plastic, making them wait. Unobtrusively, his hand, on the side of the unit away from the audience, adjusted its controls.

"Three Reechi sit facing each other on the steps of Rashta's temple," he said. "They are talking and one has a blue cloth on his head." Galuga's face darkened, and there was another wondering "Oh!" from the audience. But the priest of Rashta spoke up.

"You are fools!" he shouted to the audience. "This much had I heard of the magic eye, that it could see things that were hidden from others' sight. But how can we know the truth of this, since none of us may check? Let the magic eye tell us something we can check." And Galuga whirled, suddenly, pointing to a toy figure outlined against the sky on a distant roof-top. "What does that one, Ron Baron?"

Again Ron bent over the scanner and his fingers made adjustments.

"That one," he announced, "lays cloths to dry in the sun."

"Ho!" Galuga's shout cut across the rising murmur of the multitude. "Run, some of you, and fetch that one. We will see if the magic eye indeed saw, or whether the false priest lies."

From the far edge of the crowd, several Reechi broke off and went dashing off through the narrow streets. And the crowd settled itself, to wait.

There is nothing as unnerving as a Reechi crowd waiting for something to break. Unlike a human gathering, there is no mutter of conversation, no moving about, but only the still, stark process of waiting. Watching from the shadow of the pillared porch, Jer felt an irresistible surge of admiration for Ron. For he waited as the Reechi did, straight and still as if turned to stone, through the stretching laden minutes between the departure of the searchers, and their return.

They brought him finally, half-dragging him through the crowd, an old thin Reechi, who shook with fear at the sight of the two priests. They carried him to the empty lane between them and stood him there.

"Speak," said Galuga, "tell the truth and you will not be harmed. What were you doing on your roof? Were you laying out cloths to dry after watching?"

"No, no," quavered the old man, "I am old, I am poor. I have no cloths. Only this—" and he indicated the band of rough fiber around his middle.

"What!—" Ron took one step forward. Too late, he saw through Guluga's scheme. "Old one, come here to me. Look at me—"

"No," wailed the oldster, looking pleadingly at Galuga. "I am afraid. I am poor. I have no cloths. I was just standing in the sun!"

"The eye lied!" shouted Galuga triumphantly to the crowd. "The eye lied. The false priest lied. Itco has lied!" He raised his arms in a frenzy, beginning to move his feet in the shuffling stamping movement with which the Reechi work themselves up to a religious frenzy.

"Don't listen to him!" called Ron, desperately, as the dust boiled up around the other's stamping feet.

"Can't you see the old man is terrified of Galuga? Galuga put him on the roof to be seen by me and then deny what he was doing." His words were lost in the gathering voice of the crowd.

"Itco—has—lied," voices chanted, taking up the refrain in time to their stamping feet. "Itco—has—lied." Dust seethed and mounted over the crowd, hiding them from view, obscuring the square, rolling in choking folds up the steps. Jer rushed from the porch, grabbing Ron by the arm.

"Come back inside!" he yelled over the noise, grabbing Ron by the sleeve. "They're working up to murder!" Ron shook him off.

"They won't touch me," he yelled back. "I'm a priest."

"Some of Rashta's priests will, though," shouted Jer. And, appearing like phantoms out of the yellow dust, five Reechi in vermilion robes, headed by Galuga, came leaping up the steps.

Ron stood rooted. But Jer, whipping a tear gas grenade from his robes, pulled the pin and sent it rolling down the steps toward the charging priests. It burst, and Jer dragged Ron back from the searing fumes and through the temple door. He was swinging it shut behind them when a stone, thrown by a priestly hand, came flying through to catch Ron on the temple.

And as the big door of the temple slammed shut, Ron dropped into darkness.

He awoke to the silence and peace of his own room in the temple. For awhile he lay still, letting the memories creep back to him, remembering what had happened the day before.

It was all very hazy and confused. He remembered the stone flying at him. The next thing had been Jer bathing his forehead in the temple office. He had been sick and Jer had given him a drink. It had tasted good. He had had another. Jer had had one with him. He remembered reading the letter announcing Palet's coming. After that there was nothing left to do but get drunk. They had sat in the little office, and the hours had stretched out into a montage sequence in which Jer's black eyes stared piercingly at him across the rims of constantly refilled glasses.

He had been telling the little man, over and over again, that he did not blame the Reechi. He did not blame Galuga. It was just as fair for Galuga to run in a ringer like the old Reechi as it was for he, Ron, to bamboozle the crowd with science of the thirty-first century. He had raved about dirty office politics and said that he didn't want to be Assistant Chief of Sections, anyway. He wanted to stay here with the Reechi and if the office hadn't been on his neck for more skins all the time he would have gotten along all right with the green aliens. He had sworn he was quitting the minute Palet arrived.

Now, on the morning after, the shame of these recollections made him shudder. He dragged up the forlorn hope that Jer had been equally drunk and would not remember; and tried to make himself believe it. He sat up dizzily, and made his way to the medicine chest in the infirmary, where he washed down a hangover pill with about a quart of water. Then, feeling somewhat bloated, but better, he made his way to the office.

Jer was seated at the desk, making out grading slips on the last pile of hides they had received as offerings. Ron flopped down in the chair and watched him.

"Had breakfast?" asked Jer, without looking up. Ron grimaced.

"I don't feel like it yet," he said. "Wait'll the pepper pill takes effect." A short silence fell between them. Breakfast was not the important topic and both of them knew it. Finally Ron spoke out.

"Well," he said, bitterness creeping into his voice

in spite of himself, "what's going on after my little debacle of yesterday?" Jer shoved the slips away from him and turned.

"Nothing," he said.

"Nothing?" echoed Ron.

"Nothing," repeated Jer, flatly. "Evening service last night was a bust. The only one who showed up was Kibuki, and I sent him on home. Nobody here this morning." Ron smiled a little in self-derision.

"And Palet?" he said.

"The ship's circling the planet," answered Jer. "They flashed they'd be down in about an hour."

"That's that, then," said Ron, with a sigh. "Hope I wasn't too much bother last night, Jer."

The little man grinned.

"No," he said, and added, "but you were wild. It was all I could do to stop you from writing out your resignation right then and there."

"Too bad you did," answered Ron. "I'll just have to do it this morning." Jer stared.

"You're crazy!" he said. "Where'll you find another job? They're tight as hell back on Earth right now, and you can't keep your citizenship there without one. Not with every Tom, Dick, and Harry trying to buy his way back home from the Frontier Planets. The Reechi aren't that bad, Ron."

"The Reechi aren't that bad," said Ron, soberly, "but the business of exploiting them is. I didn't see what Itco was really like while I was back in the office on Earth. It made sense, then, all this conniving and bamboozling. All this taking advantage of a people too childish to understand. But there's no point in talking, Jer. I'll be out anyway, when Palet gets here."

Jer looked away.

"Don't get sour," he said.

"I'm not sour," said Ron. "Just disappointed. I wanted to fill the quota, and I can't. I wanted the Reechi to like me, and they don't. I want to stay here, and I can't. Maybe if I had the next ten years and no Itco office breathing down my neck—" He broke off suddenly. "Where's Jubiki? I wanted him to help me pack my stuff."

"Jubiki?" repeated Jer, looking a little startled. "I haven't seen him since I sent him home last night."

"Well, he must be here," said Ron, annoyance edging his voice in spite of his efforts to keep it away. "He comes in first thing every morning. He must be around the temple somewhere."

He got up and strode out into the corridor. Jer followed him.

"Jubiki!" Ron called. The word went bounding away down the corridor to die in the little side passages and rooms. "Jubiki!"

The whirr of a buzzer sounded in the distance. Jer had stepped back into the room and pressed the button that sounded on the roof. The sound of his footsteps came back up to Ron in the silence that answered them both.

"This is ridiculous," said Ron. He looked at Jer and added wryly, "Unless Jubiki's given me up as a lost cause, too."

Jer shook his head, his eyes alert.

"He's never missed before," he answered. "Let's check up and see if he's at home." He led the way back into the office and the larger scanner set in the wall there. He spun dials and the interior of the cubicled building in which Jubiki slept came into view. Quickly the scanner's view swept up and down its halls. They were deserted.

"Not there," said Jer.

"Wait a minute," Ron shouldered the little man aside, stepping up to the scanner. "Even if he isn't there, the whole building shouldn't be empty like that." The dials flicked under his fingers and a view of the street outside took shape on the screen. It was completely empty of life.

"By the Lord!" said Ron, between his teeth, "there's

only one place that could drag them out like that!"
and the scene on the scanner spun dizzily as its view
jumped wildly through the deserted streets to the
Rashta Temple.

The square was packed.

Crowded, jammed, stifled between the buildings
that hemmed it in, the green-bodied mass shifted
and boiled as each individual fought his neighbor for
a better view. On the steps of the temple, on the
sacrificial slab of tilted stone were spreadeagled not
one, but two green bodies, awaiting the knives held
up by a chanting Galuga to the idol's face, in his
prayer for their blessing by the lust and love of Rashta.

"No wonder they're all there," said Jer. "No wonder Jubiki deserted. *Two* hunks of meat for the carver!"

"It isn't like Jubiki," Ron could not quite hide the
touch of disappointment in his voice. "There was
something a little gentle about him. He wasn't quite
as bloodthirsty as the rest. I thought that maybe—
Holy Hell!"

With one sudden savage movement he jumped the
screen closer to the sacrificial slab; and the faces of
the two tied there filled the screen.

"Jubiki!" ejaculated Jer. "And the old one that lied
about you yesterday, Ron."

The big man had already whirled from the screen.
With one yank he swung open the arms cabinet and
unhooked a gunbelt, its holster jammed with the
heavy shape of a twin-charge Gaussier. He slapped
the belt around his waist and hooked it.

"Get out of my way," he said to the little man, who
stood barring the door.

"Listen, Ron," pleaded Jer. "I know you're fond of
Jubiki. But don't you see—the Conventions—if you
use that gun—"

"Get out of my way!"

"Listen, Ron. Wait a second. I'll tell you—"

Ron's fist moved in a blurring arc. It smashed
against Jer's head, throwing him back against the

wall. He slumped to the floor, the whites of his eyes
half-showing through closing lids. A little trickle of
blood welled from the lower corner of his mouth.

Ron stepped over him and was gone.

In the silent office, Jer lay still for several minutes.
Then he groaned and opened his eyes woozily. Pushing against the wall with one hand, he struggled to a
sitting position. He wiped at the blood on his mouth,
and tenderly felt his jaw. For a second he sat there,
nursing it. Then he took his hand away and, throwing back his head, went off in a burst of silent laughter, which lasted for several seconds.

Finally he sobered and got to his feet. He walked
out of the office and down to the infirmary, where he
washed the blood from his face and treated his jaw.

He had just finished injecting a local anesthetic in
the injured area when the message unit rang its alarm
bell. He laid down the syringe and went down the
hall to answer it.

An excited voice babbled at him as he opened the
receiver.

"This is Palet. That you, Ron? Jer?"

"It's me," replied Jer, shortly, and flicked on the
visio. The plump, worried features of the Assistant
Chief of Stations seemed to jump at him from the
screen.

"The ship's down," said Bug Palet. "I'm coming in
by flitter to the temple roof in about two minutes."

"I'll be there," said Jer, and flicked off.

The flitter came down like a snowflake from the
clouds. It rocked to a halt on the rooftop and the
transparent cover slid back. Bug Palet stepped out.

He was bigger and more rotund than Jer. His face
was baby-round with smooth flesh, but it showed the
first signs of a fat man going to pieces with worry
and a bad digestion. There were crow's-feet thick

around the humorless eyes, and the skin was dark beneath them. He moved in an undignified hurry.

"C'mon, c'mon," he said, grabbing Jer by the elbow and hurrying him through the roof door, and down the stairs toward the office. "Where's Ron? Better get him. We've got to get briefed on the situation here. C'mon."

Jer let himself be chivvied down to the office. But, once there, he shut the door behind them and literally shoved the other man into a chair.

"What's this?" the words came popping from Palet's mouth as he bounced on the cushions. "What're you doing? Where's Ron?"

"I'll find him for you in a minute," said Jer, without turning his head from where he was bent over the dials of the wall scanner. "He should be shooting up the temple of Rashta by this time."

"What?" the fat man bounced clear back to his feet on that one. "Shooting—but the Conventions! Central Headquarters on its way here! The fool! Let me see!" And he shoved Jer away from the instrument.

But Jer had already found the square in front of Rashta's temple and the scanner showed it empty. Dust hung thinly over it in a dispersing haze. But there was no sign of life, Reechi or human, and the sacrificial slabs were empty.

"What happened? What happened?" demanded Palet excitedly.

Jer told him.

The fat man turned livid with anger. He became so angry he forgot to jitter, and his voice slowed down to a thick, malevolent crawl.

"The stupid hick!" he said. "That's what comes of taking on a colonial. You didn't know he was born on the Outer Planets, did you, Jer?"

"Yes," said Jer.

"Huh?" said Palet. "I thought he was too ashamed to tell anybody. Well, it doesn't matter. He mucked up old Itco, and Itco'll muck him. I'll see he loses his

Earth papers for this! I'll see he's deported! Where the hell is he now? Find him!"

Jer spun the scanner dials and gave a low whistle of surprise.

"He's coming back to the temple here," he said. "There's a crowd behind him."

"C'mon!" said Palet, leaping for the door. "Show me the way to the front of this shack!"

Jer led him forward through the building and out to the wide stone steps.

"Here he comes," said Jer.

A mob of shouting Reechi boiled into the square, following the old one, Jubiki and Ron. The tall Earthman led the procession, and he walked like a conqueror across the square, to the foot of the steps, and up to stand facing the two men there. And for a minute the two of them found themselves at a loss for speech.

Ron was a wild and wonderful sight. His priestly robes had been ripped to tatters, one eye was black, his lip was cut and an assortment or other cuts and bruises were scattered over his face. But his smile was jaunty.

"You look like *hell!*" said Jer, his voice cutting through Palet's babble of astonishment.

"That's nothing," answered Ron. "You ought to see Galuga."

"Galuga!" exploded Palet. "Then you didn't shoot him? You fought with—with—"

"Four falls, catch-as-catch-can," grinned Ron. "For the first ten minutes it was all I could do to hold my own. Then I got in a lucky kick at his head. He came right back at me, but after that science began to tell. The third time I knocked him out they couldn't bring him to again. Want a blow-by-blow description?"

"But the crowd—" stammered Palet, waving an incredulous hand at the gaping green faces that pressed to the foot of the stairs.

"All for Itco now," said Ron. "I should have done it long ago. The trouble was, we were being too subtle for these Reechi. The simple thing was to fight it out. If I won, naturally, my god was stronger. If he won, his was. Why complicate the matter? All Itco needed was a display of the effectiveness of his strong right arm—yes, you fat skunk—" said Ron, turning suddenly on Palet and waving a brawny fist under the fat man's nose. The startled Assistant Chief took an abrupt step backward. "There's the strong right arm you were talking about all the time in your letters. Take a good look at it. I suppose you want to fire me now?"

"Why—" blurted Palet. "Beating up a defenseless native—the Conventions—"

"Cut it out," said Jer, speaking up. "Galuga may have been smaller, but he outweighed Ron by a good forty pounds. And these Reechi are made of spring steel."

"Well," the words came reluctantly from Palet's lips, and he darted a poisonous side-glance at Jer. "I suppose—if the Conventions haven't been broken—maybe we could keep you on, Ron. Of course, there'd be a reduction in salary and a few minor changes, but—"

"I'm glad you said that," answered Ron, his voice rising. "I'm very glad you offered that. Because now I can tell you I don't want your stinking job. And I don't want my Earth citizenship any more, either, because as soon as I get home, I'm applying for a settler's permit and coming back here. So, when the Commission arrives, I'm going to testify to just what a trading outfit like Itco does to get its skins on a planet like this, and you can kiss your trading rights good-bye!" He was shouting by the time he finished, and Palet's face was crimson.

"Why, you muddy-faced swamp-baby!" screamed the Assistant Chief. "You think you'll come back here, do you? You think you'll testify against Itco? Why, we'll bring so many charges of mismanagement and cruelty to the Reechi against you that you'll never outlive your forced labor term on the Colony Planets. Why, we've already got those letters you sent back to the office faked up so that—" he stopped, suddenly aware that he was saying more than he had intended.

"Go on," said Jer, smoothly, "so that what?" Palet turned on him like a wounded bear.

"What're you sticking your oar in for?" he roared.

Jer grinned and took off his nose.

Palet and Ron gasped together. Jer ignored them. Calmly, as if he was an actor removing makeup in his dressing room, he continued to strip off portions of his features. The lashes came away and parts of cheeks and chin. The plump lower lip was peeled away to reveal a thinner one underneath.

"If you want to be uncomfortable," he said, conversationally, turning to Ron, "try wearing skin plastic night and day for a couple of months straight." His shrewd eyes, that were all that remained familiar about his features, bored into the big man.

"Allow me to introduce myself," he said. "Cay Retver, advance agent for the Commission on Margaret IV."

"But you—" stammered Palet, "you've been with Itco for years."

"The real Jer Bessen has, of course," answered the little man. Even his voice, Ron noticed fascinatedly, had changed. It was crisper now, charged with the tones of authority. "He stopped off on his way out here at Government request. He's vacationing on Arcturus III at the moment."

"You," the fat man choked. "You were sent here to spy on us, on Itco. We'll file protest. We'll claim bias, we'll—"

"No," said the other, coolly, "not at all. My job here was only to survey the native situation and check on the qualities of Ron." His eyes swiveled to the young human. "Being planetary governor on a Class Eleven planet is a big responsibility. Think you'd care for it, Ron?"

"Huh?" said Ron, his face showing the dazed expression of an improperly poleaxed steer.

"I said," repeated Cay, speaking slowly and clearly, "would you care to accept the position of Governor of Margaret IV? I have the power to make the appointment provisionally, and of course the Commission will confirm it, since there's no competing candidate."

"I think I'm probably dreaming," said Ron dizzily, "but I'll say yes, anyway."

"Good," Cay smiled and took him by the elbow, turning him toward the Temple. "You and I had better get busy, then. There is a lot to be done before the Commission arrives." Ron followed him dazedly.

Palet, coming to himself with a start, dashed after them, clutching Cay just as they reached the temple door.

"But what about us?" he demanded squeakily. "What about Itco?"

Palet was feeling weak.

"I'm afraid I can't help you," said the little man, pausing. "The matter's entirely out of my hands. After all, whether Itco retains its trading permit here, and what's done about its practices in the past, is up to only one man—the new governor. I suggest you—" he stopped suddenly.

"Ron," he said, pulling the other around.

"What?" said Ron, still half-dazed, but turning obediently to face him.

"Look down," said the little man. "I'm afraid that strong right arm of Itco is going to be needed again. Palet's fainted."

An armada should not be too quick to claim invincibility.

Fellow of the Bees

Wheatley's Foray has always been worth a paragraph or two in the history books. As much, probably, for the reason that it is the sort of incident that glows for a moment among the dry and dusty maneuvers of humanity in general, as for the fact that in a small way it marked a turning point in history. The student of those times finds his imagination fired on the one hand by the fresh wind blowing that was the new individualism—pride of self and planet as an equal with all other peoples and planets; home-pride, hearth-pride, independence—and its impending conflict with the weathered rock that was the Empire. On the other hand he is liable to be fascinated by the picture of those two crafty and experienced oldsters, the Mark-Count Geert Von Ge Brock Til Den and Madame Lydia Lallee Rouch Wheatley, matching swords, as it were, in such highly unorthodox fashion.

Beyond this, as far as I know, no researcher has gone into any great detail. Which is a pity. In an age of great generalities we are only too likely to pay but casual attention to the particulars. We, nowadays, looking down the long, dispassionate corridor of six hundred years at Arca's perky little attempt to defy the Empire, are liable to lose sight of smaller person-

alities such as the man whose very existence on the
scene at that moment made it possible for Wheatley's
Foray to take place. I refer, of course, to that amiable
if muddle-headed gentleman, the Count and Admiral
Von Horn Ge Brod, Fellow of the Imperial Bee Society and Commander of the Imperial Fleet Arm that
was concerned in the Foray. In a sense the incident is
his story, even as it is the story of Madame Wheatley
herself. But, while "Grandma," as her fellow Arcans
called her, has got her name onto other pages of
history for different reasons, the Count and Admiral
Ge Brod makes this one appearance only, emerging
from the ruck of humanity to flash once with a doubtful gleam and then disappear for good.

For that reason I have taken the liberty of digging
him out, so to speak, brushing him off, and telling
the story from his viewpoint. In doing so, I have
unavoidably trod on the thin ice of historical fact
here and there. But in the main, the facts are correct.

The Admiral Count Von Horn Ge Brod walked the
bridge of his flagship. He was a tall, thin gentleman
in early middle age, with prematurely grey hair, a
mild eye, a habit of thinking to himself. Just at the
moment he was thinking to himself what a lonely life
it was, being an Admiral. *Nobody talks to me*, he
thought. *When I talk to them, they squeeze up on me.
They act stiff and uncomfortable.*

"Commodore—" said the Admiral.

"Yes, sir?" answered Commodore Nik Helm, looking up from the gigantic viewing screen on which
was depicted that arm of the Imperial Traansalian
Fleet which the Admiral commanded, and a fair share
of the heavens that contained it.

"Is that the planet we hit next?"

"Yes, sir," said the Commodore. "The Planet Arca."

"Tell me about it."

"A small, out-of-the-way world, sir. Settled about
two hundred years ago by a colony of spacemen. I

imagine they picked it because it was so inhospitable
they didn't expect any other group would want to
take it away from them."

"Well, *we* don't want to take it away from them,"
said the Admiral.

"No, sir."

"All we want is their able-bodied adults for space-
hands, don't we?" continued the Admiral, chuckling
in what he imagined was a fashion of easy camaradie.

"Yes, sir."

"Though why I really don't know," said the Admiral, pondering. His thoughts wandered. "Tell me, Commodore," he added. "You really don't resent the fact
that I was given Admiral's rank and put in charge of
this expedition just because my Uncle Geert has influence at court, do you?"

The Commodore's face went slightly purple. "No,
sir," he said, stiffly. "Of course not, sir. Excuse me,
sir. I really should get back to the screen."

Now, that's what I mean, thought the Admiral, as
the Commodore turned his back. *No matter what I
say, I can't seem to put them at their ease. I wish I
were back at the Imperial Planet*, his thoughts went
on, a trifle wistfully. *That new mutation of black bees
was just beginning to show results . . .*

And the Admiral wandered off down the bridge,
thinking of his apiary back on the Imperial Planet,
wondering how it was getting on since his uncle the
Mark-Count Geert Von Ge Brock Til Den had whisked
him away from it and plunged him willy-nilly into a
career with the Imperial Space Navy. So deep in his
thoughts was he that he bumped into another officer
standing at the far end of the bridge.

"Ah—excuse me, Captain," he said. "I was just
thinking of my bees."

Captain Ver Niertal, up to his ears at the moment
in the labor of directing five hundred ships of war,
ranging in size from courier to dreadnought class,
into a safe landing on the planet below them, franti-

cally signaled a subordinate to take over, and turned toward the Admiral with a desperate look of geniality on his face.

"Sir?" he said.

"Bees," repeated the Admiral, imagining the other had not heard him clearly. "You know—buzz, buzz—honey."

"Oh, yes, sir," echoed the Captain, sneaking a frantic look out of the corner of his eye at the master screen he had just abandoned. Two of the light cruisers were already out of line. "Bees."

If the Commodore's face had turned slightly purple, the Captain's was turning a rich maroon. Sadly aware that he had somehow, once again, managed to rub his subordinates the wrong way, the Admiral turned and wandered off, thinking wistfully of bees and the dear, dead days in which he had nothing to do but putter around with them.

The Third Grand Sector Fleet Arm of the Imperial Traansalian Space Navy under the command of the Right Honorable and Noble Admiral Von Horn Ge Brod, Count of the Northwest Hemisphere of the Planet Vaarhard, Suzerain of the Full Planet and Three Moons of Talko and Fellow of the Imperial Bee Society, descended on the rocky little world of Arca like a convocation of eagles into a chicken-yard. The people of Arca, of course, offered no objection. The thought of resistance was not merely foolish, it was fantastic.

"It should," said Commodore Helm to Captain Ver Niertal judiciously, as they stood on a hastily thrown-up platform in the square of Arca's main town, "be a good haul here. Did you notice the large number of trading ships all over the planet?"

"I did, sir," replied the Captain. "This world must support itself almost exclusively by trading and hauling the rest of the galaxy. That means a good crop of trained spacemen." He changed the subject abruptly. "Where's the Beekeeper?"

The Commodore frowned.

"Ver," he said. "I'm not too greatly impressed with our good admiral, myself, but I hardly think you should invent names—."

"Didn't," replied the Captain. "Every little tube-wiper in the fleet has been calling him that ever since we left Imperial Base. Hold on, there he is now, sir."

The thin, rather sad-faced figure of the Admiral could be seen approaching the platform through the air in one of the flagship's gigs. It landed and he stepped out on the platform.

"Ah, Commodore, Captain," he said, his face lighting up. "Wonderful to have solid ground underfoot again, eh? What are we supposed to do now?"

"Well, crewman, what are you waiting for?" snapped the Captain to the grinning gig pilot. "Return to the ship."

"Yessir!" said the gig pilot, and took off.

The Commodore was busily explaining to the Admiral. "The governing body of the planet is to wait on us here," said the Commodore. "They should be along at any minute. I've got a speech typed out for you here, Admiral. You simply inform them that all able-bodied adults between the ages of fifteen and thirty will be required for service in the Imperial Navy and that they'll save us and themselves trouble by cooperating."

"Dear me," said the Admiral. "Isn't that rather drastic? Fifteen to thirty, I mean. Who's going to run all these trading ships they have scattered around?"

"They'll get by until another generation grows up," answered the Commodore. "After all, the very might of the Imperium is a protection for them against any other power that might try to dominate them."

"I suppose so," began the Admiral doubtfully, "still—."

"*Buzzz!*" cried a sharp little voice.

The three men jumped. A small boy crawled out from underneath the platform.

"Lie down, you're dead," he told them. "I just blasted you with my rear Holman-Matin Difinitors."

"Run along, little boy," said the Commodore, annoyed.

"I will not," said the boy. "I blasted you and you're dead and now you can't take my daddy and mummy away." And abruptly the boy sat down on the concrete of the square and started to cry.

"Look here!" snapped the Captain. "You—."

But the Admiral was already down off the platform and in the process of picking the boy up.

"Come now," he said, rather agitatedly, "Come now—"

"I hate you," sobbed the boy.

"I'll call a crewman to take him home, sir," the Commodore said to the Admiral.

"I—I'll cross-lead your Polman generators and blow you all up." the boy choked.

"Hush, now," said the Admiral, trying to soothe him. The boy wriggled furiously.

"You think I can't, but I can!" he screamed. "We learned all about divelular generators in school and all I have to do is set up a constant field of y-sub-one in your governing arc, and I'll blow you all up."

The Commodore and the Captain exchanged startled glances.

"Where do you live, son?" asked the Admiral.

"Just a minute, sir," interrupted the Commodore, stepping forward. "Did you learn all this in school, boy?"

"I won't tell you," cried the boy bravely.

"I don't think he has to, sir," said the Captain, coming up in his turn. "It seems pretty obvious we've stumbled on a gold-mine here. If this planet teaches ship's operational theory in their grade schools, then practically everybody on the planet will have had spacetraining and we can take them clear up to the ages of fifty and draft them right into active service without anything more than a little indoctrination."

"By God, Captain!" said the Commodore. "I believe you're right!" And they both beamed on the sobbing boy with the glow of fondness a pig-raiser might radiate in the direction of a prize pig.

"What are you maundering about!" snapped the Admiral, testily. "Stop bothering the child, he's all wound up as it is—. Where do you live, son? I'll take you home."

"Won't tell!" choked the boy.

"You'll tell *me*," coaxed the Admiral. "I'm in charge here. You show me where you live and I promise neither your father nor your mother will be taken."

"But, sir—" protested the Captain.

"SHUT UP!" exploded the Admiral. "Go away and let me handle this myself!"

Somewhat stunned, the two officers retreated from the neighborhood of the platform and watched from a distance as the Admiral, after a short period of soothing, got directions from the boy and started off across the square toward the residential section of the city, still carrying the boy.

"This way?" asked the Admiral.

"Yes," said Tommy Wheatley. They were walking side by side now, with Tommy holding the Admiral's hand. He looked up now at the tall, thin figure beside him, a slight look of puzzlement on his tearstained face.

"You're a funny kind of Admiral," he said.

"No doubt," answered Von Horn Ge Brod. He sighed. "I suppose it's because I'm new to the job."

"Oh, did you just get out of school a little while ago?" said Tommy.

"School?" echoed the Admiral.

"School," answered Tommy. "Where you learned fleet management and control."

"I'm afraid I didn't learn fleet management and control," said the Admiral.

"Then how come you're an Admiral?"

"It was my uncle's idea," said the Admiral, hollowly. "I don't know anything about spaceships."

"What a *dummy*!" marveled Tommy. "Can't you even do plain-space navigation?"

"No," said the Admiral.

Tommy digested this in silence for several yards. Eventually he was moved to charity. "Oh, well," he said. "It probably isn't your fault. I guess you just weren't brought up right."

Gyneth Wheatley, looking out the front door of the plastic dome that was her home, felt the strength suddenly drain from her and fear throw cold bands about her heart. She sagged against the half-open door.

"Mother—" she said. The word came out in a shaken whisper. She wet dry lips and tried again, this time raising her voice enough so that it carried back to the kitchen. "Mother!"

There was the rapid scurry of light footsteps and Grandma Wheatley came running.

"What is it?" she snapped.

"They've got Tommy."

Grandma Wheatley followed her daughter's gaze and saw, approaching down the narrow street between the bright domes of the Arcan homes, her grandson, accompanied by a tall, thin, and slightly stoop-shouldered man in early middle age. Briskly, she elbowed past her youngest daughter and marched out to meet the oncoming pair.

"What's this now?" she demanded.

Admiral Von Horn Ge Brod looked down, a long way down, at the alert-looking little old lady with the fantastic white pompadour of hair.

"Greetings, madam," he said. "Does Tommy belong to you?"

"My grandson," she informed him.

"Then I'll leave him with you," said Von Horn. "He heard a couple of my officers talking in the square and got rather upset."

"And small wonder," said Grandma.

"I agree with you," replied the Admiral, sadly. "I don't know why we can't grow our own spacemen instead of taking the men and women from other planets. But then I never was good at understanding military matters."

Grandma cocked an interested eye at him. "You look like an Admiral of the Imperial Navy," she said.

"I am," answered Von Horn.

"But I'll be damned," said Grandma, "if you talk like one."

Von Horn looked at her in some surprise. "Do you know how Admirals talk?" he asked.

"I do," said Grandma, "having been one myself."

Von Horn peered at her. "Madam—Wheatley, is it?" he asked.

"It is," said Grandma.

"I am admittedly ignorant of almost everything connected with spaceships and space navies," said Von Horn, "but you will forgive me for saying that you look to me as little like an ex-admiral as I probably look like a practicing admiral to you."

"Young man," replied Grandma. "If half the merchant ships on this planet were armed, I'd undertake to chase you clear back to the Imperial Planet itself."

Von Horn was on the point of making some kind of rejoinder to this when he was interrupted by Tommy tugging at his hand.

"That's my auntie Gyneth," said Tommy.

"My youngest," said Grandma dryly. "Suppose you come on into the house, Admiral, and we'll see if we can't offer you a drink."

Her face was perfectly calm and her voice bland as she issued the invitation. Von Horn, being innocent as a babe unborn of the customary conduct of Imperial Officers when on sub-class planets, matched her in lack of perturbation. Tommy and Gyneth, on the other hand, fell into the open-mouthed expression of those who have just seen the Devil, complete with horns and tail, offered a friendly piece of pie. They *knew*.

"Why, thank you," said Von Horn, politely un-aware that iron-clad regulations and three hundred years of tradition were crashing into ruins about him as he stood there. "That's very kind of you. I'd be delighted."

"Grandma!" hissed Gyneth, scandalized, as Tommy led the Admiral happily into the dome and the two women followed up in the rear.

"You mind your own business, girl," said Grandma, tartly.

The Commodore looked down from the platform into the tight, pale faces of the Arcan District Repre-sentatives. He had just finished reading, in default of Von Horn's presence, the speech which he had writ-ten for the Admiral.

"Any questions?" he said, passing the copy of the speech to the Captain, who pocketed it.

"In God's name, Commodore," burst out one heavy, older man with the scars of some unknown accident grey against the whitened tan of his face. "Why don't you just turn your arms on the planet and incinerate it? It's a cleaner way of extermination."

"Your youth and your old people will be left," answered the Commodore.

"The children and the half-dead," cried a thin man, "the babies and the senile. Can they keep up our trading contracts? Arca cannot exist—"

He was drowned out in the half-wail, half-growl of protest that surged up from the representatives. The Commodore listened wearily. He had heard this same noise many times. He let it run its course for perhaps half a minute and then held up his hand.

The voice of the crowd died away to silence. Hope half-hid in fear, they listened.

"Orders are orders," said the Commodore. "As you gentlemen and ladies no doubt know. Our transports

will start loading in half an hour outside all your
principal towns and cities. Have your people at the
landing stages."

The main living room of Grandma Wheatley's dome-
shaped house had no corners in it. The floor flowed
into the walls and the walls into the ceiling in gentle
curves, so that it was something like being in the
interior of a comfortable egg. The tables and chairs
were roughhewn out of a foamy, resilient material
which gave just enough to support its burden easily.
The material was a soft grey, the walls and ceiling
and the floor covering were a grass-green.

Actually, the only two bright touches of color in
the room were the imitation fireplace where a three-
dimensional of an ancient water sailing vessel rode
eternally under full sails through the red and flicker-
ing sea of the phantom flames, and the huge star
screen on the opposite wall where a tiny white spaceship held his position forever steadfast while the galaxy unreeled around him at the touch of a button.

"An excellent beverage," said the Admiral, sipping
at the pale yellow liquid in his glass. "What is it—if I
might ask?"

"Herb wine," said Grandma.

"I beg your pardon?" said the Admiral.

"Wine," explained Grandma, "made from native
herbs—plants."

"Good Lord—*natural* wine?" ejaculated the Admiral. "This is a find." He held his glass up to the light
of the imitation fireplace and again sipped at it,
cautiously. "Why, it's a fine drink, every bit as tasty
as the synthetics I've sampled." He looked at Grandma,
puzzled. "But since you know the taste sensations
you want, why don't you just duplicate it syntheti-
cally? It'd be a great deal easier and quicker, I
imagine."

"Tradition," said Grandma.

"Tradition?" echoed the Admiral, puzzled. He cast

his mind back over the great book of Imperial History which he, like all noble children, had been forced to learn almost by heart. "I don't remember any traditions on making wine from herbs."

"Not Empire tradition," replied Grandma, looking at him shrewdly over the pale gold of the liquor in her glass. "Something older than that. Tradition going back to the old world, to Earth itself—may it one day be found again!"

The Admiral looked at her with deep interest. "And what tradition is that?" he asked.

"It's our religion," said Grandma. "The sons of Earth are scattered over half the galaxy, each with some little bits of memories of the old world." She pointed to the three dimensional of the sailing ship riding on the flames. "There's one of ours. Another's the making of herb wine. They are the keystones of something that will one day be uniquely Arcan."

"Dear me," said the Admiral. "You're going to run into trouble with the Imperial authorities if you try to be so individualistic."

"The Empire is on its way out," said Grandma. "I tell you this, I who have worn the Imperial uniform and commanded a levy fleet during the Nikalong uprising fifty of my years ago. We won—of course. Imperial fleets always win when it is a matter of men and machinery. But there—" she pointed again to the three dimensional of the boat "—and here—" she lifted her wine glass "—are the weapons that will destroy her eventually."

The Admiral tugged at his nose with a hint of embarrassment.

"You make me feel guilty," he said.

"My apologies," returned Grandma, a touch of malice sharpening the twinkle in her eyes. "How would you like to look at some others of our secret weapons? Our garden, or our bees?"

"Bees?" It had been a good number of thousands of generations since the Admiral's ancestors had been

able to prick up their ears, but it must be admitted their remote descendant made a noble attempt.

"And why not?" answered Grandma. "Would you like to see them?"

The Admiral shook with something like a fever. The abrupt wrench of his unexpected parting from his apiary on his uncle Geert's sudden orders had been, in part, its own anesthetic. The shock had numbed him until he found himself well into space with the fleet. And by that time the hopelessness of his position had transmuted his longing for the hives into a dull ache. He had thought of bees—but only with a sad sort of wistful longing. Now, with the sudden news that there were bees within viewing distance, that longing shot up into a raging hunger. Did he want to see them? What a foolish question!

"I—I—I—" stammered the Admiral, shooting to his feet. "I—I'd be delighted."

As if in a delicious dream, the Admiral let himself be led out the back door of Grandma Wheatley's dome, through a garden rank with rich beauty of color and shape, and into a short meadow where white hives on their platforms gleamed like mounds of snow, in a long double row with an avenue between; its airy length and breadth were patrolled by the busy shapes of worker bees in their multifarious comings and goings.

The Admiral stepped into that avenue; in doing so, he stepped into Paradise, which is a place where Empires and Fleets and levies from the sub-class planets do not exist. Grandma Wheatley, watching him, saw this; understanding, she made no effort to detain or follow him, preferring to leave him until that moment when, in his own good time, he should elect to return. She turned and went back through the flowers of the garden and into the main living room of her dome.

*   *   *

There were four people waiting for her there, now. Besides Tommy and Gyneth there were Corla, Grandma's oldest daughter, with her husband Jachim, these two being the parents of Tommy. Jachim's face was strained and white; Corla held Tommy in her arms.

"Who is this man you have here?" cried Jachim, as Grandma came in. "Tommy says he's promised to keep Corla and me out of the levy."

"He's a good man," said Grandma, sitting down in one of the chairs. "A political appointee, I'd guess. He knows less about the universe than Tommy does."

"But he *is* the Admiral?" There was hope in Corla's voice.

"He is," said Grandma, shortly. "But whatever he promised Tommy, you two must go when the rest go."

"If—," Jachim stared at her. "But why? If there's any chance at all—for Tommy's sake."

"Are you a fool?" demanded Grandma. "What do you think Tommy's life would be like—we won't even bother considering what yours would be like—if the planet knew his parents had been singled out for such favoritism?"

Jachim sighed and the strength seemed to go out of him. His shoulders slumped.

"I knew it was too good to be true," he said. "Then there's no hope?"

"Not for individuals," replied Grandma. "For the whole planet." She got abruptly to her feet and began to stride back and forth across the room, her lips tight and her eyes abstracted. "Let me think."

A sub-class planet was what its name implied. It was a full-size world only recently settled by a sparse scattering of human beings, who clung together in small clusters at a few points of the globe, if, indeed, they did not all settle roughly in one main area. It was this latter situation that was the case with Arca. As a result, even before the Imperial ships had landed, the Fleet Arm had been able to throw a detection screen around all of the few thousand square miles of coastal plain where the Arcan villages were located. And since that first announcement of the levy that was to be made, that screen had been shrinking, contracting on the central village, where the Flagship stood. As its rim closed in, passing over the individual villages, a little bubble of a screen was left around each one. These in turn each contracted around the Imperial transport which stood on the outskirts of each village, until every such ship was surrounded by a jostling, scared-eye mass of people swept from all the surrounding territory. Held now, penned, by a force screen as well as the detection screen, they stood helplessly while the officers of the Fleet winnowed the strong and healthy from the old, the young and the sick, and drove the former like sheep aboard the transports.

"All right! Come on out of there!"

There have possibly been ruder awakenings from Paradise, but at the moment the Admiral would have disagreed that any such thing were possible. Like the trained beekeeper he was, he had been moving quite fearlessly among the hives; he had just taken out one of the screens loaded with the black, crawling bodies of workers, and was examining them. Now, with shattered fragments of his pleasure evaporating in the sunlight around him, he lifted his head to see two Fleetmen of petty-officer rank step from the flower garden, halt abruptly on seeing him, and lower their sidearms in some confusion and a touch of fear.

"Well?" said the Admiral shortly.

"Sorry, sir," said the older of the two, a short, square-faced man. "We saw a pip on the detector screen and we thought it was one of the natives hiding out."

By sheer chance he had said exactly the wrong thing. It was, in fact, a matter of comparative values.

Every person tends to rate his own profession highest of all and grade people of other duties and persuasions on a descending scale. To the Fleetmen, quite naturally, the military ranked highest, and therefore the owner or owners of the apiary were low people in social standing and general morals. Hence the reference to a "native hiding out." To the Admiral, on the other hand, the Elect, the Chosen of God, were not men who drove spaceships or walked out of gardens with guns in their hands telling other people to come out of there, but beekeepers. To hear one so coarsely insulted, even by proxy, by a member of the laity was enough to fire even his gentle breast to anger. For perhaps the first time in his life, the Admiral felt savage.

"Excellent," he said. "You're just in time to give me a lift back to the ship. And before you go," he added, "you can put this tray back for me."

It is a curious fact, but a true one, that bees are able to tell when the human approaching them is afraid of them or not. For this reason, a self-assured beekeeper can do things with his charges that a person of lesser experience would not attempt for a very large sum of money. It is unnecessary, therefore, to go into details of the replacing of the tray. Suffice it to say that the Admiral, himself unmarked, flew back to the flagship with two Fleetmen whose faces and arms were already beginning to swell into hideous shapes.

The Fleet Arm loaded and lifted. Up it went, in a compact ball, transports in the center, warships around them, into the airless regions. At a safe distance from the planet's surface it headed out into the interstellar regions, where it would be possible to go up from normal drive into warp-drive without danger of backlash from nearby gravitic fields.

It faded away and was lost to view from Arca. The children and the old people saw it vanish.

At ten hours out from the planet, the Admiral had locked himself in his cabin. He was in bad humor and he was thinking.

Bees, he was thinking, angrily, *and why not? Am I a weakling or a Fellow of the Imperial Bee Society? Brass bound military man? Certainly not! Not built for it. Whole thing senseless. Rip people away from homes here, ship them off to be shot up there. Total result, what? Nothing. Meanwhile bees get neglected.* "And before you go (say it casually) you can put this tray back for me." *Ha! Served them right.*

Take bees. Useful. Produce honey. Feed selves and beekeepers. Take Spacemen. Unuseful. Produce damage and ruin. Eat up tax money much better devoted to bee research. Scooting all over the galaxy! Good God, who in his right mind wants to scoot anyway? Distrust scooters myself, on principle. Unstable.

Spit in Geert's eye. Hand in my resignation.

I'll do it!

—And just at that moment, the lights went out, the alarm hooter rang through the ship and the Flagship lurched to a blow that seemed to tear it apart.

"*Sabati!*" swore the Captain; which is a very impolite word indeed in lower Sirian. He shook his head dazedly and climbed to his feet. "What hit us? Are you all right, sir?" he went on, turning to the Commodore and helping the latter to his feet.

"I think so, Ver," replied the Commodore shakily, wiping a trickle of blood that was flowing from a scalp cut where his head had connected with an instrument board. "Get on stations and find out what happened."

The Captain turned toward the Communications Board. But before he could touch the first button that would connect him with his station officers, the master screen lit up and a benign-appearing little old lady—dressed in a somewhat out-of-date uniform, but unmistakably that of an Admiral of the Imperial Navy—beamed down at him.

"Your fleet is shot to hell, Captain," she said sweetly. "If you call your superior officer, we'll give you a chance to surrender. Five minutes." And the little old lady vanished from the screen.

"Shot to hell, eh?" said the Commodore, grimly. "We'll see about that." He flung himself at the communicator and began checking on the Fleet Arm.

Three of the five minutes had gone by when the Admiral arrived on the bridge at a dead run.

"What's this? What's this?" he shouted, hastily straightening his uniform. "What's going on?"

The Captain groaned, raised his eyes toward the ceiling and then turned to him patiently.

"We've been attacked, sir," he explained.

"By whom? Why? What? Where? When?" exploded the Admiral, going off like a string of firecrackers.

"I don't know, sir—" the Captain was beginning, when he was interrupted.

"By Arca," said a voice. "The Arcan Navy, to be exact." And they looked up to see on the screen the little old lady who had appeared there briefly just a few minutes before. "Your time for surrender is almost up."

The Admiral blinked into the screen. "Why— Madame Wheatley!"

"The same," answered Grandma, equitably. "At your service, Admiral."

Now we must leave the realm of historical fact for that of folk-tale and legend. The Arcans, understandably, preserved the record of that day's happenings only in the more trustworthy, if less material, strongboxes of their memories, rather than committing it to writing, a procedure which might, even several hundred years after the event, have been somewhat dangerous. And since it is folk-tale and legend, perhaps we are justified in letting our imagination play with the scene a bit.

We can imagine the crowds at each landing field,

the lined, bitter faces and the wondering young ones upturned and watching as the fleet and the transports rose, dwindled and vanished into the blue-black sky. And at last each elderly survivor taking a grandson or a granddaughter by the hand, heading blindly with uncertain step into a future of desolation and sorrow.

And then—running through the crowd—a rumor. A wild and fantastic rumor.

"—To the square—."

"Why?"

Old faces numb and hopeless.

"Grandma Wheatley—she's going to talk from the capitol—."

Young faces puzzled, looking up.

"What can she say?"

"I don't know. But come—come!"

So in each small town and village, the old and the very young streamed from the landing fields into the square where the huge general information screen was set up; moving slowly at first, in tiredness and indifference, but picking up speed as they went, as the rumors grew.

"—She's got a plan."

"What plan?"

"I don't know, but—."

"And what good are plans now?"

"It seems too late for them, but—."

"We haven't anything."

"Yes, but—."

But, *but*, BUT . . . The twelfth hour had struck. *But* there were thirteen hours, weren't there? Wild hope tugging at reluctant hearts, they quickened their paces from a walk to a run, their voices from a murmur to a babble and the crowds grew as they flooded into the squares and packed them tight. The screens hung blank before them, huge and grey. Suddenly the screens ran riot with color, which flamed for a second, then vanished, to show them the little lady that everyone on Arca knew by reputation if not by sight.

"Arcans," she said.

They waited, hardly breathing.

"Free People," she went on, "—for you have been free people until this hour—we have been subjected to an attack by the enemy."

A low moan of wonder went over the crowds.

"I say *enemy*," repeated Grandma. "You and I were born on worlds that thought of themselves as part of the Empire. We moved—those of us who were born on planets other than Arca—to this world, to establish a home of our own. Again it was within the bounds of the Empire. We thought of ourselves as belonging to the Empire.

"But we made no convenant with the Empire. We signed no treaty, agreed to no terms, accepted nothing, offered nothing. Our belonging was merely an assumption on both sides.

"Now, as a result of that assumption, Imperial ships have landed here without warning and with no right but the right of superior strength have taken away the finest among us. In doing this they have destroyed any friendship between us—any alliance. They have become the enemy."

She talked on, showing them with pictures built of her words the difference that was the way of life of the Empire's, and the way of life that was theirs. She showed them, without sparing, exactly what the loss of the men and women of space-working age would mean to Arca, to themselves and to the children. And finally she must have said something very much like this:

"Without the men and women to fulfill our trading contracts, we will die. Therefore we might as well gamble with what little we have left. I leave it up to you."

Her speech was undoubtedly a solemn one. But what followed on its heels was anything but solemn.

Of course, they agreed with her. What could they do but agree? And then the fun started.

The nearest approach to a warship on Arca were the heavy-duty, long-range cargo cruisers; the villages had a total of nearly three hundred of these. To man these they had a little under a thousand of the people over fifty who were not prohibited by absolute invalidism or some equal disability from taking off. But a cargo cruiser requires a minimum of twelve crew members, including the captain. Where were these extra hands to come from?

One guess.

The children under fifteen almost went through the roof in their excitement.

"Yipeeee!" yelled Tommy Wheatley, dancing in the square.

On all the landing fields a madman's holiday was taking place. Tottering oldsters and straining youngsters were hurrying between the towns and the ships, loading them with everything portable that could be snatched up. Clocks, chairs, vases, toys, pictures, cups, pictures, statuettes, cooking utensils, old shoes, small lamps, all the small impedimenta of housekeeping, all the lumber of civilization were snatched up and hurried out to the waiting cargo cruisers. For two hours the towns were ransacked; and then Grandma put a halt to it.

"No more time," she said crisply, in a general broadcast. "To your places. We lift in twenty minutes."

The Fleet Arm had headed directly out from Arca's sun under ordinary drive, with the purpose of putting the necessary half-light year of distance between itself and the system before dropping into warp-drive. Such a trip would take roughly twelve hours, shiptime.

The three hundred Arcan cargo ships rose in ragged formation; a scant three hours of travel brought them to a spot that their intimate knowledge of their own system told them was one where the gravitic strains of the sun and the planets would, for the short moment required for changeover, balance each other out. They arrived, they waited for a fraction of a second, they flickered and were gone.

"Did you see *me!*" screeched half a hundred young voices in exultation over half a hundred intercom systems, as the Arcan fleet resolved itself into the shadowy twilight of interdimensional travel.

So, while the Imperial Fleet Arm was plodding its half year of distance out from the sun of Arca under ordinary drive, the three hundred Arcan vessels hopped to Lyra III, which is fourteen light-years away. Here they came back into normal space and reformed their formation—taking a precious eighty minutes of time—and took off once more at right angles for Copasca, a systemless little sun in the Pelagos quadrant sixty light years from Lyra III. Once again they normaled, reformed, and turned. And this time they went half-way across the galaxy to an almost forgotten sun called Aldebaran.

At Aldebaran, after going normal, they did a right about face and found themselves at last in line and directly behind the Imperial Fleet Arm, although a little matter of some eight hundred and twenty light years separated the nose of Grandma's leading cruiser from the tip of the stern stabilizer of the most laggard Imperial scout. In three hundred cargo cruisers, three hundred experienced old fingers made identical calculations and three hundred heads nodded in unison when Grandma Wheatley came briefly onto the communication's screen to announce her own figures.

"Any disagreement?" said Grandma. And when none was forthcoming she nodded her head. "Jump in ten seconds."

Once again they went into warp drive. It was a long jump, and while no objective time went by, the greyness fleeting past the screens of the ships seemed to stretch and stretch into a small eternity.

"Break out!" ordered Grandma.

They broke. At an unmatched velocity they reappeared, a matter of scant thousands of miles in front of the Imperials. In a fraction of time too small to count, suddenly the Fleet warships were there on the screen. Grandma smiled a wintry smile.

"Bombs away," said she, with grim humor.

The Admiral turned from the screen and the sardonic eye of the old lady. Momentarily, realization of the seriousness of the situation had given him dignity and stature. Officer he might be only by virtue of a careless signature on a piece of paper, but gentleman he was by birth and training.

"Well, Commodore," he said. "What's the situation?"

The Commodore reached out to flick on a screen that would shield his words from the communicator. He turned to the Admiral, so that the movement of his lips, too, were hidden.

"I don't know what she hit us with, sir," he answered. "But half the Fleet's gone. And of the rest there isn't one ship that's not crippled."

"She mentioned something about surrender," said the Admiral.

"Yes, sir. She made that offer, sir," said the Commodore, emotionlessly.

They stood waiting, the Commodore and the Captain, looking at the Admiral and waiting for his orders. Certain things they could do, in taking over the work of their Admiral; but some things they could not, and the making of this decision was one of them. What they would have done in the Admiral's place was clear enough. They would have fought. Believing it hopeless, they would still have turned down the surrender offer and fought to the last ship. They would have done this, not because they wanted to, but because they were regular officers of the Imperial Navy. And the Imperial Navy does not surrender to cargo ships, no matter what kind of secret weapon they may have.

The Admiral looked away from the officers and back to the old lady on the screen. The switch the Commodore touched erected a wall of silence between the two. But across that wall, their eyes met and conversed quite satisfactorily.

"Commodore," said the Admiral. "I would like to talk to the enemy commander."

The Commodore reached out and touched the switch which the Admiral would have been unable to find by himself; and the wall went down.

"Well, sir?" said Madame Wheatley.

"I think I'm correct, am I not," asked the Admiral, "in supposing that your primary concern is with those of your people we have impressed?"

"That's right," said Grandma.

"I thought so," replied the Admiral. "Now, *my* primary concern is for the men of my fleet arm."

Grandma inclined her head.

"Since, therefore," the Admiral went on, "I do not want my men to suffer unnecessarily; and since I'm sure you'd rather we didn't turn our guns on the transports in retaliation for your attack, I have a counter-proposal."

"I," said Grandma, folding her hands judiciously in front of her, "would be interested to hear it."

The Admiral paused. Beside him and behind him, he could feel the silence and the waiting of the Commodore, the Captain and the other officers and men on the bridge. On all his ships, on the transports, in the ships behind Grandma, there would be waiting also, men and women, not breathing and not moving as they waited for his words, holding themselves tight for the fear or the pride, or the love that was in them. And the Admiral was not a religious man; but he said a little prayer to himself in that moment. *Great Empire and Lost Earth*, he prayed, *let this be the*

way. And then he said to himself. *Amen*, and looked
Grandma squarely in the eye.

"I will release to you the people from Arca we hold
on our transports," he said. "Provided you will let
the Fleet Arm go without further hostilities. And, as a
guarantee of good faith, I will surrender myself to
you along with the Arcan impresses, as a hostage
against any breach of this agreement or future
reprisals."

"Agreed!" said Grandma, promptly. "We will start
taking our people off your transports as soon as you
have surrendered aboard my ship."

And with that her manner relaxed and she smiled.
She said something more, one word, in so low a tone
that the officers were not able to catch it before she
had faded from the screen. Even the Admiral was not
sure he had heard aright; but it was a familiar word,
especially to him, a friendly word. It sounded to the
Admiral almost exactly like *"Bees!"*

And that is the story of Wheatley's Foray; a remarkably bloodless incident considering the times to
which it belonged, but an incident of some psycho-
political importance as far as the Empire rulers were
concerned. For that it was embarrassing we cannot
doubt—and especially so to the Mark-Count Geert
Von Ge Brock Til Den, who had the misfortune to be
related to the officer responsible for the incident.

All in all, it is clear from the study of court records
that his embarrassment was at least great enough so
that he devoted his far from inconsiderable influence
to burying the matter as deeply as possible—an
achievement carried out by two main actions, one of
which was a somewhat hasty granting of autono-
mous status to Arca, the other some statesmanlike
sleight-of-hand that appears to have changed the status of the Admiral, his nephew, somewhat miracu-
lously from that of hostage to Ambassador to the new
free planet.

The appointment as Ambassador to Arca was clearly intended to be a lifetime one. Certainly, there is no evidence that the Admiral, now Ambassador, Von Horn Ge Brod ever showed any intention of resigning his post or changing his residence from Arca. Indeed, as has been said at the beginning, after this one appearance on history's pages, he rapidly sinks out of sight again; and is only casually referred to once, some fifty years later, as the developer of a new mutated strain of bees capable of being exported to and surviving on low-gravity planets.

Madame Wheatley goes on to found the Interstellar Association of Independent Traders before dying at the ripe old age of a hundred and thirty-two. But it is not found that her descendants were in any way remarkable; and they are lost to history.

A final note deals with the weapon which permitted the Arcan cargo ships to defeat armed Navy vessels. The only authority for this is the Arcan legend; the Imperials, if they ever knew about it, having suppressed the knowledge. But it seems that what smashed beyond repair half the ships in that Fleet Arm and badly damaged the rest was a wide circle of household furniture which the Arcans set down, relatively motionless in space, shortly before the Fleet Arm smashed into them at a velocity of some thousands of miles per second.

The moral in all this, if any, is obscure. * * *

No predator, however cunning, can afford to despise its prey.

Ricochet on Miza

If you decide to go hunting the Warlin, which is an intelligent creature, it is almost necessary to know three things. First, that the female, who has the more valuable hide, will invariably be holed up somewhere while her mate is out hunting. Second, that the male is telepathically sensitive and can be dominated by the human mind. And third, that the Warlin is very good at playing dead.

Bill Raush, of course, knew all of these things, although he had never gone Warlin-hunting before. In various of Carlin City's dives and dens—for Warlin-hunting is strictly illegal—he had listened to other hunters and made due note of the mistakes which might trip up a beginner. He had heard, and believed, that the Warlin loves its mate and will go to any lengths and risks to protect her. He had memorized the countless dodges used by the creature. And he had sworn to himself that, above all, his Warlin would not trick him into losing his mental control by playing dead.

Now he crouched in a jumble of rocks, under the starlit heavens of Miza, and waited. Below him he could see what was the equivalent of a waterhole in an Earthly jungle, although the fluid in it would have poisoned a human in short order. Many creatures had already come down to drink in spite of the fact that the long Mizan night was only some three hours gone and there were another sixteen yet to go before the corrugated red sun poked above the long horizon. Unfortunately none of these had been a Warlin.

Bill shifted uncomfortably upon his rocks and cursed Miza's unfriendly atmosphere that forced him to encase himself in a rubber suit and air helmet. The process of waiting was tedious. He wanted a smoke and his back itched. And nothing could be done about these things.

So obsessed was he, in fact, with his own discomforts that he almost missed the Warlin when it did come. One second, to Bill's eyes, and it was not there. The next, and it was in plain sight, shuffling down the trail to the waterhole and looking like nothing so much as a gigantic anteater with thick, woolly fur.

Bill grinned to himself. It was a big male, half again as heavy as Bill himself, although he weighed close to a hundred kilograms. The animal was physically the match for a half a dozen men. Unfortunately, as has been mentioned, it was susceptible to mental domination. It gave Bill a dark sense of pleasure to think of that mountain of muscle and bone completely at his mercy, obeying whatever commands his whim dictated.

He crouched silently, watching the Warlin approach the side of the pool, forcing his mind to lie blank and quiet like the surface of a pool of quicksand. The Warlin must not sense his presence until it was within the minimum two meters of distance. Otherwise it might be able to fight off his commands and escape.

The Warlin stopped on the edge of the pool, raised its trunk and waved it questioningly about in the darkness. Then, satisfied that the coast was clear—indeed, outside of Bill or some other human, there

was little on Miza that could have harmed it—lowered
its head to the waterhole.

Bill leaped!

Seizing the boulder in front of him to gain lever-
age, he suddenly sent his body sailing over the edge
of rocks to land feet first beside the Warlin. The
shouted intention of his mind had gone before him to
warn the male, who whirled. But the space beside
the waterhole was too limited and the Warlin found
himself within the two-meter minimum distance at
which Bill's mind could control him.

For a second he stood there, thick trunk upraised,
half reared on his massive hind legs in the instinctive
stance of battle. Then his trunk wavered and drooped,
his front legs fell to the earth, and he dropped at
Bill's feet like a huge, shaggy dog that cringes before
its master.

"Down!" Bill was shouting in his air helmet, the
better to focus his mind. "Down! Down! Down!"

He could feel the mind of the Warlin recoil beneath
the savage pound of his thought, and the sudden
realization came to him that, emotionally, the creature could not stand it. If he kept on this way, in his
eagerness to dominate, he might easily kill this male
and then he would have a battle-scarred and dirt-
snaggled hide to take back instead of the smooth,
silky female one which would be worth a hundred
times its value.

So, exultant but wary, he relaxed and the mind of
the Warlin came up under the released pressure, came
up like a cork through water.

"I've got you now," said Bill, tightly. "You can't
get away. You can't get away. Now, take me to your
den, to your den. Do you hear me? Take me to your
den."

The mind of the Warlin shifted in sudden panic.
For a second Bill caught a flashing impression of a

dark and guarded place where there was the warmth of another body and love and peace. Then the impression was gone and only stubbornness remained.

"Take me," Bill was chanting inside the air helmet. "Take me. Take me to your den. Take me there. Take me there...."

The Warlin stood still but Bill could feel its mental opposition weakening beneath the steady forcing of his human mind. Warned by the reaction he had felt when he captured the creature, he did not insist too strongly. A dead male Warlin is of little use to a hunter. Over and over again, lightly but with firm insistence, his thought beat at the male.

"Take me there. Take me there."

Suddenly the Warlin's opposition collapsed. He stood still, trembling, and Bill felt a wave of utter despair. Then the shaggy bulk turned and ambled away from the waterhole.

Bill walked close beside, one gloved hand grasping the thick fur. The night was dark, but the Warlin went surely ahead. There was no doubt that he led the way directly to his den, for his mind was opened like a box to the eyes of the human's mind and there was no deceit there.

Now that they moved in temporary cooperation, Bill was able to sense more of what the Warlin was thinking. There was a hidden level below the surface where the creature might possibly be planning something against him, for it was not Bill's ability that bridged the gap between the two minds, but the Warlin's, an ability the creature could no more negate than he could stop breathing.

The Warlin was not frightened. As one of the largest creatures on Miza, fear was very nearly foreign to it. Nor, at the moment, did it hate Bill. At the moment its mind was filled with a sense of desolation, and an odd emotion that Bill did not at first understand. When he finally did, he chuckled in his air helmet.

The male had realized that Bill was out to kill his mate. He had realized that he could do nothing to stop the Earthman and was crying deep in his alien soul—the crying of a race that had never known tears—tearing at himself with bitter reproach and pain for being the helpless instrument of his mate's imminent capture and death.

Bill chuckled and asked:

"Damn near human, aren't you?"

A flood of black hate welled up suddenly from the other mind. Partially, the Warlin had understood him—well enough, at least, so that the comparison to a human had been comprehended. So savage, so cruel, so devastating was the reaction that it stopped Bill in his tracks and he went cold with fear. It was only sheer paralysis that enabled him to keep his grasp on the Warlin's fur.

"None of that, now!" he growled, recovering. "None of your tricks." And using his mind like a bludgeon he beat the male back into temporary submission.

They went on through the night. Bill had resigned himself to a long walk. Warlins, he knew, hunted and drank far from their dens for the maximum amount of safety. How far they had already gone he had no way of telling but it was reasonable to assume that it was quite a way. In fact it might take all night. It was even reasonable that they might walk like this for days and days.

Bill jerked himself savagely alert.

"Oh, you would, would you!" he snarled, and his fury unleashed itself to the tune of curses upon the Warlin until he felt the male's mind tremble and totter beneath his onslaught. Finally, fearful of either driving the creature insane or of killing it, he let up.

The male shivered beneath his hand and abruptly collapsed. Bill stiffened, ready to apply fresh force, then realized that the creature was exhausted by the beating it had taken and close to unconsciousness.

Bill sat down beside it, keeping his hold on the fur.

"Rest then," he said. "But don't try anything. You aren't getting away from me."

Released, the Warlin's mind dropped like a stone into the mists of sleep.

They sat for an hour by the human's watch while the Warlin slept and Bill fidgeted, jumpy and nervous under the effects of the benzedrine tablet he had taken to ensure his staying alert. At the end of that time he tugged at the handful of fur.

"Come on," he growled. "Get up."

The Warlin's mind was reluctant to abandon the comfortable oblivion of sleep. It came back to awareness slowly, with the somewhat confused impression that it was back in its den and that its mate was nipping playfully at its woolly hide. Then memory returned with a rush and its mind surged in an abrupt, insane effort to throw off the human's control.

Bill beat it down. He was becoming more expert with practice and managed to return it to submission without wearing it out so much. He pulled the male to his feet.

"Let's go," he said.

Despairingly, the Warlin led off into the darkness once more. Now, it seemed, it had truly given up, for its mind was openly, nakedly sorrowing over memories of past happinesses. As if not caring whether the human mind could read it or not, the male's memory evoked pictures of meetings with his mate, of huntings, of homecomings to the den, of past victorious fights with others of his kind and of the tumbling of his young in play between his mighty front paws.

"Cut it out," said Bill derisively, "or I'll bust right out into tears."

But the Warlin ignored him. It thought on until gradually its mind began to dull and slow down like a whirlpool coming to rest. Gradually its thoughts became less and less perceptible, more and more unintelligible and feeble, like the fragmentary mumblings of a dying man. Until they ceased altogether and the Warlin stumbled, fell suddenly, and lay still.

Bill stared down at it.

"Damn it!" he swore. "Did he kick off on me after all?"

He probed the creature's mind with his own. It gave, soggily, without resistance, but with no reaction. He kicked the inert body but there was no response. Chagrined, he was reaching for his skinning knife when remembrance of what he had heard came back to him.

"Oh?" he said with a lopsided grin. "Playing dead, huh?"

His grip tightened on the Warlin's wool, his lips skinned back over his teeth, and he began to talk.

"Get up," he said, and continued to repeat the command monotonously. "Get up. Get up. Get up. Get up."

For a long minute there was no response. Then, with what was the equivalent of a sigh, life returned to the Warlin's mind and the creature stood up.

"To your den," commanded Bill. "Go!"

They went on.

From the number of tricks the male had been playing recently, Bill reasoned, his den must not now be far off. The man exulted in the thought without bothering to hide his exultation from the creature at his side. But the Warlin no longer seemed capable of resentment, or indeed of any feeling. He plodded on mechanically, and it was not far until Bill was able to sense from his mind that the den entrance would shortly be within sight.

They were passing through a particularly rough section of country. All Miza is tumbled with rock for reasons the geologists have not been able to agree on. But this was one of those unusually bad parts where you progressed by scrambling from boulder to boulder and it was necessary to watch closely for fear of slipping into the cracks.

In spite of this the Warlin led the human on, as though in a dream. He did not even look where his massive feet must go but strode surely forward while Bill scrambled beside him. The man cursed the terrain, then reflected that it would naturally be in such inaccessible sections that the Warlins would make their dens. Cheered up by this thought, he continued without complaint. Still, it was precarious going and only his firm grip on the Warlin's wool kept him from falling more than once.

Now, with the den entrance only a short distance away, Bill began to make his plans. The female would not be too much trouble but it was smart to have everything worked out in advance. He had a smoke bomb which would drive her out into the open. It would be a simple matter to stand by the side of the hole until she came out, coughing and blinded, and then shoot her.

Credits. Bill licked his lips, tasting in anticipation the smoky Earth-bottled Scotch, the rich Venusian cigars that would be his portion once he had sold the skins. He would go back to one of the inner systems— he thought of going all the way back to Mars but that would be too expensive—and allow himself a three-month spree before coming back for another hunt. This was the kind of work for a strong man—a short term of discomfort for high rewards. Eventually he would retire when the fascination of the hunt ceased to attract him. But by that time he would be rich.

Danger!

The warning rang suddenly in his mind as he felt a sudden blaze of defiance from the Warlin beside him. His mind, caught off balance, scrambled furiously to reassert itself but as it did so he felt the creature at his side lurch away, leaving only a handful of fur in his grasp.

The Warlin leaped—away from Bill—and head foremost into the pit between two huge boulders. Bill tottered on the edge.

In a second, however, he had righted himself and a furious wave of anger flooded through him.

"You stupid fool!" he yelled at the motionless bulk of the Warlin, crouched on the floor of the pit. "Don't you know you can't get away?"

There was no response from the Warlin mind and for a second Bill thought that it had found some hole down there and escaped, that it was just his imagination seeing it in the shadows of the pit. Then he realized that the pit was all of four meters deep—too far for mental contact to be maintained unless the Warlin wanted it and the Warlin quite evidently didn't.

Bill cursed again, and peered down. Yes, the creature was there, all right. Probably waiting poised to jump him the minute he came down. Probably hoping he wouldn't dare to come down.

Bill grinned sourly. If the Warlin thought it was going to get away that easily it was mistaken. It was a dangerous thing to jump down there and risk getting his skull beaten in before he could seize control of the Warlin's mind. But what were a few risks when a fortune was at stake?

Cautiously he lowered his legs over the edge of the boulder, hung for a moment, and then let go. There was a rush of wind past his ears and he half slid, half fell to the bottom of the pit. Above his head the night sky was now a small, irregular, star-studded patch of lighter black than that which surrounded him.

He landed on his feet, gun in hand, his mind flashing out, ready to overcome the mind that faced him. But there was no response and the dark bulk of the Warlin did not come leaping at him.

Bill laughed out loud.

"Chickened out, huh?" he said. Contemptuously, he ignored the creature and looked up at the little patch of sky above him. What he saw made him swear suddenly.

In his haste to recapture the Warlin he had neglected to think of how he would get back out of the pit. Now he looked up at four meters of precipitous stone walls which were absolutely unclimbable.

For a second fear crept into his mind. Then a sudden thought sent it scurrying with its tail between its legs. He looked over at the Warlin, who still had not moved.

"You outsmarted yourself that time, sonny boy," he said. "You thought I'd be trapped down here with you. But I'm not. I'll just get you to use some of that beef and toss me up to where I can grab a hold of the edge of that boulder."

He reached out to the creature's mind. It gave, soggily, without resistance, but with no reaction. Bill sneered.

"You poor stupe," he said, "lying doggo again. Don't you remember you pulled that trick on me once before and it wouldn't work?"

Striding over to the Warlin, he kicked it viciously.

"Get up," he said, without heat, but with a bitter relentlessness. "Get up. Get up. Get up. Get up."

As has been said, the male Warlin will go to almost any lengths to protect its mate. Also, it is very good at playing dead.

Only, as Bill Raush eventually discovered, this one wasn't playing.

When law and justice collide, sometimes the only way to write straight is with crooked lines.

The Law-Twister Shorty

He's a pretty tough character, that Iron Bender—" said the Hill Bluffer, conversationally. Malcolm O'Keefe clung to the straps of the saddle he rode on the Hill Bluffer's back, as the nearly ten-foot-tall Dilbian strode surefootedly along the narrow mountain trail, looking something like a slim Kodiak bear on his hind legs. "But a Shorty like you, Law-Twister, ought to be able to handle him, all right."

"Law-Twister . . ." echoed Mal, dizzily. The Right Honorable Joshua Guy, Ambassador Plenipotentiary to Dilbia, had said something about the Dilbians wasting no time in pinning a name of their own invention on every Shorty (as humans were called by them) they met. But Mal had not expected to be named so soon. And what was that other name the Dilbian postman carrying him had just mentioned?

"Who won't I have any trouble with, did you say?" Mal added.

"Iron Bender," said the Hill Bluffer, with a touch of impatience. "Clan Water Gap's harnessmaker. Didn't Little Bite back there at Humrog Town tell you anything about Iron Bender?"

"I . . . I think so," said Mal. Little Bite, as Ambassador Guy was known to the Dilbians, had in fact told Mal a great many things. But thinking back on their conversation now, it did not seem to Mal that the Ambassador had been very helpful in spite of all his words. "Iron Bender's the—er—protector of this Gentle . . . Gentle . . ."

"Gentle Maiden. Hor!" The Bluffer broke into an unexplained snort of laughter. "Well, anyway, that's who Iron Bender's protector of."

"And she's the one holding the three Shorties captive—"

"Captive? What're you talking about, Law-Twister?" demanded the Bluffer. "She's *adopted* them! Little Bite must have told you that."

"Well, he . . ." Mal let the words trail off. His head was still buzzing from the hypnotraining he had been given on his way to Dilbia, to teach him the language and the human-known facts about the outsize natives of this Earth-like world; and the briefing he had gotten from Ambassador Guy had only confused him further.

". . . Three tourists, evidently," Guy had said, puffing on a heavy-bowled pipe. He was a brisk little man in his sixties, with sharp blue eyes. "Thought they could slip down from the cruise by spaceliner they were taking and duck into a Dilbian village for a first hand look at the locals. Probably had no idea what they were getting into."

"What—uh," asked Mal, "were they getting into, if I can ask?"

"Restricted territory! Treaty territory!" snapped Guy, knocking the dottle out of his pipe and beginning to refill it. Mal coughed discreetly as the fumes reached his nose. "In this sector of space we're in open competition with a race of aliens called Hemnoids, for every available, habitable world. Dilbia's a plum. But it's got this intelligent—if primitive—native race on it. Result, we've got a treaty with the Hemnoids restricting all but emergency contact with the Dilbians—by them or us—until the Dilbians them-

selves become civilized enough to choose either us or
the Hemnoids for interstellar partners. Highly illegal, those three tourists just dropping in like that."

"How about me?" asked Mal.

"You? You're being sent in under special emergency orders to get them out before the Hemnoids
find out they've been there," said Guy. "As long as
they're gone when the Hemnoids hear about this, we
can duck any treaty violation charge. But you've got
to get them into their shuttle boat and back into
space by midnight tonight—"

The dapper little ambassador pointed outside the
window of the log building that served as the human
embassy on Dilbia at the dawn sunlight on the cob-
blestoned Humrog Street.

"Luckily, we've got the local postman in town at
the moment," Guy went on. "We can mail you to
Clan Water Gap with him—"

"But," Mal broke in on the flow of words, "you still
haven't explained—why me? I'm just a high school
senior on a work-study visit to the Pleiades. Or at
least, that's where I was headed when they told me
my travel orders had been picked up, and I was
drafted to come here instead, on emergency duty.
There must be lots of people older than I am, who're
experienced—"

"Not the point in this situation," said Guy, puffing
clouds of smoke from his pipe toward the log rafters
overhead. "Dilbia's a special case. Age and experience don't help here as much as a certain sort of—
well—personality. The Dilbian psychological profile
and culture is tricky. It needs to be matched by a
human with just the proper profile and character,
himself. Without those natural advantages the best
of age, education, and experience doesn't help in deal-
ing with the Dilbians."

"But," said Mal, desperately, "there must be some
advice you can give me—some instructions. Tell me
what I ought to do, for example—"

"No, no. Just the opposite," said Guy. "We want you to follow your instincts. Do what seems best as the situation arises. You'll make out all right. We've already had a couple of examples of people who did, when they had the same kind of personality pattern you have. The book anthropologists and psychologists are completely baffled by these Dilbians as I say, but you just keep your head and follow your instincts. . . ."

He had continued to talk, to Mal's mind, making less and less sense as he went, until the arrival of the Hill Bluffer had cut the conversation short. Now, here Mal was—with no source of information left, but the Bluffer, himself.

"This, er, Iron Bender," he said to the Dilbian postman. "You were saying I ought to be able to handle him all right?"

"Well, if you're any kind of a Shorty at all," said the Bluffer, cheerfully. "There's still lots of people in these mountains, and even down in the lowlands, who don't figure a Shorty can take on a real man and win. But not me. After all, I've been tied up with you Shorties almost from the start. It was me delivered the Half-Pint Posted to the Streamside Terror. Hor! Everbody thought the Terror'd tear the Half-Pint apart. And you can guess who won, being a Shorty yourself."

"The Half-Pint Posted won?"

"Hardly worked up a sweat doing it, either," said the Hill Bluffer. "Just like the Pick-and-Shovel Shorty, a couple of years later. Pick-and-Shovel, he took on Bone Breaker, the lowland outlaw chief—of course, Bone Breaker being a lowlander, they two tangled with swords and shields and that sort of modern junk."

Mal clung to the straps supporting the saddle on which he rode below the Hill Bluffer's massive, swaying shoulders.

"Hey!" said the Hill Bluffer, after a long moment of silence. "You go to sleep up there, or something?"

"Asleep?" Mal laughed, a little hollowly. "No. Just thinking. Just wondering where a couple of fighters like this Half-Pint and Pick-and-Shovel could have come from back on our Shorty worlds."

"Never knew them, did you?" asked the Bluffer. "I've noticed that. Most of you Shorties don't seem to know much about each other."

"What did they look like?" Mal asked.

"Well . . . you know," said the Bluffer. "Like Shorties. All you Shorties look alike, anyway. Little, squeaky-voiced characters. Like you—only, maybe not quite so skinny."

"Skinny?" Mal had spent the last year of high school valiantly lifting weights and had finally built up his five-foot-eleven frame from a hundred and forty-eight to a hundred and seventy pounds. Not that this made him any mass of muscle—particularly compared to a nearly half-ton of Dilbian. Only, he had been rather proud of the fact that he had left skinniness behind him. Now, what he was hearing was incredible! What kind of supermen had the computer found on these two previous occasions—humans who could outwrestle a Dilbian or best one of the huge native aliens with sword and shield?

On second thought, it just wasn't possible there could be two such men, even if they had been supermen, by human standards. There had to have been some kind of a gimmick in each case that had let the humans win. Maybe, a concealed weapon of some kind—a tiny tranquilizer gun, or some such.

But Ambassador Guy had been adamant about refusing to send Mal out with any such equipment.

"Absolutely against the Treaty. Absolutely!" the little ambassador had said.

Mal snorted to himself. If anyone, Dilbian or human, was under the impression that *he* was going to get into any kind of physical fight with any Dilbian— even the oldest, weakest, most midget Dilbian on the planet—they had better think again. How he had come to be selected for this job, anyway . . .

"Well, here we are—Clan Water Gap Territory!" announced the Hill Bluffer cheerfully, slowing his pace.

Mal straightened up in the saddle and looked around him. They had finally left the narrow mountain trail that had kept his heart in his mouth most of the trip. Now they had emerged into a green, bowl-shaped valley, with a cluster of log huts at its lowest point and the silver thread of a narrow river spilling into it from the valley's far end, to wind down into a lake by the huts.

But he had little time to examine the further scene in detail. Just before them, and obviously waiting in a little grassy hollow by an egg-shaped granite boulder, were four large Dilbians and one small one.

Correction—Mal squinted against the afternoon sun. Waiting by the stone were two large and one small male Dilbians, all with the graying fur of age, and one unusually tall and black-furred Dilbian female. The Hill Bluffer snorted appreciatively at the female as he carried Mal up to confront the four.

"Grown even a bit more yet, since I last saw you, Gentle Maiden," said the native postman, agreeably. "Done a pretty good job of it, too. Here, meet the Law-Twister Shorty."

"I don't want to meet him!" snapped Gentle Maiden. "And you can turn around and take him right back where you got him. He's not welcome in Clan Water Gap Territory; and I've got the Clan Grandfather here to tell him so!"

Mal's hopes suddenly took an upturn.

"Oh?" he said. "Not welcome? That's too bad. I guess there's nothing left but to go back. Bluffer—"

"Hold on, Law-Twister!" growled the Bluffer. "Don't let Gentle here fool you." He glared at the three male Dilbians. "What Grandfather? I see three grandpas— Grandpa Tricky, Grandpa Forty Winks and—" he fastened his gaze on the smallest of the elderly males, "old One Punch, here. But none of them are Grandfathers, last I heard."

"What of it?" demanded Gentle Maiden. "Next Clan meeting, the Clan's going to choose a Grandfather. One of these grandpas is going to be the one chosen. So with all three of them here, I've got the next official Grandfather of Clan Water Gap here, too— even if he doesn't know it himself, yet!"

"Hor!" The Bluffer exploded into snorts of laughter. "Pretty sneaky, Gentle, but it won't work! A Grandfather's no good until he's *named* a Grandfather. Why, if you could do things that way, we'd have little kids being put up to give Grandfather rulings. And if it came to that, where'd the point be in having a man live long enough to get wise and trusted enough to be named a Grandfather?"

He shook his head.

"No, no," he said. "You've got no real Grandfather here, and so there's nobody can tell an honest little Shorty like the Law-Twister to turn about and light out from Clan Territory."

"Told y'so, Gentle," said the shortest grandpa in a rusty voice. "Said it wouldn't work."

"You!" cried Gentle Maiden, wheeling on him. "A fine grandpa you are, One Punch—let alone the fact you're my own real, personal grandpa! You don't have to be a Grandfather! You could just tell this Shorty and this long-legged postman on your own— tell them to get out while they were still in one piece! You would have, once!"

"Well, once, maybe," said the short Dilbian, rustily and sadly. Now that Mal had a closer look at him, he saw that this particular oldster—the one the Hill Bluffer had called One Punch—bore more than a few signs of having led an active life. A number of old scars seamed his fur; one ear was only half there and the other was badly tattered. Also, his left leg was

crooked as if it had been broken and badly set at one
time.

"I don't see why you can't *still* do it—for your
granddaughter's sake!" said Gentle Maiden sharply.
Mal winced. Gentle Maiden might be good looking
by Dilbian standards—the Hill Bluffer's comments a
moment ago seemed to indicate that—but whatever
else she was, she was plainly not very gentle, at least,
in any ordinary sense of the word.

"Why, Granddaughter," creaked One Punch mildly,
"like I've told you and everyone else, now that I'm
older I've seen the foolishness of all those little touches
of temper I used to have when I was young. They
never really proved anything—except how much wiser
those big men were who used to kind of avoid tangling with me. That's what comes with age, Granddaughter. Wisdom. You never hear nowdays of One
Man getting into hassles, now that he's put a few
years on him—or of More Jam, down there in the
lowlands, talking about defending his wrestling cham-
pionship anymore."

"Hold on! Wait a minute, One Punch," rumbled
the Hill Bluffer. "You know and I know that even if
One Man and More Jam do go around *saying* they're
old and feeble nowdays, no one in his right mind is
going to take either one of them at their word and
risk finding out if it is true."

"Think so if you like, Postman," said One Punch,
shaking his head mournfully. "Believe that if you
want to. But when you're my age, you'll know it's
just wisdom, plain, pure wisdom, makes men like
them and me so peaceful. Besides, Gentle," he went
on, turning again to his granddaughter, "you've got a
fine young champion in Iron Bender—"

"Iron Bender!" exploded Gentle Maiden. "That
lump! That obstinate, leatherheaded strap-cutter!
That—"

"Come to think of it, Gentle," interrupted the Hill
Bluffer, "how come Iron Bender isn't here? I'd have

thought you'd have brought him along instead of
these imitation Grandfathers—"

"There, now," sighed One Punch, staring off at the
mountains beyond the other side of the valley. "That
bit about imitations— That's just the sort of remark I
might've taken a bit of offense at, back in the days
before I developed wisdom. But does it trouble me
nowdays?"

"No offense meant, One Punch," said the Bluffer.
"You know I didn't meant that."

"None taken. You see, Granddaughter?" said One
Punch. "The postman here never meant a bit of offense; and in the old days I wouldn't have seen it
until it was too late."

"Oh, you make me sick!" blazed Gentle Maiden.
"You all make me sick. Iron Bender makes me sick,
saying he won't have anything against this Law-
Twister Shorty until the Law-Twister tries twisting
the Clan law that says those three poor little orphans
belong to me now!" She glared at the Bluffer and
Mal. "Iron Bender said the Shorty can come find
him, any time he really wanted to, down at the harness shop!"

"He'll be right down," promised the Bluffer.

"Hey—" began Mal. But nobody was paying any
attention to him.

"Now, Granddaughter," One Punch was saying, reprovingly. "The Bender didn't exactly ask you to
name him your protector, you know."

"What difference does that make?" snapped Gentle
Maiden. "I had to pick the toughest man in the Clan
to protect me—that's just common sense; even if he
is stubborn as an I-don't-know-what and thick-headed
as a log wall! I know my rights. He's got to defend
me; and there—" she wheeled and pointed to the
large boulder lying on the grass, "—there's the stone
of Mighty Grappler, and here's all three of you, one
of who's got to be a Grandfather by next Clan
meeting—and you mean to tell me none of you'll

even say a word to help me turn this postman and this Shorty around and get them out of here?"

The three elderly Dilbian males looked back at her without speaking.

"All right!" roared Gentle Maiden, stamping about to turn her back on all of them. "You'll be sorry! All of you!"

With that, she marched off down the slope of the valley toward the village of log houses.

"Well," said the individual whom the Hill Bluffer had called Grandpa Tricky, "guess that's that, until she thinks up something more. I might as well be ambling back down to the house, myself. How about you, Forty Winks?"

"Guess I might as well, too," said Forty Winks.

They went off after Gentle Maiden, leaving Mal—still on the Hill Bluffer's back—staring down at One Punch, from just behind the Bluffer's reddish-furred right ear.

"What," asked Mal, "has the stone of what's-his-name got to do with it?"

"The stone of Mighty Grappler?" asked One Punch. "You mean you don't know about that stone, over there?"

"Law-Twister here's just a Shorty," said the Bluffer, apologetically. "You know how Shorties are—tough, but pretty ignorant."

"Some *say* they're tough," said One Punch, squinting up at Mal, speculatively.

"Now, wait a minute, One Punch!" the Hill Bluffer's bass voice dropped ominously an additional half-octave. "Maybe there's something we ought to get straight right now! This isn't just any plain private citizen you're talking to, it's the official postman speaking. And *I* say Shorties're tough. *I* say I was there when the Half-Pint Posted took the Streamside Terror; and also when Pick-and-Shovel wiped up Bone Breaker in a sword-and-shield duel. Now, no disrespect, but if you're questioning the official word of a government mail carrier—"

"Now, Bluffer," said One Punch, "I never doubted you personally for a minute. It's just everybody knows the Terror and Bone Breaker weren't either of them pushovers. But you know I'm not the biggest man around, by a long shot; and now and then during my time I can remember laying out some pretty good-sized scrappers, myself—when my temper got away from me, that is. So I know from personal experience not every man's as tough as the next—and why shouldn't that work for Shorties as well as real men? Maybe those two you carried before were tough; but how can anybody tell about this Shorty? No offense, up there, Law-Twister, by the way. Just using a bit of my wisdom and asking."

Mal opened his mouth and shut it again.

"Well?" growled the Bluffer underneath him. "Speak up, Law-Twister." Suddenly, there was a dangerous feeling of tension in the air. Mal swallowed. How, he thought, would a Dilbian answer a question like that?

Any way but with a straight answer, came back the reply from the hypnotrained section of his mind.

"Well—er," said Mal, "how can I tell you how tough I am? I mean, what's tough by the standards of you real men? As far as we Shorties go, it might be one thing. For you real men, it might be something else completely. It's too bad I didn't ever know this Half-Pint Posted, or Pick-and-Shovel, or else I could kind of measure myself by them for you. But I never heard of them until now."

"But you think they just *might* be tougher than you, though—the Half-Pint and Pick-and-Shovel?" demanded One Punch.

"Oh, sure," said Mal. "They could both be ten times as tough as I am. And then, again— Well, not for me to say."

There was a moment's silence from both the Dilbians, then the Bluffer broke it with a snort of admiration.

"Hor!" he chortled admiringly to One Punch. "I guess you can see now how the Law-Twister here got his name. Slippery? Slippery's not the word for this Shorty."

But One Punch shook his head.

"Slippery's one thing," he said. "But law-twisting's another. Here he says he doesn't even know about the stone of Mighty Grappler. How's he going to go about twisting laws if he doesn't know about the laws in the first place?"

"You could tell me about the stone," suggested Mal.

"Mighty Grappler put it there, Law-Twister," said the Bluffer. "Set it up to keep peace in Clan Water Gap."

"Better let me tell him, Postman," interrupted One Punch. "After all, he ought to get it straight from a born Water Gapper. Look at the stone there, Law-Twister. You see those two ends of iron sticking out of it?"

Mal looked. Sure enough, there were two lengths of rusty metal protruding from opposite sides of the boulder, which was about three feet in width in the middle.

"I see them," he answered.

"Mighty Grappler was just maybe the biggest and strongest real man who ever lived—"

The Hill Bluffer coughed.

"One Man, now . . ." he murmured.

"I'm not denying One Man's something like a couple of big men in one skin, Postman," said One Punch. "But the stories about Mighty Grappler are hard to beat. He was a stonemason, Law-Twister; and he founded Clan Water Gap, with himself, his relatives, and his descendants. Now, as long as he was alive, there was no trouble. He was Clan Water Gap's first Grandfather, and even when he was a hundred and ten nobody wanted to argue with him. But he worried about keeping things orderly after he was gone—"

"Fell off a cliff at a hundred and fourteen," put in the Bluffer. "Broke his neck. Otherwise, no telling how long he'd have lived."

"Excuse me, Postman," said One Punch. "But I'm telling this, not you. The point is, Law-Twister, he was worried like I say about keeping the Clan orderly. So he took a stone he was working on one day—that stone there, that no one but him could come near lifting—and hammered an iron rod through it to make a handhold on each side, like you see. Then he picked the stone up, carried it here, and set it down; and he made a law. The rules he'd made earlier for Clan Water Gappers were to stand as laws, themselves—as long as that stone stayed where it was. But if anyone ever came along who could pick it up all by himself and carry it as much as ten steps, then that was a sign it was time the laws should change."

Mal stared at the boulder. His hypnotraining had informed him that while Dilbians would go to any lengths to twist the truth to their own advantage, the one thing they would not stand for, in themselves or others, was an out-and-out lie. Accordingly, One Punch would probably be telling the truth about this Mighty Grappler ancestor of his. On the other hand, a chunk of granite that size must weigh at least a ton—maybe a ton and a half. Not even an outsize Dilbian could be imagined carrying something like that for ten paces. There were natural flesh-and-blood limits, even for these giant natives—or were there?

"Did anybody ever try lifting it, after that?" Mal asked.

"Hor!" snorted the Bluffer.

"Now, Law-Twister," said One Punch, almost reproachfully, "any Clan Water Gapper's got too much sense to make a fool of himself trying to do something only the Mighty Grappler had a chance of doing.

That stone's never been touched from that day to this—and that's the way it should be."

"I suppose so," said Mal.

The Bluffer snorted again, in surprise. One Punch stared.

"You giving up—just like that, Law-Twister?" demanded the Bluffer.

"What? I don't understand," said Mal, confused. "We were just talking about the stone—"

"But you said you supposed that's the way it should be," said the Bluffer, outraged. "The stone there, and the laws just the way Mighty Grappler laid them down. What kind of a law-twister are you, anyway?"

"But . . ." Mal was still confused. "What's the Mighty Grappler and his stone got to do with my getting back these three Shorties that Gentle Maiden says she adopted?"

"Why, that's one of Mighty Grappler's laws—one of the ones he made and backed up with the stone!" said One Punch. "It was Mighty Grappler said that any orphans running around loose could be adopted by any single woman of the Clan, who could then name herself a protector to take care of them and her! Now, that's Clan law."

"But—" began Mal again. He had not expected to have to start arguing his case this soon. But it seemed there was no choice. "It's Clan law if you say so; and I don't have any quarrel with it. But these people Gentle Maiden's adopted aren't orphans. They're Shorties. That's why she's going to have to let them go."

"So that's the way you twist it," said One Punch, almost in a tone of satisfaction. "Figured you'd come up with something like that. So, you say they're not orphans?"

"Of course, that's what I say!" said Mal.

"Figured as much. Naturally, Gentle says they are."

"Well, I'll just have to make her understand—"

"Not her," interrupted the Bluffer.

"Naturally not her," said One Punch. "if *she* says they're orphans, then its her protector you've got to straighten things out with. Gentle says 'orphans,' so Iron Bender's going to be saying 'orphans,' too. You and Iron Bender got to get together."

"And none of that sissy lowland stuff with swords and shields," put in the Hill Bluffer. "Just honest, man-to-man, teeth, claws, and muscle. You don't have to worry about Iron Bender going in for any of that modern stuff, Law-Twister."

"Oh " said Mal, staring.

"Thought I'd tell you right now," said the Bluffer. "Ease your mind, in case you were wondering."

"I wasn't, actually," said Mal, numbly, still trying to make his mind believe what his ears seemed to be hearing.

"Well," said One Punch, "how about it, Postman? Law-Twister? Shall we get on down to the harness shop and you and Iron Bender can set up the details? Quite a few folks been dropping in the last few hours to see the two of you tangle. Don't think any of them ever saw a Shorty in action before. Know I never did myself. Should be real interesting."

He and the Hill Bluffer had already turned and begun to stroll down toward the village.

"Interesting's not the word for it," the Bluffer responded. "Seen it twice, myself, and I can tell you it's a sight to behold. . . ."

He continued along, chatting cheerfully while Mal rode along helplessly on Dilbian-back, his head spinning. The log buildings got closer and closer.

"Wait—" Mal said desperately, as they entered the street running down the center of the cluster of log structures. The Bluffer and One Punch both stopped. One Punch turned to gaze up at him.

"Wait?" One Punch said. "What for?"

"I—I can't," stammered Mal, frantically searching for an excuse, and going on talking meanwhile with the first words that came to his lips. "That is, I've got my own laws to think of. Shorty laws. Responsibilities. I can't just go representing these other Shorty orphans just like that. I have to be . . . uh, briefed."

"Briefed?" The Bluffer's tongue struggled with pronunciation of the human word Mal had used.

"Yes—uh, that means I have to be given authority—like Gentle Maiden had to choose Iron Bender as her protector," said Mal. "These Shorty orphans have to agree to choose me as their law-twister. It's one of the Shorty freedoms—freedom to not be defended by a law-twister without your consent. With so much at stake here—I mean, not just what might happen to me, or Iron Bender, but what might happen to Clan Water Gap laws or Shorty laws—I need to consult with my clients, I mean these other Shorties I'm working for, before I enter into any—er—discussion with Gentle Maiden's protector."

Mal stopped speaking and waited, his heart hammering away. There was a moment of deep silence from both the Bluffer and One Punch. Then One Punch spoke to the taller Dilbian.

"Have to admit you're right, Postman," One Punch said, admiringly. "He sure can twist. You understand all that he was talking about, there?"

"Why, of course," said the Bluffer. "After all, I've had a lot to do with these Shorties. He was saying that this isn't just any little old hole-and-corner tangle between him and Iron Bender—this is a high-class hassle to decide the law; and it's got to be done right. No offense, One Punch, but you, having been in the habit of getting right down to business on the spur of the moment all those years, might not have stopped to think just how important it is not to rush matters in an important case like this."

"No offense taken, Postman," said One Punch, easily. "Though I must say maybe it's lucky you didn't know me in my younger, less full-of-wisdom days. Because it seems to me we were *both* maybe about to rush the Law-Twister a mite."

"Well, now," said the Bluffer. "Leaving aside that business of my luck and all that about not knowing you when you were younger, I guess I have to admit perhaps I *was* a little on the rushing side, myself. Anyway, Law-Twister's straightened us both out. So, what's the next thing you want to do, Law-Twister?"

"Well . . ." said Mal. He was still thinking desperately. "This being a matter that concerns the laws governing the whole Water Gap Clan, as well as Shorty laws and the stone of Mighty Grappler, we probably ought to get everyone together. I mean we ought to talk it over. It might well turn out to be this is something that ought to be settled not by a fight but in—"

Mal had not expected the Dilbians to have a word for it; but he was wrong. His hypnotraining threw the proper Dilbian sounds up for his tongue to utter.

"—court," he wound up.

"Court? Can't have a court, Law-Twister," said One Punch. He and the Hill Bluffer had stopped in the middle of the village street when Mal started talking. Now a small crowd of the local Dilbians was gathering around them, listening to the conversation.

"Thought you knew that, Law-Twister," put in the Bluffer, reprovingly. "Can't have a Clan court without a Grandfather to decide things."

"Too bad, in a way," said One Punch with a sigh. "We'd all like to see a real Law-Twister Shorty at work in a real court situation, twisting and slickering around from one argument to the next. But, just as the Bluffer says, Twister, we've got no Grandfather yet. Won't have until the next Clan meeting."

"When's that?" asked Mal, hastily.

"Couple of weeks," said One Punch. "Be glad to wait around a couple of weeks far as all of us here're concerned; but those Shorty orphans of Gentle Maiden's are getting pretty hungry and even a mite thirsty. Seems they won't eat anything she gives them; and they even don't seem to like to drink the well water,

much. Gentle figures they won't settle down until
they get it straight that they're adopted and not going
home again. So she wants you and Iron Bender to
settle it right now—and, of course, since she's a member of the Clan, the Clan backs her up on that."

"Won't eat or drink? Where are they?" asked Mal.

"At Gentle's house," said One Punch. "She's got
them locked up there so they can't run back to that
box they came down in and fly away back into the
sky. Real motherly instincts in that girl, if I do say so
myself who's her real grandpa. That, and looks, too.
Can't understand why no young buck's snapped her
up before this—"

"You understand, all right, One Punch," interrupted
an incredibly deep bass voice; and there shouldered
through the crowd a darkly brown-haired Dilbian,
taller than any of the crowd around him. The speaker
was shorter by half a head than the Hill Bluffer—the
postman seemed to have the advantage in height on
every other native Mal had seen—but this newcomer
towered over everyone else and he was a walking
mass of muscle, easily outweighing the Bluffer.

"You understand, all right," he repeated, stopping
before the Bluffer and Mal. "Folks'd laugh their heads
off at any man who'd offer to take a girl as tough-
minded as Gentle, to wife—that is, unless he had to.
Then, maybe he'd find it was worth it. But do it on
his own? Pride's pride. . . . Hello there, Postman. This
the Law-Twister Shorty?"

"It's him," said the Bluffer.

"Why he's no bigger'n those other little Shorties,"
said the deep-voiced Dilbian, peering over the Bluffer's shoulder at Mal.

"You go thinking size is all there is to a Shorty,
you're going to be surprised," said the Bluffer. "Along
with the Streamside Terror and Bone Breaker, as I
recollect. Twister, this here's Gentle's protector and
the Clan Water Gap harnessmaker, Iron Bender."

"Uh—pleased to meet you," said Mal.

"Pleased to meet you, Law-Twister," rumbled Iron Bender. "That is, I'm pleased now; and I hope I go on being pleased. I'm a plain, simple man, Law-Twister. A good day's work, a good night's sleep, four good meals a day, and I'm satisfied. You wouldn't find me mixed up in fancy doings like this by choice. I'd have nothing to do with this if Gentle hadn't named me her protector. But right's right. She did; and I am, like it or not."

"I know how you feel," said Mal, hastily. "I was actually going someplace else when the Shorties here had me come see about this situation. I hadn't planned on it at all."

"Well, well," said Iron Bender, deeply, "you, too, eh?"

He sighed heavily.

"That's the way things go, nowdays, though," he said. "A plain simple man can't hardly do a day's work in peace without some maiden or someone coming to him for protection. So they got you, too, eh? Well, well—life's life, and a man can't do much about it. You're not a bad little Shorty at all. I'm going to be real sorry to tear your head off—which of course I'm going to do, since I figure I probably could have done the same to Bone Breaker or the Streamside Terror, if it'd ever happened to come to that. Not that I'm a boastful man; but true's true."

He sighed again.

"So," he said, flexing his huge arms, "if you'll just light down from your perch on the postman, there, I'll get to it. I've got a long day's work back at the harness shop, anyway; and daylight's daylight—"

"But fair's fair," broke in Mal, hastily. The Iron Bender lowered his massive brown-furred hands, looking puzzled.

"Fair's fair?" he echoed.

"You heard him, harnessmaker!" snapped the Bluffer, bristling. "No offense, but there's more to something like this than punching holes in leather.

Nothing I'd like to see more than for you to try—just try—to tear the head off a Shorty like Law-Twister here, since I've seen what a Shorty can do when he really gets his dander up. But like the Twister himself pointed out, this is not just a happy hassle—this is serious business involving Clan laws and Shorty laws and lots of other things. We were just discussing it when you came up. Law-Twister was saying maybe something like this should be held up until the next Clan meeting when you elect a Grandfather, so's it could be decided by a legal Clan Water Gap court in full session."

"Court—" Iron Bender was beginning when he was interrupted.

"We will *not* wait for any court to settle who gets my orphans!" cried a new voice and the black-furred form of Gentle Maiden shoved through the crowd to join them. "When there's no Clan Grandfather to rule, the Clan goes by law and custom. Law and custom says my protector's got to take care of me, and I've got to take care of the little ones I adopted. And I'm not letting them suffer for two weeks before they realize they're settling down with me. The law says I don't have to and no man's going to make me try—"

"Now, hold on there just a minute, Gentle," rumbled Iron Bender. "Guess maybe I'm the one man in this Clan, or between here and Humrog Peak for that matter, who could make you try and do something whether you wanted it or not, if he wanted to. Not that I'm saying I'm going to, now. But you just remember that while I'm your named protector, it doesn't mean I'm going to let you order me around like you do other folk—any more than I ever did."

He turned back to the Bluffer, Mal, and One Punch.

"Right's right," he said. "Now, what's all this about a court?"

Neither the Bluffer nor One Punch answered immediately—and, abruptly, Mal realized it was up to him to do the explaining.

"Well, as I was pointing out to the postman and One Punch," he began, rapidly, "there's a lot at stake, here. I mean, we Shorties have laws, too; and one of them is that you don't have to be represented by a law-twister not your choice. I haven't talked to these Shorties you and Gentle claim are orphans, so I don't have their word on going ahead with anything on their behalf. I can't do anything important until I have that word of theirs. What if we—er—tangled, and it turned out they didn't mean to name me to do anything for them, after all? Here you, a regular named protector of a maiden according to your Clan laws, as laid down by Mighty Grappler, would have been hassling with someone who didn't have a shred of right to fight you. And here, too, I'd have been tangling without a shred of lawful reason for it, to back me up. What we need to do is study the situation. I need to talk to the Shorties you say are orphans—"

"No!" cried Gentle Maiden. "He's not to come *near* my little orphans and get them all upset, even more than they are now—"

"Hold on, now, Granddaughter," interposed One Punch. "We all can see how the Twister here's twisting and slipping around like the clever little Shorty he is, trying to get things his way. But he's got a point there when he talks about Clan Water Gap putting up a named protector, and then that protector turns out to have gotten into a hassle with someone with no authority at all. Why they'd be laughing at our Clan all up and down the mountains. Worse yet, what if that protector should lose—"

"*Lose?*" snorted Iron Bender, with all the geniality of a grizzly abruptly wakened from his long winter's nap.

"That's right, harnessmaker. *Lose!*" snarled the Hill Bluffer. "Guess there just might be a real man not too far away from you at this moment who's pretty sure you *would* lose—and handily!"

Suddenly, the two of them were standing nose to nose. Mal became abruptly aware that he was still seated in the saddle arrangement on the Bluffer's back and that, in case of trouble between the two big Dilbians, it would not be easy for him to get down in a hurry.

"I'll tell you what, Postman," Iron Bender was growling. "Why don't you and I just step out beyond the houses, here, where there's a little more open space—"

"Stop it!" snapped Gentle Maiden. "Stop it right now, Iron Bender! You've got no right to go fighting anybody for your own private pleasure when you're still my protector. What if something happened, and you weren't able to protect me and mine the way you should after that?"

"Maiden's right," said One Punch, sharply. "It's Clan honor and decency at stake here; not just your own feelings, Blender. Now, as I was saying, Law-Twister here's been doing some fine talking and twisting, and he's come up with a real point. It's as much a matter to us if he's a real Shorty-type protector to those orphans Maiden adopted, as it is to him and other Shorties—"

His voice became mild. He turned to the crowd and spread his hands, modestly.

"Of course, I'm no real Grandfather," he said. "Some might think I wouldn't stand a chance to be the one you'll pick at that next Clan meeting. Of course, some might think I would, too—but it's hardly for me to say. Only, speaking as a man who *might* be named a Grandfather someday, I'd say Gentle Maiden really out to let Law-Twister check with those three orphans to see if they want him to talk or hassle, for them."

A bass-voiced murmur of agreement rose from the

surrounding crowd, which by this time had grown to a respectable size.

For the first time since he had said farewell to Ambassador Joshua Guy, Mal felt his spirits begin to rise. For the first time, he seemed to be getting some control over the events which had been hurrying him along like a chip swirling downstream in the current of a fast river. Maybe, if he had a little luck, now—

"Duty's duty, I guess," rumbled Iron Bender at just this moment. "All right then, Law-Twister—now, stop your arguing. Gentle, it's no use—you can see your fellow Shorties. They're at Gentle's place, last but one on the left-hand side of the street, here."

"Show you the way, myself, Postman," said One Punch.

The Clan elder led off, limping, and the crowd broke up as the Hill Bluffer followed him. Iron Bender went off in the opposite direction, but Gentle Maiden tagged along with the postman, Mal, and her grandfather, muttering to herself.

"Take things kind of hard, don't you, Gentle?" said the Hill Bluffer to her, affably. "Don't blame old Iron Bender. Man can't expect to win every time."

"Why not?" demanded Gentle. "I do! He's just so cautious, and slow, he makes me sick! Why can't he be like One Punch, here, when *he* was young? Hit first and think afterward—particularly when I ask him to? Then Bender could go around being slow and careful about his own business if he wanted; in fact, I'd be all for him being like that, on his own time. A girl needs a man she can respect; particularly when there's no other man around that's much more than half-size to him!"

"Tell him so," suggested the Bluffer, strolling along, his long legs making a single stride to each two of Gentle and One Punch.

"Certainly not! It'd look like I was giving in to him!" said Gentle. "It may be all right for any old ordinary girl to go chasing a man, but not me. Folks know me better than that. They'd laugh their heads off if I suddenly started going all soft on Bender. And besides—"

"Here we are, Postman—Law-Twister," interrupted One Punch, stopping by the heavy wooden door of a good-sized log building. "This is Gentle's place. The orphans are inside."

"Don't you go letting them out, now!" snapped Gentle, as Mal, relieved to be out of the saddle after this much time in it, began sliding down the Bluffer's broad back toward the ground.

"Don't worry, Granddaughter," said One Punch, as Mal's boots touched the earth. "Postman and I'll wait right outside the door here with you. If one of them tries to duck out, we'll catch him or her for you."

"They keep wanting to go back to their flying box," said Gentle. "And I know the minute one of them gets inside it, he'll be into the air and off like a flash. I haven't gone to all this trouble to lose any of them, now. So, don't you try anything while you're inside there, Law-Twister!"

Mal went up the three wooden steps to the rough plank door and lifted a latch that was, from the standpoint of a human-sized individual, like a heavy bar locking the door shut. The door yawned open before him, and he stepped through into dimness. The door swung shut behind him, and he heard the latch being relocked.

"Holler when you want out, Law-Twister!" One Punch's voice boomed through the closed door. Mal looked around him.

He was in what was obviously a Dilbian home. A few pieces of heavy, oversize furniture supplemented a long plank table before an open fireplace, in which, however, no fire was now burning. Two more doors, also latched, were of rooms beyond this one.

He crossed the room and tried the right-hand door at random. It gave him a view of an empty, kitchenlike room with what looked like a side of beef hanging from a hook in a far corner. A chopping block and a wash trough of hollowed-out stone furnished the rest of the room.

Mal backed out, closed the door, and tried the one on his left. It opened easily, but the entrance to the room beyond was barred by a rough fence of planks some eight feet high, with sharp chips of stone hammered into the tops. Through the gap in the planks, Mal looked into what seemed a large Dilbian bed chamber, which had been converted into human living quarters by the simple expedient of ripping out three cabin sections from a shuttle boat and setting them up like so many large tin boxes on the floor under the lofty, log-beamed roof.

At the sound of the opening of the door, other doors opened in the transplanted cabin sections. As Mal watched, three middle-aged people—one woman and two men—emerged each from his own cabin and stopped short to stare through the gaps in the plank fence at him.

"Oh, no!" said one of the men, a skinny, balding character with a torn shirt collar. "A kid!"

"Kid?" echoed Mal, grimly. He had been prepared to feel sorry for the three captives of Gentle Maiden, but this kind of reception did not make it easy. "How adult do you have to be to wrestle a Dilbian?"

"Wrestle . . . !" It was the woman. She stared at him. "Oh, it surely won't come to that. Will it? You ought to be able to find a way around it. Didn't they pick you because you'd be able to understand these natives?"

Mal looked at her narrowly.

"How would you have any idea of how I was picked?" he asked.

"We just assumed they'd send someone to help us who understood these natives," she said.

Mal's conscience pricked him.

"I'm sorry—er—Mrs. . . . ." he began.

"Ora Page," she answered. "This—" she indicated

the thin man, "is Harvey Anok, and—" she nodded at
the other, "Zora Rice." She had a soft, rather gentle
face, in contrast to the sharp, almost suspicious face
of the Harvey Anok and the rather hard features of
Zora Rice; but like both of the others, she had a
tanned outdoors sort of look.

"Mrs. Page," Mal said. "I'm sorry, but the only
thing I seem to be able to do for you is get myself
killed by the local harnessmaker. But I do have an
idea. Where's this shuttle boat you came down in?"

"Right behind this building we're in," said Harvey,
"in a meadow about a hundred yards back. What
about it?"

"Good," said Mal. "I'm going to try to make a
break for it. Now, if you can just tell me how to take
off in it, and land, I think I can fly it. I'll make some
excuse to get inside it and get into the air. Then I'll
fly back to the ambassador who sent me out here,
and tell him I can't do anything. He'll have to send in
force, if necessary, to get you out of this."

The three stared back at him without speaking.

"Well?" demanded Mal. "What about it? If I get
killed by that harnessmaker it's not going to do you
any good. Gentle Maiden may decide to take you
away and hide you someplace in the mountains, and
no rescue team will ever find you. What're you waiting for? Tell me how to fly that shuttle boat!"

The three of them looked at each other uncomfortably and then back at Mal. Harvey shook his head.

"No," he said. "I don't think we ought to do that.
There's a treaty—"

"The Human-Hemnoid Treaty on this planet?"
Mal asked. "But I just told you, that Dilbian harnessmaker may kill me. You might be killed, too. Isn't it
more important to save lives than worry about a
treaty at a time like this?"

"You don't understand," said Harvey. "One of the
things that Treaty particularly rules out is anthropologists. If we're found here—"

"But I thought you were tourists?" Mal said.

"We are. All of us were on vacation on a spaceliner tour. It just happens we three are anthropologists, too—"

"That's why we were tempted to drop in here in the first place," put in Zora Rice.

"But that Treaty's a lot more important than you think," Harvey said. "We can't risk damaging it."

"Why didn't you think of that before you came here?" Mal growled.

"You can find a way out for all of us without calling for armed force and getting us all in trouble. I know you can," said Ora Page. "We trust you. Won't you try?"

Mal stared back at them all, scowling. There was something funny about all this. Prisoners who hadn't worried about a Human-Hemnoid Treaty on their way to Dilbia, but who were willing to risk themselves to protect it now that they were here. A Dilbian female who wanted to adopt three full-grown humans. Why, in the name of all that was sensible? A village harnessmaker ready to tear him apart, and a human ambassador who had sent him blithely out to face that same harnessmaker with neither advice nor protection.

"All right," said Mal, grimly. "I'll talk to you again later—with luck."

He stepped back and swung closed the heavy door to the room in which they were fenced. Going to the entrance of the building, he shouted to One Punch, and the door before him was opened from the outside. Gentle Maiden shouldered suspiciously past him into the house as he emerged.

"Well, how about it, Law-Twister?" asked One Punch, as the door closed behind Gentle Maiden. "Those other Shorties say it was all right for you to talk and hassle for them?"

"Well, yes ..." said Mal. He gazed narrowly up into the large furry faces of One Punch and the Bluffer,

trying to read their expressions. But outside of the
fact that they both looked genial, he could discover
nothing. The alien visages held their secrets well
from human eyes.

"They agreed, all right," said Mal, slowly. "But
what they had to say to me sort of got me thinking.
Maybe you can tell me—just why is it Clan Water
Gap can't hold its meeting right away instead of two
weeks from now? Hold a meeting right now and the
Clan could have an elected Grandfather before the
afternoon's half over. Then there'd be time to hold a
regular Clan court, for example, between the election
and sunset; and this whole matter of the orphan
Shorties could be handled more in regular fashion."

"Wondered that, did you, Law-Twister?" said One
Punch. "It just crossed my mind earlier you might
wonder about it. No real reason why the Clan meeting couldn't be held right away, I guess. Only, who's
going to suggest it?"

"Suggest it?" Mal said.

"Why, sure," said One Punch. "Ordinarily, when a
Clan has a Grandfather it'd be up to the Grandfather
to suggest it. But Clan Water Gap doesn't have a
Grandfather right now, as you know."

"Isn't there anyone else to suggest things like that
if a Grandfather isn't available?" asked Mal.

"Well, yes." One Punch gazed thoughtfully away
from Mal, down the village street. "If there's no Grandfather around, it'd be pretty much up to one of the
grandpas to suggest it. Only—of course I can't speak
for old Forty Winks or anyone else—but I wouldn't
want to be the one to do it, myself. Might sound like I
thought I had a better chance of being elected Grandfather now, than I would two weeks from now."

"So," said Mal. "You won't suggest it, and if you
won't I can see how the others wouldn't, for the same
reason. Who else does that leave who might suggest
it?"

"Why, I don't know, Law-Twister," said One Punch,

gazing back at him. "Guess any strong-minded member of the Clan could speak up and propose it. Someone like Gentle Maiden, herself, for example. But you know Gentle Maiden isn't about to suggest anything like that when what she wants is for Iron Bender to try and take you apart as soon as possible."

"How about Iron Bender?" Mal asked.

"Now, he just might want to suggest something like that," said One Punch, "being as how he likes to do everything just right. But it might look like he was trying to get out of tangling with you—after all this talk by the Bluffer, here, about how tough Shorties are. So I don't expect Bender'd be likely to say anything about changing the meeting time."

Mal looked at the tall Dilbian who had brought him here.

"Bluffer," he said, "I wonder if you—"

"Look here, Law-Twister," said the Hill Bluffer severely. "I'm the government postman—to all the Clans and towns and folks from Wildwood Valley to Humrog Peak. A government man like myself can't go sticking his nose into local affairs."

"But you were ready to tangle with Iron Bender yourself, a little while ago—"

"That was personal and private. This is public. I don't blame you for not seeing the difference right off, Law-Twister, you being a Shorty and all," said the Bluffer, "but a government man has to know, and keep the two things separate."

He fell silent, looking at Mal. For a moment neither the Bluffer nor One Punch said anything; but Mal was left with the curious feeling that the conversation had not so much been ended, as left hanging in the air for him to pick up. He was beginning to get an understanding of how Dilbian minds worked. Because of their taboo against any outright lying, they were experts at pretending to say one thing while actually saying another. There was a strong notion in Mal's mind now that somehow the other two were simply waiting for him to ask the right question—as if he had a handful of keys and only the right one would unlock an answer with the information he wanted.

"Certainly is different from the old days, Postman," said One Punch, idly, turning to the Bluffer. "Wonder what Mighty Grappler would have said, seeing Shorties like the Law-Twister among us. He'd have said something, all right. Had an answer for everything, Mighty Grappler did."

An idea exploded into life in Mal's mind. Of course! That was it!

"Isn't there something in Mighty Grappler's laws," he asked, "that could arrange for a Clan meeting without someone suggesting it?"

One Punch looked back at him.

"Why, what do you know?" the oldster said. "Bluffer, Law-Twister here is something to make up stories about, all right. Imagine a Shorty guessing that Mighty Grappler had thought of something like that, when I'd almost forgotten it myself."

"Shorties are sneaky little characters, as I've said before," replied the Bluffer, gazing down at Mal with obvious pride. "Quick on the uptake, too."

"Then there is a way?" Mal asked.

"It just now comes back to me," said One Punch. "Mighty Grappler set up all his laws to protect the Clan members against themselves and each other and against strangers. But he did make one law to protect strangers on Clan territory. As I remember, any stranger having a need to appeal to the whole Clan for justice was supposed to stand beside Grappler's stone—the one we showed you on the way in—and put his hand on it, and make that appeal."

"Then what?" asked Mal. "The Clan would grant his appeal?"

"Well, not exactly," said One Punch. "But they'd be obliged to talk the matter over and decide things."

"Oh," said Mal. This was less than he had hoped

for, but still he had a strong feeling now that he was on the right track. "Well, let's go."

"Right," said the Bluffer. He and One Punch turned and strolled off up the street.

"Hey!" yelled Mal, trotting after them. The Bluffer turned around, picked him up, and stuffed him into the saddle on the postman's back.

"Sorry, Law-Twister. Forgot about those short legs of yours," the Bluffer said. Turning to stroll forward with One Punch again, he added to the oldster, "Makes you kind of wonder how they made out to start with, before they had flying boxes and things like that."

"Probably didn't do much," offered One Punch in explanation, "just lay in the sun and dug little burrows and things like that."

Mal opened his mouth and then closed it again on the first retort that had come to his lips.

"Where you off to with the Law-Twister now, One Punch?" asked a graying-haired Dilbian they passed, whom Mal was pretty sure was either Forty Winks or Grandpa Tricky.

"Law-Twister's going up to the stone of Mighty Grappler to make an appeal to the Clan," said One Punch.

"Well, now," said the other, "guess I'll mosey up there myself and have a look at that. Can't remember it ever happening before."

He fell in behind them, but halfway down the street fell out again to answer the question of several other bystanders who wanted to know what was going on. So it was that when Mal alighted from the Bluffer's back at the stone of Mighty Grappler, there was just he and the Bluffer and One Punch there, although a few figures could be seen beginning to stream out of the village toward the stone.

"Go ahead, Law-Twister," said One Punch, nodding at the stone. "Make that appeal of yours."

"Hadn't I better wait until the rest of the Clan gets here?"

"I suppose you could do that," said One Punch. "I was thinking you might just want to say your appeal and have it over with and sort of let me tell people about it. But you're right. Wait until folks get here. Give you a chance to kind of look over Mighty Grappler's stone, too, and put yourself in the kind of spirit to make a good appeal. . . . Guess you'll want to be remembering this word for word, to pass on down the line to the other clans, won't you, Postman?"

"You could say I've almost a duty to do that, One Punch," responded the Bluffer. "Lots more to being a government postman than some people think. . . ."

The two went on chatting, turning a little away from Mal and the stone to gaze down the slope at the Clan members on their way up from the village. Mal turned to gaze at the stone, itself. It was still inconceivable to him that even a Dilbian could lift and carry such a weight ten paces.

Certainly, it did not look as if anyone had ever moved the stone since it had been placed here. The two ends of the iron rod sticking out from opposite sides of it were red with rust, and the grass had grown up thickly around its base. That is, it had grown up thickly everywhere but just behind it, where it looked like a handful of grass might have been pulled up, recently. Bending down to look closer at the grass-free part of the stone, Mal caught sight of something dark. The edge of some indentation, almost something like the edge of a large hole in the stone itself—

"Law-Twister!" The voice of One Punch brought Mal abruptly upright. He saw that the vanguard of the Dilbians coming out of the village was almost upon them.

"How'd you like me to sort of pass the word what this is all about?" asked One Punch. "Then you could just make your appeal without trying to explain it?"

"Oh—fine," said Mal. He glanced back at the stone. For a moment he felt a great temptation to take hold

of the two rust-red iron handles and see if he actually
could lift it. But there were too many eyes on him
now.

The members of the Clan came up and sat down,
with their backs straight and furry legs stuck out
before them on the grass. The Bluffer, however, remained standing near Mal, as did One Punch. Among
the last to arrive was Gentle Maiden, who hurried up
to the very front of the crowd and snorted angrily at
Mal before sitting down.

"Got them all upset!" she said, triumphantly. "Knew
you would!"

Iron Bender had not put in an appearance.

"Members of Clan Water Gap," said One Punch,
when they were all settled on the grass and quiet,
"you all know what this Shorty, Law-Twister here,
dropped in on us to do. He wants to take back with
him the orphans Gentle Maiden adopted according
to Clan law, as laid down by Mighty Grappler. Naturally, Maiden doesn't want him to, and she's got her
protector, Iron Bender—"

He broke off, peering out over the crowd.

"Where is Iron Bender?" the oldster demanded.

"He says work's work," a voice answered from the
crowd. "Says to send somebody for him when you're
all ready to have someone's head torn off. Otherwise,
he'll be busy down in the harness shop."

Gentle Maiden snorted.

"Well, well. I guess we'll just have to go on without
him," said One Punch. "As I was saying, here's Iron
Bender all ready to do his duty; but as Law-Twister
sees it, it's not all that simple."

There was a buzz of low-toned, admiring comments
from the crowd. One Punch waited until the noise
died before going on.

"One thing Law-Twister wants to do is make an
appeal to the Clan, according to Mighty Grappler's
law, before he gets down to tangling with Iron
Bender," the oldster said. "So, without my bending

your ears any further, here's the Law-Twister himself, with tongue all oiled up and ready to talk you upside down, and roundabout— Go ahead, Law-Twister!"

Mal put his hand on the stone of Mighty Grappler. In fact, he leaned on the stone and it seemed to him it rocked a little bit, under his weight. It did not seem to him that One Punch's introductory speech had struck quite the serious note Mal himself might have liked. But now, in any case, it was up to him.

"Uh—members of Clan Water Gap," he said. "I've been disturbed by a lot of what I've learned here. For example, here you have something very important at stake—the right of a Clan Water Gap maiden to adopt Shorties as orphans. But the whole matter has to be settled by what's really an emergency measure—that is, my tangling with Iron Bender—just because Clan Water Gap hasn't elected a new Grandfather lately, and the meeting to elect one is a couple of weeks away—"

"And while it's not for me to say," interrupted the basso voice of the Hill Bluffer, "not being a Clan Water Gapper myself, and besides being a government postman who's strictly not concerned in any local affairs—I'd guess that's what a lot of folks are going to be asking me as I ply my route between here and Humrog Peak in the next few weeks. 'How come they didn't hold a regular trial to settle the matter, down there in Clan Water Gap?' they'll be asking. 'Because they didn't have a Grandfather,' I'll have to say. 'How come those Water Gappers are running around without a Grandfather?' they'll ask—"

"All right, Postman!" interrupted One Punch, in his turn. "I guess we can all figure what people are going to say. The point is, Law-Twister is still making his appeal. Go ahead, Law-Twister."

"Well ... I asked about the Clan holding their meeting to elect a Grandfather right away," put in Mal. A small breeze came wandering by, and he felt it surprisingly cool on his forehead. Evidently there was a little perspiration up there. "One Punch here said it could be done all right, but it was a question who'd want to *suggest* it to the Clan. Naturally, he and the other grandpas who are in the running for Grandfather wouldn't like to do it. Iron Bender would have his own reasons for refusing; and Gentle Maiden here wouldn't particularly want to hold a meeting right away—"

"And we certainly shouldn't!" said Gentle Maiden. "Why go to all that trouble when here we've got Iron Bender perfectly willing and ready to tear—"

"Why, indeed?" interrupted Mal in his turn. He was beginning to get a little weary of hearing of Iron Bender's readiness to remove heads. "Except that perhaps the whole Clan deserves to be in on this— not just Iron Bender and Maiden and myself. What the Clan really ought to do is sit down and decide whether it's a good idea for the Clan to have someone like Gentle Maiden keeping three Shorties around. Does the Clan really want those Shorties to stay here? And if not, what's the best way of getting rid of these Shorties? Not that I'm trying to suggest anything to the Clan, but if the Clan should just decide to elect a Grandfather now, and the Grandfather should decide that Shorties don't quality as orphans—"

A roar of protest from Gentle Maiden drowned him out; and a thunder of Dilbian voices arose among the seated Clan members as conversation—argument, rather, Mal told himself—became general. He waited for it to die down; but it did not. After a while, he walked over to One Punch, who was standing beside the Hill Bluffer, observing—as were two other elderly figures, obviously Grandpas Tricky and Forty Winks—but not taking part in the confusion of voices.

"One Punch," said Mal, and the oldster looked down at him cheerfully, "don't you think maybe you should quiet them down so they could hear the rest of my appeal?"

"Why, Law-Twister," said One Punch, "there's no point you going on appealing any longer, when everybody's already decided to grant what you want. They're already discussing it. Hear them?"

Since no one within a mile could have helped hearing them, there was little Mal could do but nod his head and wait. About ten minutes later, the volume of sound began to diminish as voice after voice fell silent. Finally, there was a dead silence. Members of the Clan began to reseat themselves on the grass, and from a gathering in the very center of the crowd, Gentle Maiden emerged and snorted at Mal before turning toward the village.

"I'm going to go get Bender!" she announced. "I'll get those little Shorties up here, too, so they can see Bender take care of this one and know they might just as well settle down."

She went off at a fast walk down the slope—the equivalent of about eight miles an hour in human terms.

Mal stared at One Punch, stunned.

"You mean," he asked him, "they decided not to do anything?"

A roar of explaining voices from the Clan members drowned him out and left him too deafened to understand them. When it was quiet once more, he was aware of One Punch looking severely down at him.

"Now, you shouldn't go around thinking Clan Water Gap'd talk something over and not come to some decision, Twister," he said. "Of course, they decided how it's all to go. We're going to elect a Grandfather, today."

"Fine," said Mal, beginning to revive. Then a thought struck him. "Why did Gentle Maiden go after Iron Bender just now, then? I thought—"

"Wait until you hear," said One Punch. "Clan Water Gap's come up with a decision to warm that slippery little Shorty heart of yours. You see, everyone decided, since we were going to elect a Grandfather ahead of time, that it all ought to be done in reverse."

"In reverse?"

"Why, certainly," said One Punch. "Instead of having a trial, then having the Grandfather give a decision to let you and Iron Bender hassle it out to see whether the Shorties go with you or stay with Gentle Maiden, the Clan decided to work it exactly backward."

Mal shook his head dizzily.

"I still don't understand," he said.

"I'm surprised—a Shorty like you," said One Punch, reprovingly. "I'd think backward and upside down'd be second nature to a Law-Twister. Why, what's going to happen is you and Bender'll have it out *first*, then the best decision by a grandpa'll be picked, then the grandpa who's decision's been picked will be up for election, and the Clan will elect him Grandfather."

Mal blinked.

"Decision . . ." he began feebly.

"Now, my decision," said a voice behind him, and he turned around to see that the Clan's other two elderly members had come up, "is that Iron Bender ought to win. But if he doesn't, it'll be because of some Shorty trick."

"Playing it safe, eh, Forty Winks?" said the other grandpa who had just joined them. "Well, *my* decision is that with all his tricks, and tough as we've been hearing Shorties are, that the Law-Twister can't lose. He'll chew Iron Bender up."

The two of them turned and looked expectantly at One Punch.

"Hmm," said One Punch, closing one eye and squinting thoughtfully with the other at Mal. "My decision is that the Law-Twister's even more clever and sneaky than we think. My decision says Twister'll come up with something that'll fix things his way so that they never will tangle. In short, Twister's going to win the fight even before it starts."

One Punch had turned toward the seated crowd as he said this, and there was another low mutter of appreciation from the seated Clan members.

"That One Punch," said Grandpa Tricky to Forty Winks, "never did lay back and play it safe. He just swings right in there twice as hard as anyone else, without winking."

"Well," said One Punch himself, turning to Mal, "there's Gentle Maiden and her orphans coming up from the village now with Iron Bender. You all set, Law-Twister?"

Mal was anything but set. It was good to hear that all three grandpas of Clan Water Gap expected him to come out on top; but he would have felt a lot better if it had been Iron Bender who had been expressing that opinion. He looked over the heads of the seated crowd to see Iron Bender coming, just as One Punch had said, with Gentle Maiden and three, small, human figures in tow.

His thoughts spun furiously. This whole business was crazy. It simply could not be that in a few minutes he would be expected to engage in a hand-to-hand battle with an individual more than one and a half times his height and five times his weight, any more than it could be that the wise men of the local Clan could be betting on him to win. One Punch's prediction, in particular, was so farfetched. . . .

Understanding suddenly exploded in him. At once, it all fitted together: the Dilbian habit of circumventing any outright lie by pretending to be after just the opposite of what an individual was really after; the odd reaction of the three captured humans who had not been concerned about the Human-Hemnoid Treaty of noninterference on Dilbia when they came *into* Clan Water Gap territory, but were willing to pass up a chance of escape by letting Mal summon armed human help to rescue them, now that they were here. Just suppose—Mal thought to himself feverishly—just suppose everything is just the opposite of what it seems ...

There was only one missing part to this whole jigsaw puzzle, one bit to which he did not have the answer. He turned to One Punch.

"Tell me something," he said, in a low voice. "Suppose Gentle Maiden and Iron Bender *had* to marry each other. Do you think they'd be very upset?"

"Upset? Well, no," said One Punch, thoughtfully. "Come to think of it, now you mention it, Law-Twister—those two are just about made for each other. Particularly seeing there's no one else made big enough or tough enough for either one of them, if you look around. In fact, if it wasn't for how they go around saying they can't stand each other, you might think they really liked each other quite a bit. Why do you ask?"

"I was just wondering," said Mal, grimly. "Let me ask you another question. Do you think a Shorty like me could carry the stone of Mighty Grappler ten paces?"

One Punch gazed at him.

"Well, you know," he said, "when it comes right down to it, I wouldn't put anything past a Shorty like you."

"Thanks," said Mal. "I'll return the compliment. Believe me, from now on, I'll never put anything past a real person like you, or Gentle Maiden, or Iron Bender, or anyone else. And I'll tell the other Shorties that when I get back among them!"

"Why thank you, Law-Twister," said One Punch. "That's mighty kind of you—but, come to think of it, maybe you better turn around now. Because Iron Bender's here."

Mal turned—just in time to see the towering figure of the village harnessmaker striding toward him, ac-

companied by a rising murmur of excitement from
the crowd.

"All right, let's get this over with!" boomed Iron
Bender, opening and closing his massive hands hungrily. "Just take me a few minutes, and then—"

"*Stop!*" shouted Mal, holding up his hand.

Iron Bender stopped, still some twenty feet from
Mal. The crowd fell silent, abruptly.

"I'm sorry!" said Mal, addressing them all. "I tried
every way I could to keep it from coming to this. But
I see now there's no other way to do it. Now, I'm
nowhere near as sure as your three grandpas that I
could handle Iron Bender, here, with one hand tied
behind my back. Iron Bender might well handle *me*,
with no trouble. I mean, he just might be the one real
man who can tangle with a Shorty like me, and win.
But, what if I'm wrong?"

Mal paused, both to see how they were reacting
and to get his nerve up for his next statement. If I
was trying something like this any place else, he
thought, they'd cart me off to a psychiatrist. But the
Dilbians in front of him were all quiet and attentive,
listening. Even Iron Bender and Gentle Maiden were
showing no indications of wanting to interrupt.

"As I say," went on Mal, a little hoarsely as a result
of working to make his voice carry to the whole
assemblage, "what if I'm wrong? What if this terrific
hassling ability that all we Shorties have gets the
best of me when I tangle with Iron Bender? Not that
Iron Bender would want me to hold back any, I know
that—"

Iron Bender snorted affirmatively and worked his
massive hands in the air.

"—But," said Mal, "think what the results would
be. Think of Clan Water Gap without a harnessmaker.
Think of Gentle Maiden here without the one real
man she can't push around. I've thought about those
things, and it seems to me there's just one way out.
The Clan laws have to be changed so that a Shorty

like me doesn't have to tangle with a Clan Gapper over this problem."

He turned to the stone of Mighty Grappler.

"So—" he wound up, his voice cracking a little on the word in spite of himself, "I'm just going to have to carry this stone ten steps so the laws can be changed."

He stepped up to the stone. There was a dead silence all around him. He could feel the sweat popping out on his face. What if the conclusions he had come to were all wrong? But he could not afford to think that now. He had to go through with the business, now that he'd spoken.

He curled his hands around the two ends of the iron rod from underneath and squatted down with his knees on either side of the rock. This was going to be different from ordinary weight lifting, where the weight was distributed on the outer two ends of the lifting bar. Here, the weight was between his fists.

He took a deep breath and lifted. For a moment, it seemed that the dead weight of the stone refused to move. Then it gave. It came up and into him until the near face of the rock thudded against his chest; the whole stone now held well off the ground.

So far, so good, for the first step. Now, for the second . . .

He willed strength into his leg muscles.

Up . . . he thought to himself . . . up. . . . He could hear his teeth gritting against each other in his head. Up . . .

Slowly, grimly, his legs straightened. His body lifted, bringing the stone with it, until he stood, swaying, the weight of it against his chest, and his arms just beginning to tremble with the strain.

Now, quickly—before arms and legs gave out—he had to take the ten steps.

He swayed forward, stuck out a leg quickly, and caught himself. For a second he hung poised, then he brought the other leg forward. The effort almost overbalanced him, but he stayed upright. Now, the right foot again ... then the left ... the right ... the left ...

In the fierceness of his effort, everything else was blotted out. He was alone with the stone he had to carry, with the straining pull of his muscles, the brightness of the sun in his eyes, and the savage tearing of the rod ends on his fingers, that threatened to rip themselves out of his grip.

Eight steps ... nine steps ... and ... ten!

He tried to let the stone down easily, but it thudded out of his grasp. As he stood half-bent over, it struck upright in its new resting place in the grass, then half-rolled away from him, for a moment exposing its bottom surface completely, so that he could see clearly into the hole there. Then it rocked back upright and stood still.

Painfully, stiffly, Mal straightened his back.

"Well," he panted, to the silent, staring Dilbians of Clan Water Gap, "I guess that takes care of that...."

Less than forty minutes later he was herding the three anthropologists back into their shuttle boat.

"But I don't understand," protested Harvey, hesitating in the entry port of the shuttle boat. "I want to know how you got us free without having to fight that big Dilbian—the one with the name that means Iron Bender?"

"I moved their law stone," said Mal, grimly. "That meant I could change the rules of the Clan."

"But they went on and elected One Punch as Clan Grandfather, anyway," said Harvey.

"Naturally," said Mal. "He'd given the most accurate judgment in advance—he'd foretold I'd win without laying a hand on Iron Bender. And I had. Once I moved the stone, I simply added a law to the ones Mighty Grappler had set up. I said no Clan Water Gapper was allowed to adopt orphan Shorties. So, if that was against the law, Gentle Maiden couldn't keep you. She had to let you go and then there was no reason for Iron Bender to want to tangle with me."

"But why did Iron Bender and Gentle decide to get married?"

"Why, she couldn't go back to being just a single maiden again, after naming someone her protector," Mal said. "Dilbians are very strict about things like that. Public opinion *forced* them to get married—which they wanted to do anyhow, but neither of them had wanted to be the one to ask the other to marry."

Harvey blinked.

"You mean," he said disbelievingly, "it was all part of a plot by Gentle Maiden, Iron Bender, and One Punch to use us for their own advantage? To get One Punch elected Grandfather, and the other two forced to marry?"

"Now, you're beginning to understand," said Mal, grimly. He started to turn away.

"Wait," said Harvey. "Look, there's information here that you ought to be sharing with us for the sake of science—"

"Science?" Mal gave him a hard look. "That's right, it was science, wasn't it? Just pure science, that made you and your friends decide on the spur of the moment to come down here. *Wasn't it?*"

Harvey's brows drew together.

"What's that question supposed to mean?" he said.

"Just inquiring," said Mal. "Didn't it ever occur to you that the Dilbians are just as bright as you are? And that they'd have a pretty clear idea why three Shorties would show up out of thin air and start asking questions?"

"Why should that seem suspicious to them?" Ora Page stuck her face out of the entry port over Harvey's shoulder.

"Because the Dilbians take everything with a grain of salt anyway—on principle," said Mal. "Because they're experts at figuring out what someone else is really up to, since that's just the way they operate, themselves. When a Dilbian wants to go after something, his first move is to pretend to head in the opposite direction."

"They told you that in your hypnotraining?" Ora asked.

Mal shook his head.

"No," he said. "I wasn't told anything." He looked harshly at the two of them and at the face of Rice, which now appeared behind Harvey's other shoulder. "Nobody told me a thing about the Dilbians except that there are a few rare humans who understand them instinctively and can work with them, only the book-psychiatrists and the book-anthropologists can't figure out why. Nobody suggested to me that our human authorities might deliberately be trying to arrange a situation where three book-anthropologists would be on hand to observe me—as one of these rare humans—learning how to think and work like a Dilbian, on my own. No, nobody told me anything like that. It's just a Dilbian sort of suspicion I've worked out on my own."

"Look here—" began Harvey.

"You look here!" said Mal, furiously. "I don't know of anything in the Outspace Regulations that let someone be drafted into being some sort of experimental animal without his knowing what's going on—"

"Easy now. Easy . . ." said Harvey. "All right. This whole thing was set up so we could observe you. But we had absolute faith that someone with your personality profile would do fine with the Dilbians. And, of course, you realize you'll be compensated for all this. For one thing, I think you'll find there's a full six-year scholarship waiting for you now, once you qualify for college entrance. And a few other things, too. You'll be hearing more about them when you get back to the human ambassador at Humrog Town, who sent you here."

"Thanks," said Mal, still boiling inside. "But next time tell them to ask first whether I want to play games with the rest of you! Now, you better get moving if you want to catch that spaceliner!"

He turned away. But before he had covered half a dozen steps, he heard Harvey's voice calling after him.

"Wait! There's something vitally important you didn't tell us. How did you manage to pick up that rock and carry it the way you did?"

Mal looked sourly back over his shoulder.

"I do a lot of weight lifting," he said, and kept on going.

He did not look back again; and, a few minutes later, he heard the shuttle boat take off. He headed at an angle up the valley slope behind the houses in the village toward the stone of Mighty Grappler, where the Bluffer would be waiting to take him back to Humrog Town. The sun was close to setting, and with its level rays in his eyes, he could barely make out that there were four big Dilbian figures rather than one, waiting for him by the stone. A wariness awoke in him.

When he came up, however, he discovered that the four figures were the Bluffer with One Punch, Gentle Maiden, and Iron Bender—and all four looked genial.

"There you are," said the Bluffer, as Mal stopped before him. "Better climb up into the saddle. It's not more than two hours to full dark, and even the way I travel we're going to have to move some to make it back to Humrog Town in that time."

Mal obeyed. From the altitude of the saddle, he looked over the Bluffer's right shoulder down at One Punch and Gentle Maiden and level into the face of Iron Bender.

"Well, good-bye," he said, not sure of how Dilbians reacted on parting. "It's been something, knowing you all."

"Been something for Clan Water Gap, too," replied One Punch. "I can say that now, officially, as the Clan Grandfather. Guess most of us will be telling the tale for years to come, how we got dropped in on here by the Mighty Law-Twister."

Mal goggled. He had thought he was past the point of surprise where Dilbians were concerned, but this was more than even he had imagined.

"*Mighty* Law-Twister?" he echoed.

"Why, of course," rumbled the Hill Bluffer, underneath him. "Somebody's name had to be changed, after you moved that stone."

"The postman's right," said One Punch. "Naturally, we wouldn't want to change the name of Mighty Grappler, seeing what all he means to the Clan. Besides, since he's dead, we can't very well go around changing his name and getting folks mixed up, so we just changed yours instead. Stands to reason if you could carry Mighty Grappler's stone ten paces, you had to be pretty mighty, yourself."

"But—well, now, wait a minute . . ." Mal protested. He was remembering what he had seen in the moment he had put the stone down and it had rocked enough to let him see clearly into the hole inside it, and his conscience was bothering him. "Uh—One Punch, I wonder if I could speak to you . . . privately . . . for just a second? If we could just step over here—"

"No need for that, Mighty," boomed Iron Bender. "I and the wife are just headed back down to the village, anyway. Aren't we, Gentle?"

"Well, *I'm* going. If you want to come too—"

"That's what I say," interrupted Iron Bender, "We're both just leaving. So long, Mighty. Sorry we never got a chance to tangle. If you ever get some spare time and a good reason, come back and I'll be glad to oblige you."

"Thanks . . ." said Mal. With mixed feelings, he watched the harnessmaker and his new wife turn and stride off down the slope toward the buildings below. Then he remembered his conscience and looked again down at One Punch.

"Guess you better climb down again," the Bluffer was saying, "and I'll mosey off a few steps myself so's not to intrude."

"Now, Postman," said One Punch. "No need for that. We're all friends here. I can guess that Mighty, here, could have a few little questions to ask or things to tell—but likely it's nothing you oughtn't to hear; and besides, being a government man, we can count on you keeping any secrets."

"That's true," said the Bluffer. "Come to think of it, Mighty, it'd be kind of an insult to the government if you didn't trust me—"

"Oh, I trust you," said Mal, hastily. "It's just that ... well ..." He looked at One Punch. "What would you say if I told you that the stone there is hollow—that it'd been hollowed out inside?"

"Now, Mighty," said One Punch, "you mustn't make fun of an old man, now that he's become a respectable Grandfather. Anybody knows stones aren't hollow."

"But what would you say if I told you that that one is?" persisted Mal.

"Why, I don't suppose it'd make much difference you just *telling* me it was hollow," said One Punch. "I don't suppose I'd say anything. I wouldn't want folks to think you could twist me that easily, for one thing; and for another thing, maybe it might come in handy some time later, my having heard someone say that stone was hollow. Just like the Mighty Grappler said in some of his own words of wisdom—'It's always good to have things set up one way. But it's extra good to have them set up another way, too. Two ways are always better than one.'"

"And very good wisdom that is," put in the Bluffer, admiringly. "Up near Humrog Peak there's a small bridge people been walking around for years. There *is* a kind of rumor floating around that it's washed out in the middle, but I've never heard anybody really say so. Never know when it might come in useful to have a bridge like that around for someone who'd never heard the rumor—that is, if there's any truth to the rumor, which I doubt."

"I see," said Mal.

"Of course you do, Mighty," said One Punch. "You understand things real well for a Shorty. Now, luckily we don't have to worry about this joke of yours that the stone of Mighty Grappler is hollow, because we've got proof otherwise."

"Proof?" Mal blinked.

"Why, certainly," said One Punch. "Now, it stands to reason, if that stone were hollow, it wouldn't be anywhere near as heavy as it looks. In fact, it'd be real light."

"That's right," said Mal, sharply. "And you saw me—a Shorty—pick it up and carry it."

"Exactly!" said One Punch. "The whole Clan was watching to see you pick that stone up and carry it. And we did."

"And that proves it isn't hollow?" Mal stared.

"Why sure," said One Punch. "We all saw you sweating and struggling and straining to move that stone just ten paces. Well, what more proof does a man need? If it'd been hollow like you say, a Shorty—let alone a mighty Shorty like you—would've been able to pick it up with one paw and just stroll off with it. But we were watching you closely, Mighty, and you didn't leave a shred of doubt in the mind of any one of us that it was just about all you could carry. So, that stone just *had* to be solid."

He stopped. The Bluffer snorted.

"You see there, Mighty?" the Bluffer said. "You may be a real good law-twister—nobody doubts it for a minute—but when you go up against the wisdom of a real elected Grandfather, you find you can't twist him like you can any ordinary real man."

"I . . . guess so," said Mal. "I suppose there's no point, then, in my suggesting you just take a look at the stone?"

"It'd be kind of beneath me to do that, Mighty," said One Punch, severely, "now that I'm a Grandfather and already pointed out how it couldn't be hollow, anyway. Well, so long."

Abruptly, as abruptly as Iron Bender and Gentle Maiden had gone, One Punch turned and strode off down the slope.

The Hill Bluffer turned on one heel, himself, and strode away in the opposite direction, into the mountains and the sunset.

"But the thing I don't understand," said Mal to the Bluffer, a few minutes later when they were back on the narrow trail, out of sight of Water Gap Territory, "is how . . . What would have happened if those three Shorties hadn't dropped in the way they did? And what if I hadn't been sent for? One Punch might have been elected Grandfather anyway, but how would Iron Bender and Gentle Maiden ever have gotten married?"

"Lots of luck to it all, I suppose you could say, Mighty," answered the Bluffer, sagely. "Just shows how things turn out. Pure chance—like my mentioning to Little Bite a couple of months ago it was a shame there hadn't been other Shorties around to watch just how the Half-Pint Posted and Pick-and-Shovel did things, back when they were here."

"You . . ." Mal stared, "mentioned . . ."

"Just offhand, one day," said the Bluffer. "Of course, as I told Little Bite, there weren't hardly any real champions around right now to interest a tough little Shorty—except over at Clan Water Gap, where my unmarried cousin Gentle Maiden lived."

"Your *cousin* . . . ? I see," said Mal. There was a long, long pause. "Very interesting."

"Funny. That's how Little Bite put it, when I told

him," answered the Bluffer, cat-footing confidently along the very edge of a precipice. "You Shorties sure have a habit of talking alike and saying the same things all the time. Comes of having such little heads with not much space inside for words, I suppose.

"You must be hammer or anvil"—unless you choose to be the blade forged between them.

An Ounce of Emotion

I

"Well? Are the ships joined—or not?" demanded Arthur Mial.

"Look for yourself!" said Tyrone Ross.

Mial turned and went on out of the room. All right, thought Ty savagely, call it a personality conflict. Putting a tag on it is one thing, doing something about it another. And I have to do something—it could just be the fuse to this nitrojelly situation he, I, and Annie are all sitting on. There must be some way I can break down this feeling between us.

Ty glanced for a moment across the spaceliner stateroom at the statistical analysis instrument, called Annie, now sitting silent and unimpressive as a black steamer trunk against a far wall.

It was Annie who held the hope of peace for thousands of cubic light years of interstellar space in every direction. Annie—with the help of Ty. And the dubious help of Mial. The instrument, thought Ty grimly, deserved better than the two particular human companions the Laburti had permitted, to bring her to them.

137

He turned back to the vision screen he had been watching earlier.

On it, pictured from the viewpoint of one of the tractor mechs now maneuvering the ship, this leviathan of a Laburti spaceliner he was on was being laid alongside and only fifty yards from an equally huge Chedal vessel. Even Ty's untrained eye could see the hair-trigger risks in bringing those hundreds of thousands of tons of mass so close together. But with the two Great Races, so-called, poised on the verge of conflict, the Chedal Observer of the Annie Demonstration five days from now could not be simply ferried from his ship to this like any ordinary passenger.

The two ships must be faced, main airlock to main airlock, and a passageway fitted between the locks. So that the Chedal and his staff could stroll aboard with all due protocol. Better damage either or both of the giant craft than chance any suspicion of a slight by one of the Great Races to a representative of the other.

For the Laburti and the Chedal were at a sparking point. A sparking point of war that—but of course neither race of aliens was concerned about that—could see small Earth drafted into the armed camp of its huge Laburti neighbor; and destroyed by the Chedal horde, if the interstellar conflict swept past Alpha Centauri.

It was merely, if murderously, ironic in this situation that Ty and Mial who came bearing the slim hope of peace that was Annie, should be themselves at a sparking point. A sparking point willed by neither—but to which they had both been born.

Ty's thoughts came back from the vision screen to their original preoccupation.

It happened sometimes, he thought. It just—happened. Sometimes, for no discernable reason, suddenly and without warning, two men meeting for the

first time felt the ancient furies buried deep in their
forebrains leap abruptly and redly to life. It was
rapport between individuals turned inside out—anti-
rapport. Under it, the animal instinct in each man
instantly snarled and bristled, recognizing a mortal
enemy—an enemy not in act or attitude, but simply
in *being*.

So it had happened with Ty—and Mial. Back on
Earth, thought Ty now, while there was still a chance
to do something about the situation, they had each
been too civilized to speak up about it. Now it was
too late. The mistake was made.

And mistake it had been. For, practical engineer
and reasonable man that Ty was, reasonable man
and practical politician that Mial was, to the rest of
mankind—to each other they were tigers. And common sense dictated that you did not pen two tigers
alone together for two weeks; for a delicate mission
on which the future existence of the human race
might depend. Already, after nine days out—

"We'll have to go meet the Chedal." It was Mial,
reentering the room. Ty turned reflexively to face
him.

The other man was scarcely a dozen years older
than Ty; and in many ways they were nearly alike.
There could not be half an inch or five pounds of
weight difference between them, thought Ty. Like
Ty, Mial was square-shouldered and leanly built. But
his hair was dark where Ty's was blond: and that
dark hair had started to recede. The face below it
was handsome, rather than big-boned and open like
Ty's. Mial, at thirty-six, was something of a wonder
boy in politics back on Earth. Barely old enough for
the senatorial seat he held, he had the respect of
almost everyone. But he had been legal counsel for
some unsavory groups in the beginning of his career.
He would know how, thought Ty watching him now,
to fight dirty if he had to. And the two of them were
off with none but aliens to witness.

*   *   *

"I know," said Ty now, harshly. He turned to follow Mial as the other man started out of the room. "What about Annie?"

Mial looked back over his shoulder.

"She's safe enough. What good's a machine to them if no one but a human can run her?" Mial's voice was almost taunting. "You can't go up with the big boys, Ross, and act scared."

Ty's face flushed with internal heat—but it was true, what Mial had said. A midget trying to make peace with giants did well not to act doubtful or afraid. Mial had courage to see it. Ty felt an unwilling touch of admiration for the man. *I could almost like him for that,* he thought—*if I didn't hate his guts.*

By the time they got to the airlock, the slim, dog-faced, and darkly-robed Laburti were in their receiving line, and the first of the squat, yellow-furred Chedal forms were coming through. First came the guards; then the Observer himself, distinguishable to a human eye only by the sky-blue harness he wore. The tall, thin form of the robed Laburti Captain glided forward to welcome him aboard first; and then the Observer moved down the line, to confront Mial.

A high-pitched chattering came from the Chedal's lipless slit of a mouth, almost instantly overridden by the artificial, translated human speech from the black translator collar around the alien's thick, yellow-furred neck. Shortly, Mial was replying in kind, his own black translator collar turning his human words into Chedal chitterings. Ty stood listening, half-selfconscious, half-bored.

"—and my Demonstration Operator." Ty woke suddenly to the fact that Mial was introducing him to the Chedal.

"Honored," said Ty, and heard his collar translating.

"May I invite you both to my suite now, immediately, for the purpose of improving our acquaintance

. . ." The invitation extended itself, became flowery, and ended with a flourish.

"It's an honor to accept . . ." Mial was answering. Ty braced himself for at least another hour of this before they could get back to their own suite.

Then his breath caught in his throat.

". . . for myself, that is," Mial was completing his answer. "Unfortunately, I earlier ordered my Operator to return immediately to his device, once these greetings were over. And I make it a practice never to change an order. I'm sure you understand."

"Of course. Some other time I will host your Operator. Shall we two go?" The Chedal turned and led off. Mial was turning with him, when Ty stepped in front of him.

"Hold on—" Ty remembered to turn off his translator collar. "What's this about your *ordering* me—"

Mial flicked off his own translator collar.

"You heard me," he said. He stepped around Ty and walked off. Ty stood, staring after him. Then, conscious of the gazing Laburti all about him, he turned and headed back toward their own suite.

Once back there, and with the door to the ship's corridor safely closed behind him, he swore and turned to checking out Annie, to make sure there had been no investigation or tampering with her innards while he was absent. Taking off the side panel of her case, he pinched his finger between the panel and the case and swore again. Then he sat down suddenly, ignoring Annie and began to think.

II

With the jab of pain from the pinched finger, an incredible suspicion had sprung, full-armed into his brain. For the first time he found himself wondering if Mial's lie to the Chedal about an 'order' to Ty had been part of some plan by the other man against Ty.

A plan that required Mial's talking with the Chedal Observer alone, before Ty did.

It was, Ty had to admit, the kind of suspicion that only someone who felt as he did about Mial could have dreamed up. And yet . . .

The orders putting the Annie Demonstration Mission—which meant Annie and Ty—under the authority of Mial had been merely a polite fiction. A matter of matching the high rank and authority of the Laburti and Chedal officials who would be watching the Demonstration as Observers. Ty had been clearly given to understand that by his own Department chief, back on Earth.

In other words, Mial had just now stopped playing according to the unwritten rules of the Mission. That might bode ill for Ty. And, thought Ty now, suddenly, it might bode even worse for the success of the Mission. But it was unthinkable that Mial would go so far as to risk that.

For, it was one thing to stand here with Annie and know she represented something possessed by neither the Laburti nor the Chedal technologies. It was all right to remind oneself that human science was growing like the human population; and that population was multiplying at close to three per cent per year—as opposed to a fraction of a per cent for the older Chedal and Laburti populations.

But there were present actualities that still had to be faced—like the size of this ship, and that of the Chedal ship now parting from it. Also, like the twenty-odd teeming worlds apiece, the thousands of years each of post-atomic civilization, the armed might either sprawling alien empire could boast.

Mial could not—would not—be playing some personal game in the face of all this. Ty shook his head angrily at the thought. No man could be such a fool, no matter what basic emotional factor was driving him.

*   *   *

When Mial returned to their stateroom suite a couple of hours later, Ty made an effort to speak pleasantly to him.

"Well?" said Ty, "how'd it go? And when am I to meet him?"

Mial looked at him coldly.

"You'll be told," he said, and went on into his bedroom.

But, in the four days left of the trip to the Laburti World, where the Demonstration was to be given before a joint audience of Laburti and Chedal Observers, it became increasingly apparent Ty was not to meet the Chedal. Meanwhile, Mial was increasingly in conference with the alien representative.

Ty gritted his teeth. At least, at their destination the Mission would be moving directly to the Human Consulate. And the Consul in charge was not a human, but a Laburti citizen who had contracted for the job of representing the Earth race. Mial could hardly hold secret conferences with the Chedal under a Laburti nose.

Ty was still reminding himself of this as the spaceliner finally settled toward their destination—a fantastic metropolis, with eight and ten thousand foot tall buildings rising out of what Ty had been informed was a quarter-mile depth of open ocean. Ty had just finished getting Annie rigged for handling when Mial came into the room.

"Ready?" demanded Mial.

"Ready," said Ty.

"You go ahead with Annie and the baggage—" The sudden, soft hooting of the landing horn interrupted Mial, and there was a faint tremor all through the huge ship as it came to rest in its landing cradle of magnetic forces; the main door to the suite from the corridor swung open. A freight-handling mech slid into the room and approached Annie.

"I'll meet you outside in the taxi area," concluded Mial.

Ty felt abrupt and unreasonable suspicion.

"Why?" he asked sharply.

Mial had already turned toward the open door through which the mech had just entered. He paused and turned back to face Ty; a smile, razor blade thin and cruel altered his handsome face.

"Because that's what I'm going to do," he said softly, and turned again toward the door.

Ty stared after him for a moment, jarred and irresolute at the sudden, fresh outbreak of hostilities, and Mial went out through the door.

"Wait a minute!" snapped Ty, heading after him. But the other man was already gone, and the mech, carrying Annie and following close behind him, had blocked Ty's path. Cold with anger, Ty swung back to check their personal baggage, including their food supplies, as another mech entered to carry these to the outside of the ship.

When he finally got outside to the disembarkation area, and got the baggage, as well as Annie, loaded on to one of the flying cargo platforms that did taxi service among the Laburti, he looked around for Mial. He discovered the other man a short distance away in the disembarkation area, talking again with a blue-harnessed, yellow-furred form.

Grimly, Ty turned on his translator collar and gave the cargo platform the address of the human Consulate. Then, he lifted a section of the transparent cover of the platform and stepped aboard, to sit down on the luggage and wait for Mial. After a while, he saw Mial break off his conversation and approach the cargo platform. The statesman spoke briefly to the cargo platform, something Ty could not hear from under the transparent cover, then came aboard and sat down next to Ty.

The platform lifted into the air and headed in between the blue and gray metal of the towers with their gossamer connecting bridges.

"I already told it where to take us," said Ty.

Mial turned to look at him briefly and almost contemptuously, then turned away again without answering.

The platform slid amongst the looming towers and finally flew them in through a wide window-opening, into a room set up with human-style furniture. They got off, and Ty looked around as the platform began to unload the baggage. There was no sign of the Laburti individual who filled the role of human Consul. Sudden suspicion blossomed again in Ty.

"Wait a minute—" He wheeled about—but the platform, already unloaded, was lifting out through the window opening again. Ty turned on Mial. "This isn't the Consulate!"

"That's right," Mial almost drawled the words. "It's a hotel—the way they have them here. The Chedal Observer recommended it to me."

"Recommended—?" Ty stared. "We're supposed to go to the Consulate. You can't—"

"Can't I?" Mial's eyes were beginning to blaze. The throttled fury in him was yammering to be released, evidently, as much as its counterpart in Ty. "I don't trust that Consulate, with its Laburti playing human Consul. Here, if the Chedal wants to drop by—"

"He's not supposed to drop by!" Ty snarled. "We're here to demonstrate Annie, not gabble with the Observers. What'll the Laburti think if they find you and the Chedal glued together half of the time?" He got himself under control and said in a lower voice. "We're going back to the Consulate, now—"

"Are we?" Mial almost hissed. "Are you forgetting that the orders show *me* in charge of this Demonstration—and that the aliens'll believe those orders? Besides, you don't know your way around here. And, after talking to the Chedal—I do!"

He turned abruptly and strode over to an apparently blank wall. He rapped on it, and flicked on his translator collar and spoke to the wall.

"Open up!" The wall slid open to reveal what was evidently an elevator tube. He stepped into it and turned to smile mockingly at Ty, drifting down out of sight. The wall closed behind him.

"Open up!" raged Ty, striding to the wall and rapping on it. He flicked on his translator collar. "Open up. Do you hear me? Open up!"

But the wall did not open. Ty, his knuckles getting sore, at last gave up and turned back to Annie.

III

Whatever else might be going on, his responsibility to her and the Demonstration tomorrow, remained unchanged. He got her handling rigging off, and ran a sample problem through her. When he was done, he checked the resultant figures against the answers to the problem already established by multiple statistics back on Earth. He was within a fraction of a per cent all the way down the line.

Ty glowed, in spite of himself. Operating Annie successfully was not so much a skill, as an art. In any problem, there were from fourteen to twenty factors whose values had to be adjusted according to the instincts and creativity of the Operator. It was this fact that was the human ace in the hole in this situation. Aliens could not run Annie—they had tried on Annie's prototypes and failed. Only a few specially trained and talented humans could run her successfully . . . and of these, Ty Ross was the master Operator. That was why he was here.

Now, tomorrow he would have to prove his right to that title. Under his hands Annie could show that a hundred and twenty-five Earth years after the Laburti and Chedal went to war, the winner would have a Gross Racial Product only eight per cent increased over today—so severe would the conflict have been. But in a hundred and twenty-five years of peaceful co-existence and cooperation, both races would have doubled their G.R.P.s in spite of having made only fractional increases in population. And machines like Annie, with operators like Ty, stood ready to monitor and guide the G.R.P. increases. No sane race could go to war in the face of that.

Meanwhile, Mial had not returned. Outside the weather shield of the wide window, the local sun, a G5 star, was taking its large, orange-yellow shape below the watery horizon. Ty made himself something to eat, read a while, and then took himself to bed in one of the adjoining bedrooms. But disquieting memories kept him from sleeping.

He remembered now that there had been an argument back on Earth, about the proper way to make use of Annie. He had known of this for a long time. Mial's recent actions came forcing it back into the forefront of his sleepless mind.

The political people back home had wanted Annie to be used as a tool, and a bargaining point, rather than a solution to the Laburti-Chedal confrontation, in herself. It was true. Ty reminded himself in the darkness. Mial had not been one of those so arguing. But he was of the same breed and occupation as they, reminded the little red devils of suspicion, coming out to dance on Ty's brain. With a sullen effort Ty shoved them out of his mind and forced himself to think of something else—anything else.

And, after a while, he slept.

He woke suddenly, feeling himself being shaken back to consciousness. The lights were on in the room and Mial was shaking him.

"What?" Ty sat up, knocking the other man's hand aside.

"The Chedal Observer's here with me." said Mial. "He wants a preview demonstration of the analyzer."

"A preview!" Ty burst up out of bed to stand facing

the other man. "Why should he get to see Annie before the official Demonstration?"

"Because I said he could." Underneath, Mial's eyes were stained by dark half-circles of fatigue.

"Well, I say he can wait until tomorrow like the Laburti!" snapped Ty. He added, "—And don't try to pull your paper rank on me. If I don't run Annie for him, who's to do it? You?"

Mial's weary face paled with anger.

"The Chedal asked for the preview," he said, in a tight, low voice. "I didn't think I had the right to refuse him, important as this Mission is. Do you want to take the responsibility of doing it? Annie'll come up with the same answers now as seven hours from now."

"Almost the same—" muttered Ty. "They're never exact, I told you that." He swayed on his feet, caught between sleep and resentment.

"As you say," said Mial, "I can't make you do it."

Ty hesitated a second more. But his brain seemed numb.

"All right," he snapped. "I'll have to get dressed. Five minutes!"

Mial turned and went out. When Ty followed, some five minutes later, he found both the other man and the alien in the sitting room. The Chedal came toward Ty, and for a moment they were closer than they had been even in the spaceliner airlock. For the first time, Ty smelled a faint, sickening odor from the alien, a scent like overripe bananas.

The Chedal handed him a roll of paper-like material. Gibberish raved from his lipless mouth and was translated by the translator collar.

"Here is the data you will need."

"Thank you," said Ty, with bare civility. He took the roll over to Annie and examined it. It contained all the necessary statistics on both the Laburti and Chedal races, from the Gross Racial Products down to statistical particulars. He went to work, feeding the data into Annie.

Time flowed by, catching him up in the rhythm of his work as it went.

His job with Annie required just this sort of concentration and involvement, and for a little while he forgot the two watching him. He looked up at last to see the window aperture flushed with yellow-pink dawn, and guessed that perhaps an hour had gone by.

He tore loose the tape he had been handling, and walked with it to the Chedal.

"Here," he said, putting the tape into the blunt, three-fingered hands, and pointing to the first figures. "There's your G.R.P. half a standard year after agreement to co-exist with Laburti.—Up three thousands of one per cent already. And here it is at the end of a full year—"

"And the Laburti?" demanded the translated chittering of the alien.

"Down here. You see . . ." Ty talked on. The Chedal watched, his perfectly round, black eyes emotionless as the button-eyes of a child's toy. When Ty was finished, the alien, still holding the tape, swung on Mial, turning his back to Ty.

"We will check this, of course," the Chedal said to Mial. "But your price is high." He turned and went out.

Ty stood staring after him.

"What price?" he asked, huskily. His throat was suddenly dry. He swung on Mial. "What price is it that's too high?"

"The price of cooperation with the Laburti!" snarled Mial. "They and the Chedal hate each other—or haven't you noticed?" He turned and stalked off into the opposite bedroom, slamming the door behind him.

Ty stood staring at the closed surface. He made a step toward it. Mial had evidently been up all night.

This, combined with the emotional situation between them, would make it pointless for Ty to try to question him.

Besides, thought Ty, hollowly and coldly, there was no need. He turned back across the room to the pile of their supplies and got out the coffeemaker. It was a little self-contained unit that could brew up a fresh cup in something like thirty seconds; for those thirty seconds, Ty kept his mind averted from the problem. Then, with the cup of hot, black coffee in his hands, he sat down to decide what to do.

Mial's answer to his question about the Chedal's mention of price had been thoughtless and transparent—the answer of a man scourged by dislike and mind-numbed by fatigue. Clearly, it could not be anything so simple as the general price of cooperation with a disliked other race, to which the Chedal Observer had been referring. No—it had to have been a specific price. And a specific price that was part of specific, personal negotiations held in secret between the alien and Mial.

Such personal negotiations were no part of the Demonstration plans as Ty knew them. Therefore, Mial was not following those plans. Clearly, he was following some other course of action.

And this, to Ty, could only be the course laid down by those political minds back on Earth who had wanted to use Annie as a pawn to their maneuvering, instead of presenting the statistical analysis instrument plainly and honestly by itself to the Laburti and the Chedal Observers.

If this was the case, the whole hope of the Demonstration hung in the balance. Mial, sparked by instinctive hatred for Ty, was opposing himself not merely to Ty but to everything Ty stood for—including the straight-forward presentation of Annie's capabilities. Instead, he must be dickering with the Chedal for some agreement that would league humanity with the Chedal and against the Laburti—a wild, unrealistic action when the solar system lay wholly within the powerful Laburti stellar sphere of influence.

A moment's annoyance on the part of the Laburti—a moment's belief that the humans had been trying to trick them and play games with their Chedal enemy—and the Laburti forces could turn Earth to a drifting cinder of a world with as little effort as a giant stepping on an ant.

If this was what Mial was doing—and by now Ty was convinced of it—the other man must be stopped, at any cost.

But how?

Ty shivered suddenly and uncontrollably. The room seemed abruptly as icy as a polar tundra.

There was only one way to stop Mial, who could not be reasoned with—by Ty, at least—either on the emotional or the intellectual level; and who held the paper proofs of authority over Ty and Annie. Mial would have to be physically removed from the Demonstration. If necessary—rather than risk the life on Earth and the whole human race—he would have to be killed.

And it would have to look like an accident. Anything else would cause the aliens to halt the Demonstration.

The shiver went away without warning—leaving only a momentary flicker of doubt in Ty, a second's wonder if perhaps his own emotional reaction to Mial was not hurrying him to take a step that might not be justified. Then, that flicker went out. With the Demonstration only hours away, Ty could not stop to examine his motives. He had to act and hope he was right.

He looked across the room at Annie. The statistical analysis instrument housed her own electrical power source and it was powerful enough to give a lethal jolt to a human heart. Her instruments and controls were insulated from the metal case, but the case itself . . .

Ty put down his coffee cup and walked over to the instrument. He got busy. It was not difficult. Half an hour later, as the sun of this world was rising out of the sea, he finished, and went back to his room for a few hours' sleep. He fell instantly into slumber and slept heavily.

IV

He jerked awake. The loon-like hooting in his ears; and standing over his bed was the darkly robed figure of a Laburti.

Ty scrambled to his feet, reaching for a bathrobe.

"What . . . ?" he blurted.

Hairless, gray-skinned and dog-faced, narrow-shouldered in the heavy, dark robes he wore, the Laburti looked back at him expressionlessly.

"Where is Demonstration Chief Arthur Mial?" The words came seemingly without emotion from the translator collar, over the sudden deep, harsh-voiced yammering from the face above it.

"I—in the bedroom."

"He is not there."

"But . . ." Ty, belting the bathrobe, strode around the alien, out of his bedroom, across the intervening room and looked into the room into which Mial had disappeared only a few hours before. The bed there was rumpled, but empty. Ty turned back into the center room where Annie stood. Behind her black metal case, the alien sun was approaching the zenith position of noon.

"You will come with me," said the Laburti.

Ty turned to protest. But two more Laburti had come into the suite, carrying the silver-tipped devices which Ty had been briefed back on Earth, were weapons. Following them came mechs which gathered up the baggage and Annie. Ty cut off the protest before it could reach his lips. There was no point in arguing. But where was Mial?

They crossed a distance of the alien city by flying platform and came at last into another tower, and a large suite of rooms. The Laburti who had woken Ty led him into an interior room where yet another Laburti stood, robed and impassive.

"These," said the Laburti who had brought Ty there, "are the quarters belonging to me. I am the Consul for your human race on this world. This—" the alien nodded at the other robed figure, "is the Observer of our Laburti race, who was to view your device today."

The word *was*, with all the implications of its past tense, sent a chill creeping through Ty.

"Where is Demonstration Chief Arthur Mial?" demanded the Laburti Observer.

"I don't know!"

The two Laburti stood still. The silence went on in the room, and on until it began to seem to roar in Ty's ears. He swayed a little on his feet, longing to sit down, but knowing enough of protocol not to do so while the Laburti Observer was still standing. Then, finally, the Observer spoke again.

"You have been demonstrating your instrument to the Chedal," he said, "previous to the scheduled Demonstration and without consulting us."

Ty opened his mouth, then closed it again. There was nothing he could say.

The Observer turned and spoke to the Consul with his translator switched off. The Consul produced a roll of paper-like material almost identical with that the Chedal had handed Ty earlier, and passed it into Ty's hands.

"Now," said the Laburti Observer, tonelessly, "you will give a previous Demonstration to me . . ."

The Demonstration was just ending, when a distant hooting called the Laburti Consul out of the room. He returned a minute later—and with him was Mial.

"A Demonstration?" asked Mial, speaking first and looking at the Laburti Observer.

"You were not to be found," replied the alien. "And I am informed of a Demonstration you gave the Chedal Observer some hours past."

"Yes," said Mial. His eyes were still dark from lack of sleep, but his gaze seemed sharp enough. That gaze slid over to fasten on Ty, now. "Perhaps we'd better discuss that, before the official Demonstration. There's less than an hour left."

"You intend still to hold the original Demonstration?"

"Yes," said Mial. "Perhaps we'd better discuss that, too—alone."

"Perhaps we had better," said the Laburti. He nodded to the Consul who started out of the room. Ty stood still.

"Get going," said Mial icily to him, without bothering to turn off his translator collar. "And have the machine ready to go."

Ty turned off his own translator collar, but stood where he was. "What're you up to?" he demanded. "This isn't the way we were supposed to do things. You're running some scheme of your own. Admit it!"

Mial turned his collar off.

"All right," he said, coldly and calmly. "I've had to. There were factors you don't know anything about."

"Such as?"

"There's no time to explain now."

"I won't go until I know what kind of a deal you've been cooking up with the Chedal Observer!"

"You fool!" hissed Mial. "Can't you see this alien's listening and watching every change your face makes? I can't tell you now, and I won't tell you. But I'll tell you this—you're going to get your chance to demonstrate Annie just the way you expected to, to Chedal

and Laburti together, if you go along with me. But
fight me—and that chance is lost. Now, *will you go?"*

Ty hesitated a moment longer, then he turned and
followed the Laburti Consul out. The alien led him to
the room where Annie and their baggage had been
placed, and shut him in there.

Once alone, he began to pace the floor, fury and
worry boiling together inside him. Mial's last words
just now had been an open ultimatum. *You're too late
to stop me now,* had been the unspoken message behind those words. *Go along with me now, or else lose
everything.*

Mial had been clever. He had managed to keep Ty
completely in the dark. Puzzle as he would now, Ty
could not figure out what it was, specifically, that
Mial had set out secretly to do to the Annie Mission.

Or how much of that Mial might already have
accomplished. How could Ty fight, completely ignorant of what was going on?

No, Mial was right. Ty could not refuse, blind, to
do what he had been sent out to do. That way there
would be no hope at all. By going along with Mial he
kept alive the faint hope, that things might yet, somehow, turn out as planned back on Earth. Even if—Ty
paused in his pacing to smile grimly—Mial's plan
included some arrangement not to Ty's personal ben-
efit. For the sake of the original purpose of the Mission, Ty had to go through with the Demonstration,
even now, just as if he was Mial's willing accomplice.

But—Ty began to pace again. There was something
else to think about. It was possible to attack the
problem from the other end. The accomplishment of
the Mission was more important than the survival of
Ty. Well, then, it was also more important than the
survival of Mial—And if Mial should die, whatever
commitments he had secretly made to the Chedal
against the Laburti, or vice-versa, would die with
him.

What would be left would be only what had been intended in the first place. The overwhelming commonsense practicality of peace in preference to war, demonstrated to both the Laburti and the Chedal.

Ty, pausing once more in his pacing to make a final decision, found his decision already made. Annie was already prepared as a lethal weapon. All he needed was to put her to use to stop Mial.

Twenty minutes later, the Laburti Consul for the human race came to collect both Ty and Annie, and bring them back to the room from which Ty had been removed, at Mial's suggestion earlier. Now, Ty saw the room held not only Mial and the Laburti Observer, but one other Laburti in addition. While across the room's width from these, were the Chedal Observer in blue harness with two other Chedals. They were all, with the exception of Mial, aliens, and their expressions were almost unreadable therefore. But, as Ty stepped into the room, he felt the animosity, like a living force, between the two groups of aliens in spite of the full moon's width of distance between them.

It was in the rigidity with which both Chedal and Laburti figures stood. It was in the unwinking gaze they kept on each other. For the first time, Ty realized the need behind the emphasis on protocol and careful procedure between these two races. Here was merely a situation to which protocol was new, with a weaker race standing between representatives of the two Great Ones. But these robed, or yellow-furred, diplomats seemed ready to fly physically at each other's throats.

IV

"Get it working—" it was the voice of Mial with his translator turned off, and it betrayed a sense of the same tension in the air that Ty had recognized between the two alien groups. Ty reached for his own collar and then remembered that it was still turned off from before.

"I'll need your help," he said tonelessly. "Annie's been jarred a bit, bringing her here."

"All right," said Mial. He came quickly across the room to join Ty, now standing beside the statistical analysis instrument.

"Stand here, behind Annie," said Ty, "so you don't block my view of the front instrument panel. Reach over the case to the data sorting key here, and hold it down for me."

"This key—all right." From behind Annie, Mial's long right arm reached easily over the top of the case, but—as Ty had planned—not without requiring the other man to lean forward and brace himself with a hand upon the top of the metal case of the instrument. A touch now by Ty on the tape control key would send upwards of thirteen thousand volts suddenly through Mial's body.

He ducked his head down and hastily began to key in data from the statistic roll lying waiting for him on a nearby table.

The work kept his face hidden, but could not halt the trembling beginning to grow inside him. His reaction against the other man was no less, but now—faced with the moment of pressing the tape control key—he found all his history and environmental training against what he was about to do. *Murder*—screamed his conscious mind—*it'll be murder!*

His throat ached and was dry as some seared and cindered landscape of Earth might one day be after the lashing of a Chedal space-based weapon. His chest muscles had tensed and it seemed hard to get his breath. With an internal gasp of panic, he realized that the longer he hesitated, the harder it would be. His finger touched and trembled against the smooth, cold surface of the tape control key, even as the fingers of his other hand continued to key in data.

"How much longer?" hissed Mial in his ear.

*   *   *

Ty refused to look up. He kept his face hidden. One look at that face would be enough to warn Mial.

What if you're wrong?—screamed his mind. It was a thought he could not afford to have, not with the future of the Earth and all its people riding on this moment. He swallowed, closed his eyes, and jammed sideways on the tape key with his finger. He felt it move under his touch.

He opened his eyes. There had been no sound.

He lifted his gaze and saw Mial's face only inches away staring down at him.

"What's the matter?" whispered Mial, tearingly.

Nothing had happened. Somehow Mial was still alive. Ty swallowed and got his inner trembling under control.

"Nothing . . ." he said.

"What is the cause of this conversation?" broke in the deep, yammering, translated voice of one of the Laburti. "Is there a difficulty with the device?"

"Is there?" hissed Mial.

"No . . ." Ty pulled himself together. "I'll handle it now. You can go back to them."

"All right," said Mial, abruptly straightening up and letting go of the case.

He turned and went back to join the Laburti Observer.

Ty turned back to his work and went on to produce his tape of statistical forecasts for both races. Standing in the center of the room to explain it, while the two alien groups held copies of the tape, he found his voice growing harsher as he talked.

But he made no attempt to moderate it. He had failed to stop Mial. Nothing mattered now.

These were Annie's results, he thought, and they were correct and undeniable. The two alien races could ignore them only at the cost of cutting off their noses to spite their faces. Whatever else would come from Mial's scheming and actions here—this much from Annie was unarguable. No sane race could ignore it.

When he finished, he dropped the tape brusquely on top of Annie's case and looked directly at Mial. The dark-haired man's eyes met his, unreadably.

"You'll go back and wait," said Mial, barely moving his lips. The Laburti Consul glided toward Ty. Together they left and returned to the room with the baggage, where Ty had been kept earlier.

"Your device will be here in a moment," said the Laburti, leaving him. And, in fact, a moment later a mech moved into the room, deposited Annie on the floor and withdrew. Like a man staring out of a daze, Ty fell feverishly upon the side panel of the metal case and began unscrewing the wing nuts securing it.

The panel fell away in his hands and he laid it aside. He stared into the inner workings before him, tracing the connections to the power supply, the data control key, and the case that he had made earlier. There were the wires, exactly as he had fitted them in; and there had been no lack of power evident in Annie's regular working. Now, with his fore-finger half an inch above the insulation of the wires, he traced them from the data control key back to the negative power lead connection, and from the case toward its connection, with the positive power lead.

He checked, motionless, with pointing finger. The connection was made to the metal case, all right; but the other end of the wire lay limply along other connections, unattached to the power lead. He had evidently, simply forgotten to make that one, final, and vital connection.

Forgotten . . . ? His finger began to tremble. He dropped down limply on the seat-surface facing Annie.

He had not forgotten. Not just . . . forgotten. A man did not forget something like that. It was a lifetime's moral training against murder that had tripped him up. And his squeamishness would, in the long run, probably cost the lives of everyone alive on Earth at this moment.

He was sitting-staring at his hands, when the sound of the door opening brought him to his feet. He whirled about to see Mial.

It was not yet too late. The thought raced through his brain as all his muscles tensed. He could still try to kill the other man with his bare hands—and that was a job where his civilized upbringing could not trip him up. He shifted his weight on to his forward foot preparatory to hurling himself at Mial's throat. But before he could act, Mial spoke.

"Well," said the dark-haired man, harshly, "we did it."

Ty froze——checked by the single small word, *we.*

"We?" He stared at Mial, "did what?"

"What do you think? The Chedal and the Laburti are going to agree—they'll sign a pact for the equivalent of a hundred and twenty-five years of peaceful cooperation, provided matters develop according to the instrument's estimates. They've got to check with their respective governments, of course, but that's only a formality—" he broke off, his face tightening suspiciously. "What's wrong with you?" His gaze went past Ty to the open side of Annie.

"What's wrong with the instrument?"

"Nothing," said Ty. His head was whirling and he felt an insane urge to break out laughing. "—Annie just didn't kill you, that's all."

"Kill me?" Mial's face paled, then darkened. "You were going to kill me—with that?" He pointed at Annie.

"I was going to send thirteen thousand volts through you while you were helping me with the Demonstration," said Ty, still light-headed, "—if I hadn't crossed myself up. But you tell me it's all right, anyway. You say the aliens're going to agree."

"You thought they wouldn't?" said Mial, staring at him.

"I thought you were playing some game of your own. You said you were."

"That's right," said Mial. Some of the dark color faded from his face. "I was. I had to. You couldn't be trusted."

"*I* couldn't be trusted?" Ty burst out.

"Not you—or any of your bunch!" Mial laughed, harshly. "Babes in the woods, all of you. You build a machine that proves peace pays better than war, and think that settles the problem. What would have happened without someone like me along—"

"You! How they let someone like you weasel your way in—"

"Why you don't think I was assigned to this mission through any kind of accident, do you?" Mial laughed in Ty's face. "They combed the world to find someone like me."

"Combed the world? Why?"

"Because you *had* to come, and the Laburti would only allow two of us with the analyzer to make the trip," said Mial. "You were the best Operator. But you were no politician—and no actor. And there was no time to teach you the facts of life. The only way to make it plain to the aliens that you were at cross purposes with me was to pick someone to head this Mission whom you couldn't help fighting."

"Couldn't help fighting?" Ty stood torn with fury and disbelief. "Why should I have someone along I couldn't help fighting—"

"So the aliens would believe me when I told them your faction back on Earth was strong enough so that I had to carry on the real negotiations behind your back."

"What—real negotiations?"

"Negotiations," said Mial, "to decide whose side we with our Annie-machines and their Operators would be on, during the hundred and twenty-five

years of peace between the Great Races." Mial smiled
sardonically at Ty.

"Side?" Ty stood staring at the other man. "Why
should we be on anyone's side?"

"Why, because by manipulating the data fed to the
analyzers, we can control the pattern of growth; so
that the Chedal can gain three times as fast as the
Laburti in a given period, or the Laburti gain at the
same rate over the Chedal. Of course," said Mial,
dryly, "I didn't ever exactly promise we could do
that in so many words, but they got the idea. Of
course, it was the Laburti we had to close with—but
I dickered with the Chedal first to get the Laburti
price up."

"What price?"

"Better relationships, more travel between the
races."

"But—" Ty stammered. "It's not true! That about
manipulating the data."

"Of course it's not true!" snapped Mial. "And they
never would have believed it if they hadn't seen you—
the neutralist—fighting me like a Kilkenny cat." Mial
stared at him. "Neither alien bunch ever thought
seriously about not going to war anyway. They each
just considered putting it off until they could go into
it with a greater advantage over the other."

"But—they can't *prefer* war to peace!"

Mial made a disgusted noise in his throat.

"You amateur statesmen!" he said. "You build a
better mousetrap and you think that's all there is to
it. Just because something's better for individuals, or
races, doesn't mean they'll automatically go for it.
The Chedal and Laburti have a reason for going to
war that can't be figured on your Annie-machine."

"What?" Ty was stung.

"It's called the emotional factor," said Mial, grimly.
"The climate of feeling that exists between the Chedal

and the Laburti races—like the climate between you and me."

Ty found his gaze locked with the other man's. He opened his mouth to speak—then closed it again. A cold, electric shock of knowledge seemed to flow through him. Of course, if the Laburti felt about the Chedal as he felt about Mial . . .

All at once, things fell together for him, and he saw the true picture with painfully clear eyes. But the sudden knowledge was a tough pill to get down. He hesitated.

"But you've just put off war a hundred and twenty-five years!" he said. "And both alien races'll be twice as strong, then!"

"And we'll be forty times as strong as we are now," said Mial, dryly. "What do you think a nearly three percent growth advantage amounts to, compounded over a hundred and twenty-five years? By that time we'll be strong enough to hold the balance of power between them and force peace, if we want it. They'd like to cut each other's throats, all right, but not at the cost of cutting their own, for sure. Besides," he went on, more slowly, "if your peace can prove itself in that length of time—now's its chance to do it."

He fell silent. Ty stood, feeling betrayed and ridiculed. All the time he had been suspecting Mial, the other man had been working clear-eyed toward the goal. For if the Laburti and the Chedal felt as did he and Mial, the unemotional calm sense of Annie's forecast never would have convinced the aliens to make peace.

Ty saw Mial watching him now with a sardonic smile. He thinks I haven't got the guts to congratulate him, thought Ty.

"All right," he said, out loud. "You did a fine job—in spite of me. Good for you."

"Thanks," said Mial grimly. They looked at each other.

"But—" said Ty, after a minute, between his teeth, the instinctive venom in him against the other man rushing up behind his words, "I still hate your guts! Once I thought there was a way out of that, but you've convinced me different, as far as people like us are concerned. Once this is over, I hope to heaven I never set eyes on you again!"

Their glances met nakedly.

"Amen," said Mial softly. "Because next time *I'll* kill *you.*"

"Unless I beat you to it," said Ty.

Mial looked at him a second longer, then turned and quit the room. From then on, and all the way back to Earth they avoided each other's company and did not speak again. For there was no need of any more talk.

They understood each other very well.

Only a truly civilized being is fit to judge a wild one.

Roofs of Silver

"Because you're a fool, brother," said Moran.

The words hung on the hot air between them. A small breeze blew through the rectangular window aperture in the thick mud wall to the rear. Through the window could be seen a bit of a garden, a few blue mountain flowers, and the courtyard wall of mud. The breeze disturbed the air but did not cool the room. In an opposite wall the hide curtain did not quite cover the doorway. The curtain's much-handled edge was scalloped and worn thin. Hot sunlight from the square came through the gap. Beasts like Earth donkeys, with unnatural-looking splayed hooves, drowsed around the fountain in the center of the square.

"Why don't you call me a donkey?" said Jabe, looking at them.

"Fair enough," said Moran. He sat, gowned and fat among his grain sacks, his slate balanced on his knees, his creased fingers of both hands white with chalk. "Because it's just what you aren't. Any more than those variforms out there are, no matter what they're called."

Jabe moved uneasily. His spurs clinked.

"You think I'm overadapted?" he said.

"No. You're just a fool," said Moran. "As I said and keep saying. You've been here ten years. You started out a liberal and you've become conservative. When you started to work with these settlers, the returns weren't in yet."

"It's not a hundred per cent," said Jabe.

"How can it be?" said Moran. "But what's a statistical chance of error of three per cent?"

"I can't believe it," said Jabe. "I might have believed it, back on Earth, when these people were just population figures to me. Now, I've lived with them ten years. I can't believe it."

"I've lived with them, too."

"Eight years," said Jabe.

"Long enough. I didn't marry into them, though. That's why my eyes are still clear."

"No," said Jabe. He beat his hands together softly with a curious rhythmic and measured motion until he became suddenly aware of Moran's eyes upon them, and checked their motion, guiltily.

"No," he said again, with an effort. "It can't be true. It must be sociological."

"Indigenous."

"I can't believe that," said Jabe.

"You aren't arguing with me, man," said Moran. "You're arguing with a ten-year survey. I showed you the report. It's not a matter of living conditions or local superstitions. It's a steady, progressive deterioration from generation to generation. Already the shift is on from conscience to taboo."

"I haven't seen it."

"You've got a single point of view. And a technologically high level of community at that mine."

"No," said Jabe, shifting his weight from one foot to the other, and looking down at Moran. "Report or no report, I'm not condemning a world full of human beings."

Moran sat heavily among the grain sacks.

"Who's condemning?" he said. "It's just quarantine for the present, and you and I and the rest of the agents have to go back."

"You could hold up the report."

"No," said Moran. "You know better than that."

"It could be stolen. The agent bringing it to you could have been knifed."

"No. No," said Moran. "The report goes in." He looked with a twist of anger on his face at Jabe. "Don't you think I feel for them? I've been here almost as long as you have. It's just quarantine for a time—fifty years, maybe."

"And after the fifty years runs out?"

"We'll figure out something in that much time."

"No," said Jabe. "No more than they did on Astarte, or on Hope. They'll sterilize."

"Rather than let them breed back down into the animal."

"There's no danger of that here, I tell you," said Jabe.

"Report says there is," said Moran. "I'm sending it in. It has to be done."

"Earth has to protect Earth, you mean."

Moran sighed heavily.

"All right," he said. "I'm through talking about it. You get yourself ready to leave, along with the other agents—though if you take my advice, the kindest thing you can do for that wife of yours is to leave right now, just vanish."

"I don't think I'll go," said Jabe. "No." His spurs clinked again. "I'm not leaving."

"I haven't any more time to waste with you," said Moran. He twisted around and pulled one of the grain sacks out of position. Behind it was revealed a black board with several buttons and dials upon it. He pressed a button and turned a dial. He spoke to the board.

"Survey ship? I've got an agent here who——"

Jabe leaned down and forward, and struck. Moran choked off in midsentence and stiffened up. His fat

arm came back and up, groping for the knife hilt
standing out between his shoulder blades. Then he
fell forward, half covering the black board.

"Moran?" said the board in a small, buzzing voice.
"Moran? Come in, Moran. . . ."

Two hours later, out on the desert with Alden Mann
who had come into the city with him to buy medi-
cines for the mine, Jabe stopped automatically to
rest the horses, and Alden drew up level with him.

"Something on your mind, Jabe Halvorsen?" said
Alden.

"Nothing," said Jabe. "No, nothing." He looked
into Alden's frank, younger face, made himself smile,
and went back to staring out past Alden at the sherry-
colored, wavering distance of the hot sandy plain.
Behind him, to the right of their road was the edge of
the cultivated area with palmlike trees about thirty
feet high.

"Let me know, if," said Alden, cheerfully, as he got out
his pipe and began to fill it, throwing one leg over his
saddlehorn. The spur below the floppy leather pantleg
flashed the sun for a moment in Jabe's eyes.

"If, I will," answered Jabe automatically. Alden, he
thought, was the closest thing to an actual friend
that he had. Moran he had known for a long time,
but they had not really been close. They had been
relatives in a foreign land.

Jabe lit his own pipe. He did not feel guilt, only a
hollow sick feeling over the killing of Moran. Over
the necessity of his killing Moran. He thought there
would be no immediate danger from it. The knife
was a city knife he had bought there an hour before
for the purpose. He had worn gloves. He had taken
Moran's purse, the report, and nothing else. The survey ship would not be able to identify him as the
murderer and send men to arrest him in much less
than three months. He should be able to do some-

thing in three months. If he did, after that nothing mattered.

It was good that he had suspected the report's coming. He puffed on his pipe, staring at the sandy distance. He knew where they had gone wrong. But Moran was proof of the fact that argument would be useless. They wanted something concrete.

"I was wild out here, once," said Jabe, to Alden.

"Yeah," Alden glanced at him, with some sympathy. "Nobody holds it against you any more."

"I still don't belong."

"For me, you do. And for Sheila." Alden blew smoke at him. "When your son's born he'll have a place on the staff of the mine."

"Yes," said Jabe. His thoughts veered. "You people never had much to do with the wild ones."

"Oh, we shoot a few every year."

"Did you ever keep any for a while? Just to get a notion of what makes them tick?"

"No," said Alden. "We're miners with work to do. If one gets caught, he's hung; and we're back on the job in an hour."

"You didn't hang me."

"That was different," said Alden. "You came in with that trader's packtrain, and when it was time to leave Sheila spoke for you."

"You didn't maybe take me for a trader crewman, myself?"

"Oh no," said Alden. "We knew. You can tell, a wild one."

"I'm surprised," said Jabe, a little sadly, "you'd want to risk it."

"If Sheila spoke for you—" Alden shrugged. He stared at Jabe. "What got you thinking of wild ones?"

"Nothing," said Jabe. "The sand, I guess."

It was not true, of course. What had started him was the knowledge of his advantage over Moran and the rest. All the other agents on this world had played one role, one character. By chance of luck, or fate, it had fallen on him to play two. He had not meant to be taken up by the community around the silver mine back in the mountains. It had merely happened. Love had happened—to himself as well as Sheila. And the survey ship, concerned only with its routine hundred-year check on this planetful of emigrants from old Earth, had okayed his change of status.

The result, he thought now, as the smoke of the pipe came hot from low in the bowl of it, almost burned out, was that he had two points of view where Moran and the rest had one. Two eyes instead of one, binocular vision instead of the one-dimensional view a single seeing organ could achieve. There was a recessive strain cropping up on this world, all right, but it was carried and spread by the wild ones—the degenerate individuals that had neither clan nor community to uphold them.

And the check to it, he was sure, was right in his own adopting community. The tight-held social unit of the mine people, who had preserved their purity of strain by keeping the degenerates killed off and at a distance. There was no doubt in his mind that if he had been actually a wild one Sheila would never have been attracted to him, or he to her. It was because, though she did not know it, he was unalloyed with the spreading degeneracy of this world—as she herself was pure, untainted silver like that the mine refinery turned out of the common, mingled ore of the mountains—that she had demanded him of the trader.

He knocked his pipe out on his boot. And there was the answer, he thought. A natural tendency to breed for the best that was a counterforce to what Moran and the others had discovered. In the long run, the superior, pure breed would kill off the degenerates. All he had to do was prove it to the survey ship.

Only for that he needed a specimen of each type. One of the mine people would not be hard to come by. But he would need one of the wild ones as well.

After that, it was up to the testing facilities of the survey to monitor and make findings. But the findings could only substantiate what he already knew.

And that was the important thing. For himself, he had burnt his bridges with the knife he had driven into Moran. But Sheila and his unborn son would be safe.

"Let's get on," he said to Alden. Alden knocked out his own pipe and the two horses went forward once more. The gait of their wide hooves—not splayed so badly as were the hooves of the donkeys but spread for the sand as camel hooves are spread—was smooth. Jabe wondered how it could be done—attracting one of the wild ones. He and Alden would be passing through wild territory in the early part of the mountains. But bait was needed.

After a while a thought came to him. He reached down and unhooked one of the large silver buckles from his boot. Alden, riding a little ahead, did not notice. As they rode on, Jabe set himself to rubbing the buckle to a high shine on the pant's leg hidden from Alden by the horse's bulk.

When they saw the first low crests of the mountains rising ahead of them, Jabe stuck the buckle into the headband of his wide-brimmed hat—on the side away from Alden.

When darkness came, they camped. They were only a few hours from the mine, but they were deep in the mountains. In a little shallow opening in the rocks, all but clear of scrub variform pine and native bush, they lit a fire and ate. Alden rolled himself early in his blankets, but Jabe sat up, feeding the fire and frowning into its licking flames.

He had not even reached for the chunk of dead limb an hour or so later. He had only thought about it—his hand had not yet moved—but some preliminary tensing of the body must have given him away, because the voice, dry as the desert wind that had followed them all through the day, whispered suddenly in his ear.

"Don't move, mister."

He did not move. His rifle was lying across his spread knees, its trigger guard scant inches from his right index finger, but the whisper had come from the dark immediately behind him, and a thrown knife takes very little time to cover the distance a whisper can carry, even in the stillness of a mountain night. He glanced past the flames of the fire to where the dim shape of the blanket-wrapped body of Alden lay like a long, dark log against the further rim of darkness. But whether Alden slept or waked, whether he had heard the whisper or not, the young miner gave no sign of being aware of what was happening.

"Reach out with your right arm. Slow," said the whisperer. "Fill me a cup of that coffee and hand it back. And don't you turn, mister."

Jabe moved slowly as he had been told. The last word had been pronounced *turun*. The accentual difference from the speech of Alden announced a wild one, one of the groupless wandering savages roaming about the deserted lands. The speaker behind Jabe—was it a man, or a woman?—used his words like a child, with sing-song cadences.

Slowly and steadily, Jabe passed back the full cup without turning. He felt it taken from him and heard the soft noise of drinking.

"Fill again, mister." The cup was sitting again, empty, at his side. "Fill yourself, too."

Jabe obeyed.

"What do you want?" he asked, when he had his own hot, full cup between his hands. He stared into the flames, waiting for the answer.

"Some things. That silver do-thing in your hat. Some talk. You riders from that mine town?"

"Yes," said Jabe. He had been easing his hand, a millimeter at a time toward the rifle on his knees. He found himself whispering his answer. If Alden still slumbered, so much the better. The rifle on his knees was like any that the mine people carried, but there was an anesthetic cartridge in its chamber now instead of an ordinary shell.

"It's them goats you're after?"

"Goats?" said Jabe. The community of the mine kept goats for hide and meat. He had been set to guarding some himself in the beginning, before his marriage ceremony with Sheila. Usually the old people watched them. "Some strays?"

"They aren't not strays," came back the answer. "One's eat and the other two butchered ready to eat. They's mine now."

"You stole them."

"Was you never hungry, mister?"

"Yes," said Jabe. "I was wild once, myself."

He sat waiting for the response to that. It was one of the things he had hoped would help. In addition to the bullet that was not a bullet in his gun, there were other things that belonged to him as an agent. There was a match box in his pocket that was not a match box, but an emotional response recorder. A moment's cooperation, a moment's relaxation from the wild one behind him was all that he needed. A chance to bring the rifle to bear. And meanwhile, the recorder was running. He had started it the minute Alden had rolled up and turned away in his blankets.

"Then you know," said the whisperer. "You know it, then." There was a moment of pause. "It's rich you is, down there at that mine. I seen the packtrains come and go. I seen the goats. And I seen you all down there, all rich with silver."

"The silver," said Jabe, "you like the silver?"

"Mighty rich, you is. All that silver."

"We have to mine for it," said Jabe. "We have to make it." He could not feel the recorder in his pocket, but he knew it was there, taking down the colors of the wild one's responses. "It isn't just there to be picked up."

"Yeah," there was something almost like a whispery chuckle behind him. "I found her so, watching. I couldn't walk down in through your gates, not me. But I took t'myself a high place and watched—all day—the fire going in the tall building and the bright silver things about the town. And the women with silver on them, so that they shine here and there in the sun, coming and going down there 'tween the houses. And the houses, all the big ones and the little ones with roofs of silver."

"Roofs—?" said Jabe, and then to his mind's eye came a picture of the corrugated metal sheathing, dating indestructibly back over a hundred years to the first coming of the settlers to this world, and the first establishment of the mine. "But they're——"

"What, mister?"

"Part of the buildings," said Jabe, "that's all. . . ."

A whispery laugh sounded in his ear.

"Don't fear, mister. I tell you something. If it were me comin' in with horses and men to take all you got, I wouldn't let nobody touch them roofs, but leave them there for the sun to shine on. I never seen nothing so fine, so fine anywhere, as them roofs of silver all to-shine in the sun." The whisper changed a little in tone, suddenly. "You feel that way too, don't you, mister?"

"Yes," said Jabe, out of a suddenly dry throat. "Oh, yes. The roofs—the roofs, all silver."

"I tell you what," said the whisperer. "I take this from your hat"—Jabe felt the buckle lightly plucked from his hatband—"and I got some other little silver bits from your saddles. But I want you to know, I'm going to make me little houses and roof them houses with the silver, just like yours, and come day put them out for the sun to bright-shine on. So you know your silver, it in the sun."

"Good," said Jabe, whispering. His throat was still dry.

"And now mister ... don't move," said the voice from behind him, "I got to——"

The whispered words ceased suddenly. Caught in a sudden cold ecstasy of fear, Jabe sat frozen, the breath barely trickling in and out of his throat. *For Sheila*, he prayed internally, *for all of them at the mine—not now. Don't let me be killed now. . . .* The long seconds blew away into silence. Then, a far shout broke the plaster cast of his tension.

"Alden! Jabe! Coming up!"

In one motion, Jabe snatched up his rifle and whirled to face the darkness beyond the firelight behind him. But it hung there before him emptily. And even as he relaxed and turned away from it, there rode up from the other side of the fire three of the mine men on nervous horses, their rifle barrels gleaming in the light of the fire.

"We were after a goat lifter, and the hounds started baying off this way. We rode over from our camp," said Jeff Connel, the assay engineer, as he led the way in. His long dark face gleamed under gray hair as he looked down into Jabe's face. "What's the matter with Alden, sleeping like that?"

"Alden!" Jabe turned and stepped over the fire to shake his friend out of his blankets. Alden rolled over at the first touch, his head lolling backward.

His throat had been neatly cut.

Their return to the mine with Alden's body took place in silence. Jabe rode in their midst, aware of their attitude, whether right or wrong. When two men went out from the mine together on a journey, one was responsible for the other, no matter what the circumstances. He could accept that; it was part of their customs. But what touched him with coldness now was the fact that he seemed to feel suspicion in them. Suspicion of the fact that it had been him who lived, while Alden was murdered.

That suspicion might block his chance of getting a

clean recording from one of them to place in comparison with the recording he had made of the wild one. And the recording was all he had, now. Back by the fire he had been full of hope. If he could have captured the wild one and compared his recording with Alden's when he awoke Alden to tell him of the capture. . . . But there had never been any hope of waking Alden.

Yet, there was a sort of chill hope still in him. He did have the recording he had made. And he had himself to make a recording of for control purposes. It was not impossible; it was still quite possible that he could get a parallel recording yet from one another of the mine people. It was a field sort of expedient, but the survey ship could not ignore it. If they were faced with three recordings of responses to parallel situations, and there was an identity between the two belonging to Jabe and one of the mine people, and a variance between those two and the wild one, they would have to check further.

With luck, they would send down assistance to capture at least one miner and one savage and take them, drugged, to the ship for full tests. And then. . . .

The sad caravan carrying Alden's body had wound its way through the mine streets picking up a cortege of women and children, for the available men were out on the hunt as the three who had come on Jabe and Alden had been. At the mine manager's house they stopped, brought in the body of Alden and told their story. Lenkhart, the mine manager, stood with his gray eyes in a bearded face, watching Jabe as they talked. But he said nothing in blame—if nothing in comfort. He beat his hands together with a curious rhythmic and measured motion, and dismissed them to their homes.

Sheila was kinder.

"Jabe!" she said, and held him, back at last in the privacy and safety of their own home. "It might have been you killed!"

"I know," he said. He sat down wearily. "But it was Alden."

"Oh, that animal!" said Sheila with sudden violence. "That *animal*! They ought to burn him at the pass and leave him there as a warning to the rest!"

He felt a certain sense of shock.

"Sheila," he said. She looked at him. She was a slim, tall girl with heavy, black hair. Under that hair her eyes seemed darker in this moment than he had ever seen them before, and almost feverish. "He didn't burn Alden. Alden probably never even woke up."

"But he's an animal—a wild animal!" she said again. "If he is a man, that is. It might be one of those horrible women. Was it a woman, Jabe?"

He caught a new note of hatred in the question, the thought that it might have been a woman. He had never seen her like this; he had not known she could be so dangerous where things close to her were concerned. He thought of the child she was carrying, and a little fear came for a moment into the back of his mind.

"I don't think so. No," he said. He felt the lie like a heavy weight on him. For it had been impossible to tell the sex of the whisperer. Weariness swept over him like a smothering wave. "Let's go to bed."

In the obscurity and privacy of their bed, later, she held him tightly.

"They'll get him tomorrow," she whispered. And she was fiercely loving. Later, much later, when he was sure that she slept heavily, he rose quietly in the dark and went into the living room-dining room of their three-room cottage, and extracting the recorded strip from the imitation match box, processed it. In the little light of an oil lamp, he held it up to examine it behind closed shades. And his breath caught for a second.

An angry fate seemed to pursue him. The strip was a long band of colors, a code for emotional profile that he could read as well as the men up on the

survey ship. And the profile he read off now was that
of a lone savage all right, but by some freak of luck
one with crippled but burning talents—talents far
surpassing even Jabe's own. In the range of artistic
perception, the profile of the whisperer shone power-
fully with a rich and varied spectrum of ability and
desire wherever the silver roofs had been mentioned.

Dropping the proof of a bitter exception to all he
knew about the wild ones, Jabe beat his hands together with the measured rhythm that signalled frus-
tration among the people of the mine.

In the morning, the men that could be spared formed
for the posse in the open space below the mine buildings and above the houses. There were some forty of
them, including Jabe; all superbly mounted, all armed
with rifles, side-arms and knives. Every two-man unit
had a saddle radio. The hounds, leashed, bayed and
milled in their pack.

Standing on the platform from which mine meetings were held, the mine manager laid out the orders
of the hunt. A senior engineer for many years before
he had become manager, Lenkhart was stooped and
ascetic-looking with his long gray beard.

"Now," he said to them, "man or woman, he can't
have gone far since last night if he's on foot. And a
man on horseback doesn't need to steal goats. You'll
stay in contact with radios at all times. At the sign of
any marauder or his trail, fire two spaced shots in
the air. If you hear the shots fired by someone else,
wait for radio orders from the senior engineer of your
group before moving in. Any questions?"

There were none. To Jabe, watching, there was a
heart-warming quality in the cool, civilized way they
went about it. He was paired, himself, with Sheila's
father for the hunt. He reined over next to the older
man and they all moved out together. The hounds,
loosed at last from their leashes, yelped and belled,
streaming past them.

They moved as a group for the first two hours, back to the camp where Alden had been killed. From there they fanned out, picked up the trail of the whisperer, running northwest and quartering away from the mining town. A little later, they lost the trail again and they split up into pairs, each pair with a hound or two, and began to work the possible area.

Sheila's father had said little or nothing during the early part of the ride. And Jabe had been busy thinking of his own matters. There must, he had told himself desperately again and again after the moment of discovering the freakish quality of the whisperer's profile, be some way yet of saving the situation. Now, as they turned into a maze of small canyons, hope on the wings of an idea suddenly returned to him.

He had been assuming that the whisperer's profile was useless as a means to point up the relative purity of one of the mine people. But this need not be so. The recorder took down only what it was exposed to. If he could make a recording of the whisperer where roofs of silver and all the area of the whisperer's artistic perception was carefully avoided the wild one would show in the color code as only the lonely savage he was. All the primitiveness, the bluntedness of the whisperer would be on show—his degeneracy in all other fields. A recording of any of the other mine people, and a recording of Jabe, matched with this second attempt, would show Jabe and the mine person's profile falling into one separate class, and the whisperer's into another. Better yet—the whisperer would be executed when he was caught. There would then be no chance of the survey ship sending down to make other recordings of the whisperer as a check. All that was necessary was to find the chance to make the second recording, under conditions that would be favorable. And if the whisperer was captured and held for a day or so while a trial was being set up, the chance would be there for the finding. . . .

"Jabe," said Sheila's father. "Pull up."

Jabe reined his horse to a halt and turned to face his father-in-law. Tod Harnung had called a halt in a little amphitheater of scrub pine and granite rock. As Jabe watched, the older man threw one leg over his saddle and began to fill his pipe. Like all who had achieved the status of engineer he wore a beard, and his beard had only a few streaks of gray in it. His straight nose, his dark eyes like Sheila's above the beard, were not unkind as they looked at Jabe now.

"Smoke if you like," he said.

"Thank you, sir," said Jabe. Gratefully, he got out his own pipe and tobacco, which he had not dared reach for before. The "sir" no longer stuck in his throat as it had in his first days among these people. He understood these signs of authority in a small, compact society which had persisted virtually unchanged since the planet's first settlement, a hundred and sixteen years before. It was such things, he was convinced, that had kept the pure silver of their strain unalloyed by the base metals of the disintegrating wild ones and the softening people of the desert and lower lands. By harshness and rigidity they had kept themselves shining bright.

Even, he thought, lighting his pipe—and it was a suddenly startling thought—in comparison to the very Earth strain in the survey ship now presuming to sit in judgment upon them. For the first time Jabe found himself comparing his own so-called "most-civilized" Earth strain with these hard-held descendants of pioneers. In such as Moran, in agents and sociologists, even in himself, wasn't there a softness, a selfish blindness bolstered by the false aid of many machines and devices?

He thought of himself as he had been ten years ago. Even five years ago. He was still largely of Earth then, still hesitant, fumbling and unsure. He could never then have reacted so swiftly, so surely, and so decisively to Moran's announcement about the report. Above all, he could not have killed Moran, even if he had seen the overwhelming necessity of it. This world, and in particular, the people of the mine here, had pared him down to a hard core of usefulness.

"—Sir?" he said, for Sheila's father had just spoken to him again. "I didn't catch just what you said, Mr. Harnung."

"I said—you don't by any chance know this killer, do you?"

Jabe looked sharply up from the pipe he was just about to light. He sat in his saddle, the pipe in one hand, the match in the other.

"Know him?" said Jabe.

"Do you?"

"Why—no!" said Jabe. "No sir. Of course not. I don't. Why should I?"

Tod Harnung took his own pipe out of his bearded mouth.

"Sheila's my only child," he said. "I've got a grandson to think of."

"I don't understand," said Jabe, bewildered.

The dark eyes looked at him above the beard.

"My grandson," said Harnung, harshly, "will one day be an engineer like I am. There's going to be no stain on his reputation, nothing to make him be passed over when a vacancy occurs in one of the senior positions." There was a moment's silence.

"I see," said Jabe. "You mean, me."

"There'll be no fault about his mother's line. I'm responsible for that," said Harnung. "I've always hoped there would be no fault about his father to be remembered against him, either."

Jabe felt himself stirred by a profound emotion.

"I swear," he said, "I never saw or heard that wild one before in my life! Alden was my friend—you know that!"

"I always thought so," said Harnung.

"You know," said Jabe, reining his horse close to the older man, "you know how much Sheila means to me, what you all mean to me. You know what it's meant for me to be accepted here as Sheila's husband among people"—Jabe's voice cracked a little in spite of himself—"people with a firm, solid way of life. People who know what they are and what everybody else is. All my life I wanted to find people who were sure of themselves, sure of the way the universe works and their own place in it. I always hated the business of not being completely sure, of only being mostly right, of having to guess and never having anyone in authority to turn to. And do you think," cried Jabe, "I'd throw that away, all that, for some moronic savage?"

He stopped, shaking a little, and wiped his mouth with the back of his hand. For a moment, he thought he had said too much. But then Harnung's eyes, which had been steady on him, relaxed.

"No," said Harnung, "I don't believe you would." He nodded at Jabe's pipe. "Go ahead and light up there. I had to make sure, Jabe. I have my responsibility as Sheila's father."

"Yes, sir. I understand." Fingers still trembling a little, Jabe got his pipe lit. He drew the smoke gratefully deep into his lungs.

"Very well, then," said Harnung. "As soon as you've finished your pipe, we'll get on."

"Sir!" said Jabe. An idea had just come to him. He took his pipe out of his mouth, and turned quickly to the other man. "I just thought of something."

Harnung peered at him.

"Yes?"

"I just remembered something that killer said. . . ." Jabe put his hand on the pommel of Harnung's saddle to hold the two horses together as they began to grow restive with the halt. "He said he'd been watching the town from some high place close at hand. Now we've circled almost a full turn back toward the town. Right ahead of us is a spot where we can cut over to the rock faces north of town. I'll bet that's where he's holed up."

Harnung frowned.

"He'd have had to cut back through us earlier to be there now," the older man said. "How could he have cut through us—and past the hounds?"

"Some of these desert runners could do it," Jabe said. "Believe me, sir, I know from when I was one of them. It's worth a try. And if I'm the one to lead us to where we capture him. . . ."

Harnung scratched his beard with the stem of his pipe.

"I don't know," he said. "I'll have to radio and ask permission for you and me to try it. And if we get it, we'll be leaving a hole in the search pattern when we drop out. If it turned out later he got away through that hole. . . ."

"I give you my word, sir—"

"All right," said Harnung, abruptly. "I'll do it." He picked up his radio set from the saddle before him and rang the senior engineer of the search. He listened to the answering voice for a minute.

"All right," he said at last, and put the radio back. "Come on, Jabe."

They reined their horses around and went off in a new direction. The impatient bitch hound that had been waiting with them leaped hungrily ahead once more, the red tongue lolling out of her mouth.

They angled their approach so as to come up on the blind side of the heights of rock north of the mine town. It was past noon when they reached the first of these and they began slowly to work around the perimeter of the rocks. This part of the mountain was all narrow canyons and sudden upthrusts of granite. The sun moved slowly, as slowly as they, across the high and cloudless sky above, as they prospected without success.

It was not until nearly midafternoon that the hound, running still ahead of them up a narrow cut in the rock, checked, stiffened, and whimpered, lifting her nose in the air. She turned sharply and trotted up a slope to the right, where she paused again, sniffing the breeze.

The two men looked off in the direction she pointed.

"The Sheep's Head," said Jabe. "Sir, he's up on the Sheep's Head. He has to be. And there's only one way down from there."

"He couldn't see much from there unless he wanted to climb away out . . . well, let's look," said Harnung. They put their horses to a trot and went up the slope to emerge from the canyon and cut to their right up around an overhanging lump of bare rock that was the base of the granite pinnacle known from its shape as the Sheep's Head.

The hound was eager. A sharp command from Harnung held her to no more than the customary five yards in front of the horses' heads, but she shivered and danced with the urge to run. Breasting a steeper slope as they approached the top of the pinnacle, the two riders were forced to slow to a walk. The bald dome of the Sheep's Head was just a short distance vertically above them.

They were perhaps a hundred feet from a view of the summit, when the hound suddenly belled, loud and clear. Looking up together, they saw a flicker of movement disappearing over the shoulder of the Sheep's Head. Harnung and Jabe angled their horses off in that direction, but when Jabe would have forced his animal to a trot Harnung laid his hand on the reins.

"We'll catch him now," he said. "A walk's good enough."

"Yes sir," said Jabe.

They walked their horses on up to the crest of the rise, the hound dancing ahead of them. As they came level with the top they found themselves at the head

of a long gully cutting away down from the side of
the Sheep's Head, out toward a smaller pinnacle of
rock. A few short yards to the right of them, they saw
all the litter of a cold camp, the half-demolished
carcasses of the missing goats, and some little, toy-
like objects the tops of which caught the glitter of the
sun. Jabe reined his horse over to them, and reached
down. They were all attached to a smoothed piece of
wood, and they came up as a group as he leaned
from his saddle to scoop them in. Sitting in the saddle, he stared at them. Proof of the artistic perception he had read in the whisperer's profile glowed
before him. They were tiny models of buildings with
pieces of silver fitted onto them for roofs. And it was
not just that they were well made—it was more than
that. Some genius of the maker had caught the very
feel and purpose of the mine and the life of their
people, in their making.

"Jabe!" snapped Harnung. "Come along!"

Jabe turned his horse to join the older man, slipping the piece of wood with the house models into
his saddle bag. They headed together at a steady trot
up the slope and down into the mouth of the gully.

Harnung was talking into the radio, the black bush
of his bearded lips moving close to its mouth-piece.

"The rest'll move in behind us," he said to Jabe,
replacing the radio on his saddle. "But we'll be the
ones to take him. Let's go."

They trotted down the gully, which deepened now
and narrowed. Its walls rose high around them. The
winding semilevel upon which they traveled was clear
except for the occasional rock or boulder. The almost
vertical rock of the walls was free of vegetation except for the occasional clump of brush. After a little
distance, they came to another gully cutting off at
near right angles; and the hound informed them with
whines and yelps that the fugitive had taken this new
way.

They followed.

Coming around a corner suddenly, they faced him at last. There had been no place else for him to go. This gully was blind. He stood with his back against the farther rock of the gully's end, a long knife balanced in one hand in throwing position—a thin, gangling figure in scraggly beard and dirt-darkened hide clothing. At the sight of them, he flipped his hand with the knife back behind his head ready to throw, and Harnung shot him through the shoulder to bring him down.

They brought their prisoner back to the town as the last rays of the sunset were fading from the peaks where he had secretly looked down on the life of the mine. They locked him in a toolshed behind the ore-crushing mill and split up among their various homes. Word had gone in ahead of how the wild one had been taken. Sheila was waiting in their living room for Jabe. She opened her arms to him.

"Jabe!" she said. "You did it! It was *you* that led them to him!" She hugged him, but something he was holding got in her way. "What's that?"

"Nothing." He reached out and dropped the piece of wood with the little silver-roofed houses on it down on the table beside her. "He used my silver buckle to make the roofs on them—the buckle he took from me when Alden was killed." He put his arms around her, and kissed her.

"Eat now," she said, leading him to the table. "You haven't had anything decent since breakfast." He let her steer him to his chair. She had set the table as if for a celebration," with a fresh tablecloth and some blue mountain flowers in a vase.

She sat with him. She had waited to eat until he should get back. She wanted to know all about the hunt. He listened to her questions and, a little uneasily, thought he caught an echo of the doubt that had been in the mind of her father, a doubt about his loyalty to the mine people. She did not doubt now, but earlier she must have, he thought, and now she was trying to make up for it. She came back again and again to the matter of the marauder's execution.

"... I suppose it'll be hanging, though burning's too good for someone like——"

"Sheila!" he put his coffee cup down again in the saucer so hard some of it spilled. "Can't you at least wait until I'm done eating?"

She stared at him.

"What's the matter?" she wanted to know.

"Nothing. Nothing. ..." He picked up the cup carefully again, but it trembled slightly in his hand in spite of all he could do. "We have to be just, that's all. It's a matter of justice with this man."

"But he killed Alden!" Her eyes were quite large, and he moved uncomfortably under their look.

"Of course. Of course ..." he said. "A murderer has to be punished. But you have to remember the man's limitations. He isn't like you or me—or Alden was. He hasn't any sense of right or wrong as we know it. He operates by necessity, by taboo, or superstition. That's why"—he looked appealingly at her— "we mustn't lose our own perspective and get down to his own animal level. We have to execute him—it's necessary. But we shouldn't hate him for being something he can't control."

"But Alden was your friend!" she said. "Doesn't that mean anything to you, Jabe? What's all this about the creature mean, beside the fact Alden was your friend?"

"I know he was my friend!" Even as he lost his temper with her, he knew it was the wrong thing to do, the wrong way to handle the situation. "Do you think I don't know—he was the only friend I had in this place! But I happen to know what it's like to be like that man we've got locked up in the toolshed."

"You were never like that!" she cried.

"I was."

"You were a freighter on a pack train. You had a

job. You weren't a crawling thief or murderer like that——"

"But you remembered that I might have been. Didn't you?" He half rose from the table, shouting. He wanted to throw the accusation squarely in her face. "Last night you remembered that——"

"No!" she cried, suddenly, jumping to her feet. "*You* had to make me do that! And not last night. Just now! You had to mention yourself in the same breath with that animal, that crawling beast in the shape of a man!"

"He is not," said Jabe, trying to make an effort to speak slowly and calmly, "an animal yet. He is only on the way to being one. We who can still think like human beings——"

"Human!" she cried. "He's a filthy, wild animal and he doesn't deserve to be hung. Why do you say he isn't? Why is it everything that's perfectly plain and straight and right to everybody else gets tangled up when you start hashing it over? Alden was your friend and this wild one killed him. It doesn't seem bad enough that creature already stole goats that took the food out of people's mouths——maybe even the mouth of your own son, next winter——"

"Why, there's not going to be any shortage of food——" he began, but she had gone right on talking.

"——not even that. But he killed your friend. And you say he ought to be dealt with, but you want me to feel bad about it at the same time. Nothing I do ever is right, according to you! I'm always wrong, always wrong, according to you! If you feel like that all the time why did you marry me in the first place?"

"You know why I married you——"

"No I don't!" she cried. "I never did!" And she turned and ran from him, suddenly. The bedroom door slammed behind him, and he heard the bolt to it snap shut.

Silence held the house. He got up and went across to the cupboard on the opposite wall. He opened it and took out a small thick bottle of the whisky made at the mine still. For a moment he held it, and then he put it back. Reason returned to him. He felt for the recorder in his pocket. It was there, and he turned toward the door.

Quietly, he let himself out of the house.

The toolshed where the whisperer was held was unguarded and locked only by a heavy bar across the door on the outside. In the darkness, he merely lifted the bar from the door and stepped inside. For a moment he could see nothing; and then as his eyes adjusted to the deeper gloom, the lights on the outer wall of the ore-crushing mill, striking through the gaps between the heavy planks of the toolshed wall, showed him the wild one, tightly bound.

"Hello," he said, feeling the word strange on his lips. A gaunt whisper replied to him.

"I mighty thirsty, mister."

He heard the words with a feeling of shock. He went back outside the shed to a pipe down the hill, filled the tin cup hanging from it and brought it back. The prisoner drank, gulping.

"I thank you, mister."

"That's all right," he said. Reaching in his pocket, he started the recorder. He searched for the expression on the prisoner's face in the darkness, but all he could make out was a vague blur of features and any expression was hidden. It did not matter, he thought.

Skillfully, he began to question the prisoner. . . .

He woke with a sudden jerk and came fully awake. For a second he felt nothing, and then the cruel, dry hands of a hangover clamped unyieldingly upon his head and belly. He could not remember for a moment what had happened. He lay still, on his back, staring at the ceiling above his bed and trying to remember what had happened. Bright sunlight was coming around the edges of the curtain on the window, and Sheila was not in the bed with him.

He must be late for work—but Sheila would never have permitted that. He tried once more to put the previous evening together in his mind, and slowly, it came back.

He had got a good recording from the wild one. He had not even had to look at it to know that it was what he wanted. The prisoner was like any creature in a trap, and there was nothing in him of the dangerous perception Jabe had found earlier. He had got a good recording, and after it was over he had cautioned the prisoner against telling anyone else about the interview. But it did not really matter whether the prisoner spoke or not. They would think, whoever heard it, that Jabe had simply stumbled in on the man while drunk—to taunt or bully him.

For Jabe had made sure that he was drunk, later. But first he had made a parallel recording of himself and one of the supervisors on night shift at the ore-crusher mill, and broadcast the results of all three to the survey ship from a transmitter hidden behind his own house. Then he had gone over to the bachelors' barracks to make sure of his alibi for the evening. There was always a group drinking at the barracks and it was the natural place for a husband who had just had a fight with his wife.

When he stumbled home at last, he had found the bedroom door unbolted.

Now, lying in the bed, he wondered again at the lateness of the morning hour. A thought came to him. Perhaps he had been allowed the day off by the mine manager because of his usefulness in capturing the prisoner. He listened, but could not hear Sheila in the next room. He rolled over and saw a note from her on the bedside table.

"*—Back soon, darling. Breakfast on the stove to warm.*"

Things were evidently well once more between them. He thought of the three profiles safely messaged off to the survey ship the night before and a great sense of relief and happiness rose in him. He rolled out of bed and headed for the shower.

By the time he was showered, dressed, and shaved, the hangover had all but disappeared. He drew the curtain on the bedroom window and looked out on a midmorning bright with the clear mountain sunshine. Up the little slope behind the house, near the storage shed where his transmitter was hidden, a clump of the same blue flowers Sheila had filled into the vase the evening before were growing wild. Their heads stirred in the small breeze passing by, and they struck him suddenly as a token of good luck.

He turned away from the window, walked across the bedroom, and pushing open the door to the main room of the house, stepped into it. The room was clean, tidied-up, and empty of Sheila's presence, but he had not taken more than a step into it before he was aware of his invisible visitors.

The first glimpse showed only a sort of waveriness of the air in two corners of the room—and that was all anyone but he, or one of the other agents, would have seen. He, however, now that he had become aware of them, felt a small device implanted in the bone of his skull begin to operate. The waveriness fogged, then cleared, and he saw watching him two men from the survey ship, both armed and in uniform. They were, it seemed to him, remarkably young-looking, and he did not know their names. But there was nothing so surprising in that, for the personnel of the ship had turned over a number of times since he had first been landed on this world.

"Well, this is quick," he said. The lips of one of them moved and a voice sounded inside Jabe's ear.

"I'm afraid you're under arrest," the voice said. "You'll have to come up with us."

"Under arrest?"

"For the killing of"—the one speaking hesitated for a tiny moment—"your brother."

"Brother. . . ." Jabe stopped suddenly. About him

everything else seemed to have halted, too. Not merely the room and the people in it, but the world in its turning beneath them seemed to have stopped with the word he had just heard. "Brother? . . . Oh, yes. Moran." The world and all things started to move again. He felt strangely foolish to have hesitated over the word. "Moran Halvorsen. We were never very close. . . ." His mind cleared suddenly. "How did you find out so soon it was me?" he asked.

Outside, at some little distance off, there was a sudden outburst of cheering. It seemed to come from the open space where they had gathered yesterday for the hunt. It drowned out the answer of the man from the ship.

"What?" Jabe had to ask.

"I say," said the other, "your profile was one of the three you sent up to the ship, some hours ago. It showed aberrancies of pattern. It was too much of a coincidence, taken with the recent death of—Moran Halvorsen. We checked, and there was a good deal of indication it was you."

"I see," said Jabe. He nodded. "I—expected it," he said, "but not so soon."

"Shall we go, then?" said the man from the ship.

"Could we wait a few minutes? A minute or two?" said Jabe. He turned to look out the window. "My wife . . . she ought to be back in just a few minutes."

The man from the ship glanced at his watch, and then over at his partner. Jabe could feel rather than hear them inside his ear speaking to each other on another channel.

"We can wait a few minutes, I guess," said the one who had done all the talking. "But just a few."

"She'll be right back, I'm sure," said Jabe. He moved to the window, looking out on the narrow, sloping cobble-stoned street before the row of houses. "You'll make sure she doesn't see me go?"

"Sure," said the man from the ship. "We can take

care of that all right. She'll just forget you were here when she got here."

"Thank you," said Jabe. "Thanks. . . ." He turned away from the window. People were beginning to hurry down the street from the direction of the open space, but he did not see Sheila. He moved back into the room, and caught sight of the board with the little model houses, still on the table.

"I'll take this," he said, picking it up. He turned to the one who had been doing the speaking. "So the three recordings got through all right?"

The other two looked at each other.

"Yes—" said one. There was a sudden, rapid step outside the house. The door burst open and Sheila almost ran in. Her face was flushed and happy.

"Jabe!" she cried. "We're going to have a dance! Isn't that wonderful? Manager Lenkhart just announced it! Did you get your breakfast yet? How do you like the holiday?" She spun about gleefully. "And—guess?"

"What?" he said, filling his eyes with the sight of her.

"Why, they're going to burn him after all! Up at the pass. Isn't that marvelous? And we'll all have an outdoor dinner up there, and burn him just as it starts to get dark, then everybody comes back here for the dance. Isn't that wonderful, Jabe? We haven't had a dance for so long!"

He stood staring at her.

"Burn?" he said stupidly. "Burn? But why——"

"Oh, *Jabe!*" she pirouetted about to face him. "Because we haven't caught one like this for such a long time, of course." She held out her arms to him. "Everybody thought because production in the mine wasn't up last month Manager Lenkhart wouldn't let us have anything but an ordinary hanging. But the staff engineers pleaded with him and said how badly everybody needed a holiday—so we got the whole thing." She reached for him, but he stepped back,

instinctively. "Burning, and picnic, and dance! Jabe—"
she said, stopping, and looking at him in some puzzlement. "What's wrong? Aren't you happy. . . ."

The word died suddenly on her lips. Suddenly she
stopped moving. She stood arrested, like a wax figure in a museum—only her chest moved slightly with
her breathing. Jabe made a move toward her, but
one of the armed men stopped him.

"No," said the voice in his head. "She's in stasis
now, until we leave. Better not touch her."

Jabe turned numbly toward them.

"No . . ." he said. "I sent recordings that proved
these people were different. You know about them.
What she says isn't what it sounds like. I tell you,
those recordings——"

"I'm sorry," said the voice. Both men were looking
at him with something like pity on their faces. "You're
overadapted, Jabe. You must have suspected it yourself. You couldn't seriously believe that thousands of
men working over a ten-year period could come to a
wrong conclusion. Or that that report Moran was
going to send in would be the only way we'd have of
knowing about things here——"

"I tell you, no!" said Jabe, breaking in. "I *know*
these people here. They're different. Maybe I am a
little . . . overadapted. But these people operate according to standards of justice and conscience. It's
not just taboo and ritual, not just——"

"Come along, Jabe," said the voice and the two
men moved in on him. "You'll have a chance to talk
later."

"No," he said, backing away from them. People
were beginning to stream past outside the front window. Jabe evaded the two men and went to the door,
opening it. At the top of the street, leading from the
square, two of the bachelors appeared carrying rifles.
The prisoner walked silently between them.

"Jabe—" began the voice in his head.

"I tell you, no!" said Jabe, desperately. "Sheila's

expecting. She makes things sound different than they are."

"Oh, Jabe!" said one of two women, hurrying past. "Did you hear about the jam? You'll have to tell Sheila!"

"Jam?" said Jabe, stupidly.

"That marauder. They asked him what he wanted and he wanted bread and jam for a last meal. Imagine. Two pounds he ate! Not my jam, thank goodness——"

"Come on, Etty!" said the other woman. "All the good places'll be gone. . . ." They hurried off.

The two bachelors with the rifles and the prisoner were only a few steps behind the women.

"Wait—" said Jabe, desperately.

The bachelors stopped at this command from a senior and married man. The prisoner also stopped. He had not been cleaned up, in his ragged suit of badly tanned hide, except for a clean white bandage on his arm. The whites of his eyes were as clear as a child's and his beard was the soft silk of adolescence. All three of them looked inquiringly at Jabe.

"Wait," said Jabe again, unnecessarily. He appealed to the nearest bachelor. "Why's Manager Lenkhart doing this?"

The bachelor frowned, looked at the other bachelor, then back at Jabe. He guffawed in uneasy fashion.

"What was his reason?" said Jabe.

The bachelor shrugged elaborately. He looked at the ground, spat, and kicked a pebble aside.

"We've got to get going," said the other bachelor. He looked over at the prisoner, who had moved aside to reach up and feel the low edge of the metal roof on Jabe's cottage, the roof made of corrugated aluminum.

"Silver," he said, glancing a moment at Jabe. "It's mighty rich—and fine."

The bachelors guffawed again. They took the prisoner's elbows and marched him off, down the slope of the road.

"You see there? You see?" said Jabe, staring after them, but speaking to the invisible warders just behind him. "He thought the sheet metal was silver, that the roofs were made of silver. There's your true degenerate. But the men with him——"

"Let's go, Jabe," said the voice gently in his head. He felt the warders take hold of him on either side. Invisibly, they led him out into the street, on the same way down which the other prisoner had already gone. He felt the uselessness of it all suddenly cresting over him like a wave, the sudden realization that there was no hope and there had never been any hope, no matter how he had tried to delude himself. He had known it from the beginning, but something in him would not let him admit the truth about these people—about his own wife, and his own child soon to be born—to himself.

From the beginning he had known that there was no saving them. Yet he had tried, anyway—had killed his own brother in an attempt he knew was quite hopeless, to save a people who were already regressing to the animal. Why? Why had he done it? He could not say.

All he knew was that there had never been any choice about it—for him. He had done what he had to do.

"Come along now," said the gentle voice in his head. Dumbly, and plodding like a donkey, he let them lead him as they would. To where, it no longer mattered.

Can the frenzy of conflict ever end in "calm of mind all passion spent"?

The Invaders

I

Hector McGarrity looked at Tica and assumed his sternest expression.

"You realize," Hector said, "if you intend to play the part of my assistant on Lamia, you'll have to take orders like everybody else." From the easy chair in which she was sitting, Tica turned her face up to him. It was a fine boned, perfectly controlled face that would have been pretty had there been a little more warmth of expression on it.

"Of course," she said.

He considered her dispassionately. Tica Smith, a junior planetary representative at twenty-four and a political enemy of the branch of Central Headquarters under which he worked; a frighteningly precocious child dedicated to the abstract virtues in a universe of concrete vices. For the past five days he had made a number of efforts to soften her shell of theories before it should be cruelly shattered by the reality that awaited them both on Lamia. They had been absolutely without success. She considered herself his enemy and had wangled the right to come with him to the threatened world solely to acquire

197

ammunition for her battle to destroy him and the system of Assigned Defense Commanders of which he was the working unit. She disbelieved or discounted anything he said.

He permitted a small corner of annoyance to touch his mind. It was almost the ultimate in emotion that training and time had left him. This annoyance was followed almost immediately by a wisp of ironic humor. Though she did not know it, he was being gentle with her. It was the first time in fifteen years he had been gentle with anyone.

"I'll see you again when it's time to land," he said, abruptly, and, turning on his heel, opened the door of her stateroom and stepped out into the long central corridor of the liner. He closed it behind him. Turning to the left, he went forward toward the control room.

He strode along the echoing steel corridor, a heavy-shouldered still-faced giant of a man, moving lithely with the ease of the strict physical conditioning that was required of him. His highly trained body was remote from the cold center of his mind. And it needed to be. For his decisions meant life or death to the people of the far flung colonies he defended, from time to time, when raiding alien groups broke through the Frontier Guard. It was as if his body housed two brains—one, the director of the bone-and-muscle fighting machine that walked the corridor—the other, the remote thinker that meditated on the present situation.

Briefly, the matter was simple. A spearhead of the Spindle ships had penetrated the defending stations of the Beltane quadrant. These swift, voracious aliens, by far the most common and the trickiest of the unknown races that made attempted raids on the little human space-area, would try a hit-and-run plundering of any one of a number of Colony planets in the vicinity. Hector, among other Assigned Defense Commanders, had been sent out to one of the threatened colonies to take charge of matters there and direct the colonists in case they should be the target of the invaders' attack.

So much for that. It was a job Hector was trained to do, and had done a dozen times in the past fifteen years. What complicated the situation was the presence of Tica. She headed a Government Committee that was probing the Defense Commander setup with the hope of destroying it. Their motives in doing so were almost unselfish and badly mistaken.

Theoretically, their claim that the unlimited powers accorded to a Defense Commander on assignment were a danger to Colony freedom, was sound. In practice, it had been proved that Colonies were almost never capable of supplying the proper sort of trained leadership in such a crisis. Still, people sitting at far away government desks and luncheon tables would argue the fact. Therefore Tica's presence. Therefore, loomed a very real danger that she would disagree with some of Hector's actions on Lamia and, by revealing her own position, create a dangerous division of authority.

Colonists at odds with Hector might appeal to Tica, as visiting junior representative, to override his decisions. She would have no legal right to do so, but— Hector's face went a little grim—it might come to killing. Again, theoretically he would be within his rights, but he had no illusions as to what would happen in practice to the Assigned Defense Commander who shot down a visiting elected representative of a populated planet.

He had reached the control room door. Now he shut the problem from his mind, and pushed it open, stepping inside. A young second officer sat at the navigator's board. Hector went directly to him, ignoring the captain who stood across the room, and looked over the gold-braided shoulder.

"How soon before we land?" Hector asked.

From across the room, the captain turned an angry face toward Hector. The *Mariana* was a passenger liner. She had been hauled off her regular route under peremptory government orders to deliver Hector and Tica Smith to Lamia. The passengers aboard were nervous and the captain had been bearing the brunt of their complaints. To be ignored in his own control room was a further annoyance.

"It's customary to knock, Mr. McGarrity," he said, "when a passenger comes into the control room." Hector ignored him.

"How long?" he repeated to the second officer.

The young officer flushed, but did not turn his head or reply. He was feeling a natural sympathy for his captain, whose rebuke to Hector had emboldened him He picked up a hand calculator.

ınside himself, Hector sighed softly. He put one large hand on the back of the chair and spun it around so that the boy faced him. While the white face stared, he drew the gun that he wore quite openly in the holster at his side.

"Sonny," he said, quietly, hefting the heavy weapon casually in his hand, "do you realize that I could smash your face in with the butt of this and be strictly within my rights?"

The blood drained from the young officer's face and neck. For a moment his nerve held, then it broke.

"About an hour," he said. Hector nodded and turned away. As he walked out through the door, the second's eyes went in hurt amazement to the captain. The captain avoided his gaze, turning his head away.

It was always the same, thought Hector, wearily, walking in the direction of the passenger lounge. There was always the position to uphold. He remembered the motto of the training halls, during his five grueling years of preparation for the job. "To be wrong is to be dead." It was literally true during the last stages of the training. When you take over an unfamiliar people in a situation that requires unthinking obedience on a few days notice, there must be no doubt in their minds that you are all-powerful, that you can do no wrong. Now he had a further chore to do. The second's defiance and the captain's hostility were an index of the attitudes of the passengers. If their resentment should be in any way communicated to the colonists during the brief landing, there would be trouble. He turned into the lounge.

There was a good handful of people there, some at the bar, most seated at tables, drinking. Frightened and angry glances rested on him as he came in, and a low mutter of talk broke out.

Hector ignored them. Paying no attention to the bartender he went behind the bar and picked up a bottle at random. Without offering to pay, he took a glass and carried both to an empty table. He sat down, poured the glass full and drank.

He sat there, with grim amusement, while the tension grew. The muttered voices rose and fragments of wrathful speech came clearly to his ears. Finally one man jumped to his feet and strode over to Hector's table. He put both hands on the edge and leaned forward.

"Listen!" he said tightly. "We've been talking it over. It's not fair to the passengers of this ship to run the risk of landing on Lamia. There's no reason you and Representative Smith can't take a lifeboat down."

Hector refilled his glass.

"Damn it!" shouted the man who was tall and slim, with a touch of the first gray hair of middle age, and an air of authority about him. "Listen to me when I talk to you." And he reached out to grab the arm that was raising Hector's glass to his lips.

Like a flash Hector's other hand moved in a swift blur of motion, and there was an odd, crunching sound as it closed over the grabbing hand. Then he let go, and the man stood staring in shocked disbelief at fingers that stood at odd angles to his palm with the white bone showing through.

"You broke it," he said stupidly.

Hector drank.

"You broke it!" repeated the man. It was almost a wail. With a sudden, choked sound, he turned and ran out through the door of the lounge, holding his injured hand in the other one.

For a long second, the stillness of death held the lounge; then swiftly passengers began to leave. Hector's job was done. There was no resentment now among the passengers to communicate to the colonists. Only fear.

A little bitterly, Hector drank.

Forty minutes later, the alarm bell sounded. Hector braced himself in the chair for the slight shock of the landing, then rose to his feet. He made his way to the open port and found Tica Smith there, waiting. Beneath her dark hair, her face was as calm as ever, but her brown eyes were chill.

"You might be interested to know," she said. "I heard about what you just did." He nodded briefly, abstractedly, dismissing the matter.

"Follow me down," he told her, "and don't say anything unless one of the welcoming committee speaks to you."

"Very well," she said coldly, picking up her luggage case, and followed him down the steps to the landing field, and the people who waited there.

There were five of them: a thin, ineffectual looking man in his sixties; a thickset man of middle age and better than average height; a strange-looking individual in rough clothes with a knife at his side and long brown hair and beard framing a narrow nose and keen brown eyes; and a nondescript young man with a portable pickup transmitter slung from his shoulders.

It was to him that Hector walked immediately, ignoring the others. He had been talking down into the pickup in easy conversational tones. Now, seeing Hector, he hurried what he had to say.

"—and here he is now, folks. Commander Hector McGarrity, whom you—"

Hector pushed him away from the portable set, cutting off the flow of words. He stood squarely in front of the pickup, knowing that throughout the city behind him, his words and appearance would be filling the screens of any set now working.

"Listen to me," he said briefly. "I want your attention. This planet is now under martial law. You will all go home, and stay home, unless your job is essential to city operation. Inside the next two hours, I will come on the air again to give you detailed directions as to what you must do. Until then, stay off the streets and make sure you can easily be located. That's all."

He turned away from the pickup and started away across the field. Tica and the rest followed him, all except the young man with the pickup, who stood where he was, following them out of sight with the scanning unit of the pickup.

"Where's the car?" said Hector, abruptly. The thickset man pointed toward a ground vehicle, parked some distance off to their right. Hector changed direction.

"Let me introduce myself," panted the thickset man, hurrying to keep pace with Hector's long strides; "I'm Governor Gideon Stern. This is Mayor Hemple—"

"Save it!" said Hector, curtly. "When we get to the governor's house, we can talk. Right now, I want a look at the city."

He strode on.

II

At top speed, they drove through Lamia City. Hector rode in front with the governor, who was driving, and kept up a steady barrage of questions. What was

their water supply? Did they have a militia? Sewage
disposal? Which of the buildings had reinforced walls?

"But surely," protested Gideon Stern, his ruddy
face paling, "you won't let it come to street fighting?"

"Maybe," said Hector laconically; and took up his
questions, again.

The car was crowded. In the back seat, wedged in
between the brown-bearded man and the thin city
mayor, Tica held her luggage case on her knees and
strove to maintain her customary coolness. The two
who shared the seat with her showed no inclination
to talk to each other; which puzzled her. The bearded
man was quietly abstract, the mayor clearly in a
state bordering on nervous collapse. She could feel
the slight trembling in the bony arm that pressed
against her side. He aroused her sympathy, even as
the other's unconcern irritated her. Before she could
stop to remember what Hector had told her, she
spoke to him.

"I imagine you're terribly worried," she began, "facing the threat of an invasion so suddenly this way."
He turned a grateful glance toward her and the words
came spilling out.

"You don't know the half of it!" he began. "We've
been waiting—"

"Quiet back there!"

It was Hector's voice, coolly authoritative from the
front seat, and it sliced off the mayor's flow of words
abruptly. He stiffened and sat in silence. Tica bit her
lip angrily.

The back seat rode in silence until they reached the
governor's house.

They went immediately to the office, where they
took chairs in a rough circle, all except Hector who
stood facing them, and the bearded man who seemed
to prefer to remain standing.

"All right," said Hector, crisply. "Now the intro-
ductions." He pointed in turn to the Governor and

the Mayor. "You're Stern, and he's Hemple. You?" He stabbed a finger at the brown-bearded man.

"J. J.," came the prompt answer.

"He's one of the bush-runners," interposed Stern, hastily. "Sort of a representative of the hunters and trappers. He—they—sent him in to see if there was anything they could do to help."

"All right." Hector nodded. He turned to Tica. "Tica Smith, my assistant," he said briefly.

"Just a minute!" Tica had been boiling inside ever since Hector had summarily cut short her conversation in the car. "When I agreed to be known as your assistant, I didn't intend the truth to be kept from the local authorities." She sent a challenging stare at Hector.

"Very well," he answered evenly. She could not tell from his face whether he was angry or not. "This is Miss Tica Smith, Junior Representative from the planet Arco, who has come along as a government observer."

"How do you do," said Stern brightening. "I'm glad the government has seen fit to send Miss Smith along."

"Yes, yes, indeed!" echoed Hemple. The bush-runner said nothing, and Tica, looking at him, was prodded into further action.

"And one more thing," she said. "Since this is a government matter, I think we should dispense with pet names or abbreviations." She turned squarely toward the bushrunner. "What's your full name?"

"J. J.," he answered, bending his bright eyes on her.

Her temper snapped. "Don't be ridiculous," she said. "You must have a full name." The hint of a thin smile touched the man's lips, half-hidden beneath the beard.

"I guess," he said, coolly, "you never learned your manners, Miss." The words took her breath away.

"Why—" she began furiously, when she could speak again. But Hector interrupted.

"That's enough," he said, crisply. "For the information of all of you, Miss Smith is an observer only. She has nothing to do with the action I take; and no authority." Tica choked back her rage. He was speaking no more than the truth. "Now, we'll get down to business. I understand your one piece of heavy armament is a late-model K-4 rock-anchored space rifle, ten miles from the city. You also have some two thousand portables and hand-guns arsenaled in the K-4's dome. Is that right?"

"Yes," bleated Hemple. "But—"

"That's right, that's right," interrupted Stern, quickly.

"You have gun assistants for the K-4 who have been trained in its use?"

"Yes," said Stern.

"But no militia?"

"Well, no," answered the perspiring governor, "but the bushrunners—"

"Are the bushrunners," interrupted J. J., suddenly with a snap. "Just so you get things straight, Commander, the boys aren't worried about themselves. We could fade off into the bush and those raiders'd never find us. We'll still help, but we aren't doing all the work for these fat citizens. So you and these two figure things out and tell us what you want. If we like it, we'll do it. If we don't, you can whistle for all the help you'll get." Hector looked at him.

"We'll see," he said noncommittally. He turned back to the two officials.

"Can you think of anything we haven't discussed that concerns the defensive effort the city might put up?"

"No," said Stern, and the mayor nodded by way of agreement.

"All right," said Hector. "Then hook me up with the local station, and I'll make my broadcast."

What he said was brief and to the point:

"All able-bodied men over sixteen and the single able-bodied women over the same age will remain in the city, in their own homes as much as possible, and await further orders. All others will prepare for evacuation, taking warm clothing, bedding, and food for two weeks. Nothing else. I repeat, nothing else. This city is under martial law and any attempt to smuggle valuables out will be regarded as looting and punished as such. As soon as each evacuee is ready, he or she is to notify the mayor's office. By tomorrow morning at the latest you will be moved out back into the bush. All sales of liquor are hereby discontinued, and all other business establishments are closed except for the sale of food and clothing. Stay in your homes; stay close to your receivers; and wait further orders."

He clicked off the pickup into which he had been talking; and turned back to the four occupants of the room.

"Miss Smith and I will stay here," he said to Stern. "You'll arrange to have rooms fixed for us."

"Of course," said the Governor.

"Very well," said Hector. He moved over to the desk and picked up a stylus in one large hand, and drew a sheet of paper toward him. "You, J. J., can arrange for guides to take the evacuees back into the bush?" The bushrunner nodded.

"We'll do that," he said.

"And you, Stern," the stylus in Hector's hand raced over the paper, "this is an official order authorizing you to withdraw the portables and handguns from the K-4 housing and distribute them to the able-bodied men and women in the city. Take ten men out to the space rifle and—"

"I knew it! I knew it!" The anguished tones of the mayor brought all eyes toward him. He ignored them, concentrating on Stern. "I told you, Gideon. I told you he'd want those before we could get that beast out of the gun-housing—"

"Shut up, you fool!" answered the governor, roughly. "I never expected to use them, anyway." He turned calmly enough to meet Hector's demanding stare. "The truth of it is, Commander, that you aren't going to be able to defend Lamia with the weapons and people here. One of our local species of animal that has the uncomfortable power of—er—shocking people, has taken up its residence in the housing and can't be gotten out. And no one can get in while it's there." Hector felt a little white flame of anger flare coldly in the back of his mind.

"You deliberately let me broadcast without knowing this?" he said.

"Frankly, yes," said Stern. His face was smooth now. "You see, I've heard about Miss Smith's committee. I've even listened in on some of the broadcast meetings over the ultrawave. And I agree with her. There's no reason why untrained men and women should have to risk their lives and possessions when we have a Space Fleet to do the job for them. Now, in this case, all the weapons are in the space rifle housing and the housing can't be entered. The only thing you can do, Commander, is to broadcast for a Fleet defense unit to be stationed here at the planet until the emergency is past." He smiled, a little smugly.

Hector smiled a wintry smile in his direction.

"How much do you know about Fleet movements, Stern?" he asked. The governor shrugged.

"Nothing, naturally," he answered. "I've got nothing to do with military matters."

"Then I'll tell you something," said Hector. "All available Fleet units are waiting at base right now for the first news of a planetary raid. When they hear, they'll move to gather in the raiders and force them back beyond the Frontier. Until then, they'll stay where they are."

"But you can call them!" cried the governor.

"Only in an emergency," said Hector.

"But my God!" said Stern. "If this isn't an emergency, what is?"

"It's an emergency for Lamia," said Hector, "and Lamia is only of secondary importance." He got up from the desk and strode around it to stand facing Stern. The smaller man drew back. "You fat little idiot!" he said. "You and your handful of people are in the front line. Back on the Inner Worlds, there are six quadrillions of men and women and children with no protection at all. If the Raiders aren't trapped out here and killed off or forced back, they have no fleet nor weapons. Should I weaken the line that hopes to hold them? No! If we can't get at the weapons, that's our tough luck. And if you're responsible for the creature being there, then you've cut all our throats and I'll take pleasure in seeing you before a firing squad. This is no game, Stern!"

A stunned silence in the big office followed his words. Stern was shaken, Hemple on the point of collapse. Tica stared at Hector, white-faced, overwhelmed by the change from the taciturn, quiet man she had faced with confidence on the liner trip in to the planet. Only J. J. whistled softly to himself and rubbed the butt of his knife with one brown thumb.

"You know, Commander," he said, "I like the way you talk. I don't guess me and the boys will have any disagreement with anything you want to do." Hector glanced at him, and half-smiled.

"Thanks," he said.

"Nothing," said J. J. He shrugged his shoulders, turning swiftly on the paralyzed governor. "What's in there, Stern? A land-squid? A digger?" The governor shook his head, dizzily, as if coming out of a trance.

"A smuglet," he said, "I—we saw smuglet tracks leading up to the ventilator. The bars were chewed off." Hector looked at J. J.

"That sounds right," the bushrunner answered his unspoken question. "A smuglet can chew through thin steel if you give him time and you know those ventilator gratings. None of the other shockers could."

"Shockers?" demanded Hector.

"You'll see," answered J. J. "A bunch of the native animals here have some way of tickling up your nerves when you get too close. A smuglet can knock you over at fifteen yards. We better get out there and take a look-see."

III

They rode out in two cars. J. J., the Governor, with the mayor in the first, and Hector with Tica following in the second. It was the first time they had been alone together since leaving the ship and he could feel her sitting stiffly beside him as he handled the controls, betraying fear and anger. Finally she spoke.

"You could have called for help," she said. He shook his head.

"No," he replied briefly. She persisted.

"If you *had* called," she said, "they would have come, wouldn't they?" He looked at her out of the corner of his eyes.

"No," he repeated. Her temper flared.

"I think you're a glory-hunter!" she snapped. He shrugged, keeping his eyes on the road. They were out of the clean wide streets of the city now and the track they followed was rutted and hemmed with brush. Odd purple trees arced over their heads at long intervals.

"What you don't realize," he said, suddenly, impelled by the same obscure urge to justify himself that had led him to talk to her on the liner, "is the size of the human living area. As I said back in the office, there's some six quadrillion of us, settled in a number of planetary systems in an area of space roughly sixty thousand light years in diameter. One planet, one colony, a few thousand inhabitants are like one bug on the surface of the pond when the fish come in to feed. The flash of one dark shape, a ripple, and it's gone. Expendable. But if the fish can be turned back, by any sacrifice, that is the important thing.

"You sit in your Committee Room back on Earth and speak of the brave colonists, the women, the children. And you allow yourself the luxury of pity for them, thinking them somehow different, because of their position, than you. *I* tell you there is no difference. The human race has grown big enough to attract the attention of other space-going races and you, as well as these, the colonists, may live to see your birthplace flame into nothingness and the ancient mountains of Earth flowing in lava to the sea. We are a long way, maybe a million years yet, from peace and security; and maybe we'll never have it."

She looked at him oddly, reluctant to believe that he should think so deeply. His words were too much at odds with her preconceived ideas of him and the service to which he belonged. Finally she took refuge in mockery.

"My, you're a pessimist," she said with superficial banality.

He shrugged in angry disgust and drove on in silence.

The space rifle was a great dome shielding a thick muzzle—like the head of some gigantic cobra rising from the brush and purple trees. For a space of forty meters around it, the ground had been cleared. The two cars pulled up and parked.

They got out.

Two men—by their uniforms, members of the local police—were standing by the dome. They turned and hurried up to Stern as the group approached.

"Still in there, sir," said the taller one, saluting. "Jerry tried to crawl up to the door, but the smuglet must have felt him coming, and knocked him out just as he got there. We dragged him off and sent him back to headquarters."

"Oh, yes," said Stern worriedly, "This is Commander McGarrity, boys. You'll take your orders from him."

"Yes, sir," said the one he spoke to. Hector reached out and caught his shoulder with one big hand, turning him toward the dome.

"Where's the ventilator?" he asked.

"Halfway around the dome," the policeman said, pointing. Hector, following the line of his finger, saw a square opening some five feet off the ground, with some ragged ends of grating twisting out. He moved in that direction, followed by J. J.

When he got close, he could see that part of the grating had been bent and broken as well as chewed. He pointed it out to the bushrunner.

"Pretty strong," he said.

"Hefty," admitted J. J. "They weigh between ninety and a hundred and fifty pounds, grown. Feed off the bush, though; and don't do any harm, except with that shocking trick of theirs."

"What is it?" asked Hector. "Like the charge from an electric eel back on Earth?" J. J., shrugged.

"Don't know," he answered. "I don't think anyone does. Not much like the eel, though. More like the skunk—if the skunk were psychic. You don't have to do anything but get close, and it's strictly defensive. Walk up close and you'll get a tingle."

Hector turned and approached the building. He was barely three meters from it when a strange twitchiness seemed to run all over the surface of his skin. He stopped.

"Feel it?" said the bushrunner. "Now take one more step." Hector took his customary long stride forward and immediately the twitching jumped to unbearable proportions. His teeth chattered and his scalp seemed to crawl and his head began to swim dizzily. He took a hurried step backward, and the twitching dropped. He went two more steps to the rear, and it was gone.

"Does it keep that up all the time?" he said, rejoining J. J.

"Until it's dead," answered the bushrunner. Hector stood a minute, thinking. Then he turned and strode back to Stern.

"I take it the door to the housing's locked?" he said.

"Yes," answered the governor, unhappily. "I don't suppose there's any way you could fire through it, and—"

"Not through *that* shielding," said Hector, waving his hand at the dome. "Also, it would wreck the rifle controls inside."

"Maybe if we rushed it," suggested Stern. J. J., shook his head.

"Take you too long to unlock the door," he said.

"Do you have any exterminators in the city, with gas equipment?" said Hector. Stern's face lit up.

"Of course," he answered.

"Get them out here," said Hector. "And bring the fire department, too." Stern nodded and hurried off to the two-way communicator in his car.

The fire department was the first to arrive. Hector had them well-tap with power equipment to the first water level and hook the pump up. Then he directed two volunteers to run the nozzle of the hose as close to the dome as possible and direct a steady stream of water into the torn ventilator. The pump whirred, the two volunteers braced themselves, and a jet of silver water hammered into the opening.

The opening drank it up.

After half an hour, Hector called a halt. He walked close enough to the dome to satisfy himself that the smuglet was still alive and broadcasting. Then turned and came back.

"I can understand," he said to J. J., "that the animal might be undrownable. But where's the water going to?"

There was a diffident noise at the side and one of the policeman spoke up.

"Excuse me, Commander—" he said. Hector turned.

"What?" he said.

"Excuse me," the man went on. "But I've been inside the housing before, and there's a drain in there—"

"Drain!" echoed Hector, exasperatedly. He whirled on one heel and shouted. "Stern!"

The governor came running up. Hector's voice was hard.

"You don't happen deliberately to be sabotaging the defense of this colony, do you?" he said, grimly. "Why didn't you tell me there was a drain in there?" The governor's jaw fell in surprise.

"A drain!" he said. "Why that's right, there is a drain in there. I'd forgotten all about it." Hector's lips thinned, and he turned away.

"All right!" he called to the fire department crew. "Get that out of there. Where's that exterminator outfit?"

Footsteps sounded at Hector's elbow. "Right here, Commander." It was a lank old man with a leathery face. "We just arrived."

"Good," said Hector. "Have they told you about what we're trying to do here?"

"Yep," answered the oldster.

"Think you can get close enough to pump gas into that ventilator?"

"Why, sure," said the exterminator. "Jerry here'll just walk right up to that hole and put the tube in," he indicated a large, lumpish youth not much smaller than Hector. "Jerry's m'boy. Strong as a truck." Jerry grinned and picked up a bulky section of the gas generator to show how strong he was.

"Hmm," said Hector. "Well, tie a rope around him, just to make sure."

"I don't need no rope," protested Jerry. Hector looked at him. "Yes, sir, Commander," he mumbled.

A rope was tied around Jerry's ample waist, the gas generator hooked up and Jerry picked up one end of the tube.

"Do you think it'll work?" said Tica, looking up at Hector as the boy started for the ventilator. Hector shook his head.

"There's that open drain," he said, "and no one can stay up there long enough to plug the ventilator. But we may get enough—" he was watching the boy Jerry approach the ventilator. He had just slowed as if he had run into a waist-high river of invisible molasses. He was not giving up easily, however, for he continued to shuffle on, head down. He slogged his way to the opening, leaned for a moment against the dome, and slid down the smooth metal in an ungraceful faint.

"Haul him back," ordered Hector.

They pulled the large, unconscious body in hand over hand. Hector was already taking off his jacket. Tica looked at Hector with a new emotion.

"You aren't going in there?" she said, incredulously.

"Do you see anybody else offering to go?" He inquired sourly. J. J. drifted over with a word of advice.

"Don't try to run in, Commander," he drawled. "It hits you like an ax in the neck when you come into close range sudden." Hector nodded; and, taking the rope that had been disengaged from Jerry, tied it around his own broad chest, under the shoulders. He picked up the tube that Jerry had dropped, and started to walk in, letting it slide through his fingers as he approached the fallen end by the dome.

"Just hope his heart's in good shape," said J. J., with a malicious glance at Tica.

"His heart!" she echoed, spinning on him.

"Kills fellers like him, sometimes," said J. J., snapping his fingers. She turned away, controlling herself. Of course Hector's heart would be—would have to be, for the job he did—in perfect shape. Her breath came a little faster as she watched.

Hector had started for the dome with slow easy strides. When the first warning tingle touched him, he stopped and forced himself to breathe deeply. Then he stepped forward.

It was like stepping down a steep shelving beach into very cold water. With the first step the twitching tore at him, seeming to choke off his breathing. With the next, it became unbearable. His skin crawled, his throat contracted, and the dome began to spin dizzily before his eyes. A feeling of utter panic began to rise within him. He lurched forward toward the haze of the dome and the bobbing black splotch that was the ventilator hole. He was no longer conscious of the ground beneath his feet or the rope around his chest. Only a dim recognition of the tube he held in his hands stayed with him.

He took one more step and felt the wall of the dome hit him, and the end of the tube pull up from the ground and almost slip through his fingers. Every nerve in his body was screaming, leaping in protest against the outrage of the feeling that tore at him. He set his teeth in his lower lip, feeling for a second the small, sharp pain distract him from the unknown thing tearing at him. He lifted the tube, fumbled it into the opening. His arms felt like lead, but he pushed once, fighting back the black waves of unconsciousness that rose nauseatingly within him. He pushed again, and the tube slid farther into the hole. And then the black waves rose at last, fighting down the end of his resistance, and buried him deep.

IV

Several hours later Hector awoke to a dark room and the eerie shadows cast by a strange moon hurtling close and swift along the horizon. Fighting back the dragging weakness that lay like a heavy blanket on his limbs, he struggled to a sitting position.

"Hey!" he called hoarsely.

A door opened suddenly, and a shaft of brilliant light cut across him, dazzling him. He blinked in the sudden glare, hearing the light taps of a woman's heels approaching him. He recognized Tica.

"You mustn't get up," she said. He growled something unintelligible even to himself. Grasping her arm, he hauled himself upright with as little ceremony as if she had been a post. She staggered under his weight, but stood. When he had regained his feet, she put one slim arm around his waist by way of support.

She helped him into the next room. It was the office of the governor's house, back in the city and Stern, Hemple and J. J. were standing in it, looking at him curiously. He paid them no attention, but staggered across the room to the desk and sunk in a chair that was pulled up to it. The smooth plastic was cool against his legs. He glanced down.

"Get me some clothes!" he croaked. J. J. chuckled. Tica turned and went back into the bedroom. Hector's gaze swept the room and settled on Stern.

"Did I get the tube in?" he demanded.

"Oh, yes," said the Governor, nervously. "Yes, it's in. The gas is going."

"Any luck yet?"

"No." Hector let his eyes shift to the two other men.

"What are you all doing back here?" he asked. Tica came back in with his tunic and breeches. He pushed himself up from the chair and reached for them, but from sheer weakness was not able to avoid the help she offered him in putting them on.

"Well—" said Hemple, J. J. laughed.

"You don't know it, Commander," he said, "but you got a rebellion on your hands."

"What?" growled Hector.

"These two fat sheep," said J. J., jerking his thumb at Stern and Hemple, "heard a rumor on the ultra-wave that the raiders had been spotted less than twenty-four hours from here. Instead of keeping the news to themselves, they let it out and the whole town has gone wild. The citizens know, now, that the smuglet is keeping them from the weapons. Half are heading for the hills; and the other half are trying to contact the raiders on the ultra-wave and surrender."

"Surrender!" Hector turned on Stern and Hemple, steadying himself with one hand on a corner of the desk. "You damn fools! You don't surrender to the Spindle Ships, any more than you surrender to a tiger. Both simply take it as an invitation to eat you up."

"Not me—not me!" bleated Hemple. "I didn't want to surrender. But Gideon—" Stern made a little despairing jerk with his hand and the thin man's voice stopped.

"Yes," Stern said, in a low voice, "I said they should try it." The strength seemed to have gone out of him, yet at the same time a certain frankness and honesty had returned to replace it. "As you say, Commander, I'm a fool. I knew it, but I didn't want to admit it. Now I've just made a mess of things." He sat down on a chair, burying his face in his hands. "I was a fool to buy the governorship in the first place."

"Buy the governorship!" It was Tica's voice, high and shocked. J. J. chuckled maliciously in the corner; but Hector nodded.

"That explains a lot of things," he said; and his voice was somewhat kinder. He turned to Tica. "It's not unusual in some outer colonies where the governorship is more of a paper title than anything else, for men to buy up a few votes to make themselves feel good and perhaps add a little prestige to whatever business they happen to be in. Why didn't you tell me?" he went on to Stern. "It would have saved us both a lot of trouble."

The girl stared at him, astonished. "But he *is* the governor, isn't he?" asked Tica.

"He might as well be the dogcatcher for all the good he can do me," said Hector grimly. "His election was a farce; and in the eyes of the colonists, he's a farce. And Hemple?"

"My cousin," said Stern, ashamedly. He went on lamely, "We figured Lamia was growing. I would be the first governor. He would be the first mayor—"

"Forget it now," said Hector. "You can both go home—no, wait; I may have some use for you after all. J. J. said they're trying to make contact with the raiders. That means a group of them are at the ultra-wave station. Is there any way I could get there without attracting attention?"

"There's a power-tunnel there from this building," answered Stern. "But you'd never make it. They'll—"

"We'll make it," interrupted J. J. He stepped over to the window and pressed the button that rolled the wide transparent sheet back into its casing. He whistled twice into the darkness.

There was a stir outside. A leg came over the sill, followed by an arm, and a big, bald-headed man climbed into the room, followed by a boy in his teens who grinned embarrassedly at Tica and turned a bright red under her gaze.

"This is Bonny," said J. J., slapping the boy on the shoulder, "and the other one's Crocus. They can go ahead to take care of any guards at the other end of the tunnel."

"But he's just a child," said Tica, fascinatedly. Bonny turned his head away. J. J.'s, thin lips twisted a trifle sourly.

"As I said when I first saw you," he answered, "you her"I love you" was evidently never learned manners. Bonn man than most you'll ever meet." He turned to Hector. "Let's go."

Stern and Hemple led them downstairs to the mouth of the power tunnel connecting with the station, but, at Hector's order, stayed there. The others got into the two little plastic shells that floated there between the upper and lower rails of the tunnel, Bonny and Crocus in the first one—and the frail craft pillowed on its magnetic fields, rocked dangerously as the bald-headed man climbed aboard—and J. J., Hector and Tica in the second.

"Shove off," said J. J. In the car ahead, Bonny lifted the magnetic grapple that anchored his craft to a standstill and it rocketed off into the dimness of the tunnel. "One—two—three—four—five—" counted J. J., and lifted his own grapple. The three of them were slammed back into the seat as the shell leaped forward.

It was like dropping down an endless well. Their speed between the close walls that they almost, but never quite touched, was so terrific that it made Tica dizzy and she clutched automatically at Hector, closing her eyes. He felt the small, tense pressure of her hands and turned his head to look down at her dark hair, whipping free in the air that got past the visor of the shell. And he looked away again, feeling an unaccustomed uneasiness stir within him, but holding the arm she held, very still.

It was a trip measured in seconds. Nevertheless, when they got to their destination, the life-and-death struggle that preceded them was already over. Three men in the uniform of the city police were dead or dying, and Bonny was straightening up from another still figure in civilian clothes, the knife in his hand running red. Again his eyes met Tica's and again he blushed. A sudden surge of pity and horror shook her so that she, this time, turned her head away.

"Upstairs!" snapped J. J. He slid back the doors of the levitator and held them while the rest stepped into the rising pressure of the beams and were borne upward past fleeting white doors to the top of the shaft. Here, J. J. pulled back the final door and they tumbled out into the broadcast room at the top of the station.

"Hold it!" snapped the bearded bushrunner. The men around the controls froze, seeing the guns in the hands of the three men. Hector, who had not bothered to draw his own weapon, strode over to the control board and brushed the man there roughly out of the way.

"Made contact?" he demanded, harshly.

"N-no," stuttered the technician, his fear naked in his eyes.

"Good!" growled Hector. He turned away. Walking over to the transparent dome that covered the broadcast room, he looked out.

A sea of faces were upturned toward him. He marked the limits of the crowd and estimated that most of the people in the city must be grouped around below, waiting. He turned away and went back to the pickup in the middle of the room.

"Switch me onto the outside screen," he said. The man he had shoved from the controls turned slowly back to them and made some adjustments. "Am I on?"

"You're on," said J. J., from his position next to the dome. "I can just see the top of the screen from here."

From the crowd outside came a distant, muted, swelling roar to echo and verify his words. Facing the pickup, Hector held up his hand for silence; and, as the roar faded, those in the broadcast room heard the thunder of his voice from the annunciators outside the building.

"Listen to me!" he said. "You know me. All of you know me. I have spoken to you twice so far. You know what my job is here. It is to defend you from the attack of the alien. But it is more. It is also to take command of this colony and this planet and not to relinquish command until my job is done. I have, therefore, just put a halt to your attempt to surrender to the Spindle Ships.

"I will tell you why. This alien race which has just broken through the Frontier Guard and threatens you now, does not understand the concept of surrender. They have never surrendered themselves and they cannot conceive what humans mean when they attempt to surrender to them. Your surrender to them would have meant only an invitation to butchery and looting.

"Furthermore, there is no need to surrender. By the time they reach Lamia, the housing of the K-4 will be open and we will be armed to repulse them. You may have heard that all attempts to remove the smuglet have been failures. This is not true. I promise you that I will open the K-4 housing before noon tomorrow. As guarantee that this will happen, I furthermore give you my word that if the housing is not open, I will then make no further opposition to your attempts to call the alien and surrender. Until then, however, this building will be evacuated and remain sealed.

"That is all."

He stepped back from the pickup and signaled the man at the control board to cut the screen.

"It's off," said J. J., from the dome. He added, after a moment's pause, "And they're leaving."

"All right," said Hector. "Everybody downstairs. I'm going to seal this, and then I'll be right with you."

They turned and went, herding the men who had been attempting contact before them, crowded back into the levitator and dropped to the lofty entrance hall on the ground floor. In a few minutes, Hector rejoined them.

"We'll go out the front way," he said. "I want to

seal that, too." He turned to the men who had been working in the broadcast room. "You understand that none of you are to come back here?"

They muttered a sullen assent.

"Good," said Hector, and they went through the high front doors into the cool night, the stationmen fading away in the darkness, the others watching curiously as, with his handgun, Hector melted the edges of the two metal doors together.

"Now," he said, turning away. "Back to the governor's house."

Stern was still waiting for them when they returned, but Hemple had gone back to his home and wife, perhaps feeling the need for the presence of familiar things now that his world was crumpling. Stern, the somewhat stronger man of the two, and a bachelor, was sticking it out, but his face was wan as he greeted them.

"Stern," said Hector, without preliminaries, "You'd better show Miss Smith her room, and turn in yourself. It doesn't look like we can do anything until morning." Tica looked up at the hard lines of his face.

"How about you?" she asked.

"I'm going to talk some things over with J. J." His features were drawn and tired as he answered.

"I'm not tired," she said, "I'll stay up, too."

"You'll go to bed!" his voice was harsh.

"But if there's talking to be done, I want to hear it," she cried. "Remember, I'm here as an observer."

"And let me remind you," his voice boomed angrily in the echoing hallway of the governor's house, "that I am in command and you are strictly under my orders. Go to bed!" And, turning on his heel, he strode off into the office. J. J. turned and followed him. The door slammed, leaving her sick and angry.

"Miss Smith!" It was Stern's voice at her elbow,

soft, almost humble. She turned toward him. "This way, Miss Smith."

As in a dream, she followed him down the hall and off a branching corridor to a wide dim room, lit by the swiftly moving moon.

"The light—"

"Never mind the lights," she said, numbly. "I can see well enough, and I think I'll go right to sleep." He nodded, and went out.

"Good night, Miss Smith." The door closed behind him.

"Good night," she murmured automatically to the closed door. She walked across the shadowed room and sank tiredly onto the softness of the wide bed. It would be dawn in a few short hours. She leaned forward, pressing her slim fingers against her temples as if to drive back the memories of the day. The mob, Hector collapsing against the dome, the boy Bonny with his dripping knife. She lay back, head against the yielding pillow, taking her hands from her face. She was conscious of a deep dragging exhaustion and a longing to be gone, away from the harsh incomprehensible standards of this unfamiliar world. She felt as if the whole fabric of her logic had been ripped away; as if she had been staked out naked to the universe, mute and helpless. She groped for something to cling to and realized suddenly that it was Hector, and Hector alone who bridged the gap between the present situation and all the other situations she had ever known.

She tossed on the bed.

She had come out here as an observer—supposedly. Actually, she admitted to herself, she had been nothing more than a prejudiced gatherer of facts favorable to her own cause. It had been her belief that the Colonists were abused by the Assigned Defense Commanders, that the military organization robbed them of personal freedoms. She laughed, a little bitterly. Freedom? Freedom to buy offices? Free-

dom to cut throats? Those were their freedoms.
Starkly, to herself, in the darkness she faced the fact
that she had not known what she was talking about.
She realized now that the committee she headed
was a pack of fools who read statistics from sheets
of paper and thought themselves qualified to make
decisions. She would resign. She would report that,
after looking over the situation, she felt herself un-
qualified to judge the matter. And she would tell
Hector of this decision right away.

The notion was so attractive that she rose to her
feet. Almost happily, she walked across the room and
out the door into the hall. Here she paused. She had
paid little attention to which way she had come to
her bedroom in this big house and now she was
uncertain of the way back to the office. She hesitated. Then it occurred to her that Stern's room must
be close.

"Mr. Stern," she called softly. When there was no
answer, she tried again, more loudly, "Mr. Stern!"

Still there was no answer. Asleep, she thought. She
moved to the nearest door on the hallway and knocked.
There was no answer and she opened it up. It was in
perfect order and empty. She stepped back, shut the
door and tried the next one.

It was behind the fourth door that she found Stern's
bedroom. It was unmistakably his, for among the
disorder of the bed and closet she saw the discarded
clothes he had been wearing that day. Other clothing
from racks and drawers had been yanked out and
strewn around. A half-packed luggage case sat open
on the bed and a window curtain fluttered in the
breeze from the garden beyond. Stern was gone.

Tica went cold.

She had no idea of the time that she had been lying
on her bed; but it could not have been more than half
an hour. And in that short time Stern had either
left or been making hurried preparations to do so—

preparations which had been suddenly interrupted. Her over-strained nerves leaped suddenly under a spasmodic thrust of fear. What the condition of the governor's room could mean, she did not know, but on this wild, panic-ridden planet she could not do otherwise than expect the worst. The fat governor had deserted. Hector must be told.

V

Filled with this idea, Tica turned back into the corridor and ran blindly along it, hunting instinctively for the office where she had left the other two men. She blundered by open doors and around corners until eventually she stumbled on the big entrance hallway again and recognized the double doors of the office in its right hand wall. She pressed the button and they flew apart as she thrust into the room.

"Commander!" she cried.

Tica brought herself to a sudden halt. The office, too, was empty.

The calm light of the ceiling shed its even glow on the deep chairs, the desk, with its litter of papers, and the wide open window. She froze, feeling the beat of her heart step up to the frantic rhythm of a fear-crazed animal. The heartbeats shook her, standing there in silence and alone.

Then, there was the faint murmur of voices from outside. She moved swiftly to the window, telling herself that she was foolish. It was possible that they were only in the garden. Still, some instinct of caution caused her to stand to one side of the airy gap, looking out obliquely, but hiding herself from view.

Down and beyond the garden, on the road that led from the governor's house to the hills, she saw two men standing in the light of a street globe, one with the giant frame of Hector and the other with the flowing hair and beard of J. J. They had halted and were staring back, irresolute, at the house. Tica realized, suddenly, that they must have heard her call Hector's name. A tag end of their conversation came faint but clearly to her ears.

"—you think?" J. J. was saying. "We could play safe."

"No," Hector's voice was more distinct, the ring of command audible in it even at this distance, "There's no time. Let's go."

They turned away, their figures following their long shadows up the street and dwindling away toward the hills and the brush beyond. That way led to concealment and safety when the Raiders arrived; but only if enough unsuspecting people remained in town to appease their savage desires. There was no longer any doubt in Tica's mind that she and the colonists were being deliberately deserted first by their governor, and now by the bushrunners and the Commander who should have been the core of their defense. That was why she had been shunted off to a bedroom—so that her accusing voice would be among those to be silenced by the alien. That was why Stern, wiser than she in the meanness and cowardliness of men's minds, had fled, leaving his clothing half-packed behind him.

With this abrupt realization, the last of her courage washed suddenly out of her, and she crumpled on her knees by the window, sobbing.

For a long time she let the grief flow from her, unchecked. Then, gradually, as the torment of emotions within her subsided, she rose unsteadily to her feet and blew her nose. Then she walked across the room to the liquor cabinet set in one wall of the office and poured herself a strong drink of Earth brandy. She lifted the glass in cold fingers and drank.

The brandy flowed down, turning to liquid fire inside her, shocking her out of the numbness that fear had left. She gasped, and set the glass down, looking around her.

Her strength was returning, and with it, a touch of the sureness that had dictated her actions all her life and won her the planetary junior representativeship on Arco at twenty-three. The situation might or might not be hopeless for her and the unprotected city-people. There were some things still that could be done.

She stepped to the desk and the directory that lay there. She punched for the section marked CITY OF-FICES, and the directory flipped open before her. The list she wanted was pitifully small—the small column of call numbers for the Fire Department Chief, Lighting Department Chief, Heating and Power Unit Chief, and a handful of others. But Tica did not hesitate. She dialed their numbers on the Communicator and sent out her calls as quickly as possible.

Two hours later, as the first brightness of dawn streaked Lamia's sky, they were all gathered in the office, a group of worried uncertain men. She faced them with the assurance taught her by political campaigning. She had profited by the short period of time before they gathered in obedience to her summons, to change her clothes and take some benzedrine. Crisply erect, and clear-eyed, she faced them.

"I'll come straight to the point," she said. "I am Tica Smith, Junior Planetary Representative from Arco to Central Headquarters, Earth, and here are my credentials." From the desk beside her she picked up a couple of papers and handed them to the nearest man, who glanced at them, gave a short exclamation of surprise and passed them on to his neighbor. They went around the room.

Tica continued: "I came here incognito to observe the workings of the Assigned Defense Commanders System for a Committee investigating this System—a committee which I happen to head. You may have read about it, or heard some of my speeches." She paused and there were a few murmurs of assent from around the room.

"However," she went on, "the situation here has forced me to come out into the open." She paused for them to assimilate the implications of this statement, but they looked back at her, politely uncomprehending. She stiffened her resolution.

"I have been forced to take over the reins of authority here," she said. "Because the ones who should have done the job of organizing your defense have betrayed you. Your governor, Defense Commander McGarrity and the bushrunners have left you to save yourselves in whatever way you can. They've left you—run off into the bush."

Still there was no reaction from them—only the polite, dumb silence. Anger flamed up within her.

"Don't you realize what I'm saying?" she cried. "You've been abandoned. Doesn't any one of you have anything to say?" She stabbed out with her forefinger at random, pointing out the heavy, aging man who was the city Heating and Power Unit Chief. "Don't *you* have anything to say?" The man looked embarrassed.

"Well, miss," he cleared his throat, "you've got to admit it does sound kind of thin."

"Thin?" she echoed, bewildered. He cleared his throat.

"It was just a few hours ago," he said, "that the Commander promised he'd open up the rifle dome before noon."

"But he was lying!" she protested.

Her words echoed away into the silence of the room. Looking around she saw the polite disbelief written on each face.

"Are you all insane?" she said. "It was just those same few hours ago that you and the rest of the city were going against McGarrity's orders in trying to surrender to the alien."

"Oh, sure," said the Fire Department Chief. "But the governor said to surrender."

"The governor!" echoed Tica. "Stern? The man who bought his votes to get into office? Don't tell me you had any faith in him!"

"I guess not," said the Fire Chief, stubbornly, "but somebody's gotta take charge. Anyway, it's none of my business." And, rising, he turned toward the door.

In a flash she saw it, the key to these incomprehensible colonists of the Outer Planets. They were a little people, bewildered and scared. They expected to be led. They wanted to be led. For no one of them had the courage and belief in his own ability to take control of the rest. Seeing it, a sudden weight lifted off her. Now the situation had become clear and simple again, and she knew what to do.

"Stop," she said crisply; and the Fire Chief halted. "I am in charge here now. All of you are under my orders. I intend to notify the nearest Military Headquarters of the defection of the Defense Commander and demand protection for Lamia. I will take the responsibility for the unsealing of the ultra-wave station; and the rest of you will supply me with the men to operate it."

Swiftly she issued her directions. . . .

The morning sun was high in the sky before they had torched through the outer doors of the ultra-wave station. The doors had been of heavy metal and the commercial cutters were weak compared to the ravening fury of the weapon McGarrity had used to seal them together. Stony-faced, Tica had watched her little band of men work desperately, casting sidelong glances at the rest of the city populace, which, under the pressure of a sheep-like herd instinct and a pressing fear, were drifting off toward the rifle dome to await the fulfillment of Hector's promise. More than once, Tica had been tempted to turn to the local broadcast station in a nearby building and announce to all the people what she had cautioned the utility officers to keep to themselves; but she hesitated to withdraw the straw of hope from the despairing populace. However, after she had talked to the nearest Military Headquarters, she would have another to offer in its place.

The tall doors swung inward.

Tica's little group went across the threshold with a brush. They clustered around the levitator doors, eagerness thinly veiled with restraint that Tica's presence imposed as she pushed through them and entered the levitator first, herself. They crowded in behind her.

As she rose on the pressure beams, her heart lightened for the first time since her landing, for—and she faced the fact squarely—she was like the men behind her; she had no particular wish to be responsible for the people of Lamia. Now she was scant seconds away from shifting that responsibility to the shoulders of the nearest military unit. The door of the broadcast room sank level with her and she swung it open. She had time for one lingering touch of regret that Hector had run out the way he had; for, in spite of her opinions, he had reached through to her and touched her, and she had almost begun to admire him.

Then the doors swung open and the regret was lost in horror. For Hector had sealed the station well. He had turned his handgun loose on the delicate wiring of its controls; and the place was a shambles.

Like beasts to high ground, when the spring flood freshens and spreads, the people of the city, the colonists, had been drifting all morning to the high mound of the rifle dome, towering above the brush. They had ringed it with a packed and desperate crowd, children and men and women alike. And so they waited, clinging to the hope that was beyond all reason, for some had been close to the dome and had felt the smuglet, and knew it was still alive.

It was to and through this crowd that Tica came, backed by the men who had helped to open the ultra-wave station for her. She pushed between their packed bodies to the open space that surrounded the dome and held up her hand to get their attention. It seemed to her now that there was only one thing left to be done and that was to tell them how they had been betrayed. They must be informed that Hector had never intended them to use the ultra-wave—that it was destroyed. They could do nothing now but scatter into the bush, each one taking what chance might bring him.

The crowd watched her. She mounted a small collapsible stand that the men with her had brought and took a portable annunciator in her hand.

"Listen to me," she said.

They looked at her, waiting.

"I am Tica Smith," she said, "Junior Representative from Arco. These men with me have looked at my credentials. They know I am the person I say I am. They will vouch for the fact that what I say is true. You have been betrayed by Commander McGarrity—"

"No!" It was a shrill cry of protest, almost a shriek from the edge of the crowd, and a short, stout man began to force his way through it toward the platform. For a moment he was lost in the eddy and swirl of the taller heads around him and then he burst out on the inside of the packed ring of staring people and ran toward Tica.

"Governor Stern!" she gasped.

He jerked the annunciator from her hand.

"Don't listen to her!" he shouted into it. "She doesn't know what's going on. She—" The men by Tica rolled over him in a wave, smothering him, tearing the annunciator from his hand.

"Let him talk!" said Tica, icily.

Wondering, the men who had been with her at the

breaking in of the ultra-wave plant doors, released him. He staggered to his feet, snatching back the annunciator.

"Last night," he panted, "before he sealed the ultra-wave station, Commander McGarrity called the Military Headquarters of this space sector. The aliens are coming. Detector tracers showed them heading in this direction. And the Fleet is behind them, five hours behind them. And the alien'll be here by noon. We've got to hold them off until the Fleet comes—"

There was a low moan from the crowd.

"The station will be opened," Stern went on. "Commander McGarrity has promised it!"

"Commander McGarrity has promised it!" echoed Tica scornfully, snatching the annunciator from his hand. "Let me tell you people about Commander McGarrity and his promises. Last night he promised that if the station was not open by noon, he would let you try to surrender to the Spindle Ships. But he made sure that you would not be able to do so. I and these men with me have just cut our way into the station. Would you like to know what we found there? The ultra-wave equipment was smashed beyond repair!"

Sound swelled up once more from the crowd. And this time there was a note of hysterical fear in it, and the packed bodies swayed menacingly toward Stern. Tica waved them back.

"What do you say to that?" she demanded, handing the annunciator back to him.

"He says that the dome will be opened as promised!" interrupted the thunderous voice of another annunciator from beyond the far edge of the crowd.

VI

Quickly they turned. Emerging from the bush at the edge of the cleared area was the tall figure of Hector, his clothing torn and tattered, carrying the tightly roped and squirming figure of an animal in his arms. Following him was J. J., and a swarm of the bushrunners. J. J.'s voice came clear to Tica, without the annunciator, raised in a shrill yelp of delight.

"Out of our way, you sheep, you fat sheep, or we'll carve a way through you!"

The crowd split wide and through the gap came Hector and the bushrunners. The men around Tica melted away from her as Hector came up; but he did no more than glance at her.

"Put that thing away," he said curtly, nodding at the annunciator she held in her hand. Numbly, like someone waking from a dream she set it down. He turned away, setting the bound animal in his arms on the ground. Her eyes went past him to the now unfriendly, accusing eyes of the crowd. Sick inside, she turned away.

"Don't you worry none, miss." It was barely a whisper in her ear. She turned to see the boy Bonny facing her and smiling sympathetically. A surge of gratitude swept through her and she reached impulsively for his hand, but he drew away shyly.

Hector was now squatting by the squirming beast he had carried in, and cutting some of the cords that bound it. As they fell away, the shape of it was disclosed more clearly. It had a long, weasel-like snout and body of about a hundred pounds in weight. It had six short legs, and a bushy, sinuous tail with a barb in the end which lashed angrily right and left as they freed it. Its eyes were small and yellow and malevolent, not any bit afraid, but brimful of hate and viciousness. It looked at Hector with hungry longing.

When the animal remained held only by the cords that shackled its feet and jaws, Hector rose again to his feet, lifting the annunciator to his lips.

He spoke to the crowd.

"This is what I promised you," he said. "We tried

every means we could think of to drive the smuglet out of the rifle-dome. When everything failed, this was left." He gestured to the animal at his feet. "Every species has its own natural enemy; and this, we believe, is the smuglet's." His lips smiled, a trifle grimly. "Nobody seems to know its proper name, but J. J., tells me that among his men it's known as the bush-killer."

The bush-killer stared up at him with its yellow, hate-filled eyes.

"Now we'll put it into the ventilator," he concluded, and set the annunciator down.

It took three men to pick up the squirming fury now that most of its bindings had been removed. They carried it to the edge of the smuglet's influence and set it down.

"Sticks!" called J. J. The bushrunners clustered around with long poles, sharp-pointed on the end, with which they hemmed in the bush-killer, back against the dome. "Bonny!"

The boy slipped away from Tica, to and through the pole-men and stood poised on the edge, knife in hand.

"Now!" said J. J.

With one fluid motion, Bonny leaped to the side of the bound animal. His knife flashed and in the same split second he was back behind the barrier of the encircling men. A hair's breadth behind him, the body of the now cut free bushkiller landed fair on the sharp points, then flung itself screaming away again.

For a second it crouched there, radiating hate. Then, as if it had suddenly forgotten the people around it, it stood up on its last two legs and sniffed the air daintily. Its sharp muzzle turned slowly clockwise and halted on a line with the torn ventilator opening.

Inside the dome the smuglet cried out for the first time—a lonely frightened sound.

Disinterestedly, the bush-killer dropped back to the

ground. Suddenly three of the pole-men went backward under the impact of its leaping body. But the
pole-points bore it back. Yowling with anger it paced
the narrow area.

"Close in," said J. J.

The half-circle narrowed. On its two ends, the men
could not get within two meters of the building, but
their long sharp poles bridged the gap and slowly the
bush-killer was driven back. For a moment it stood
at bay. Then, with scarcely an appearance of effort, it
turned and leaped, vanishing into the black and ragged hole in the ventilator screen.

There was a moment of silence. Hector shoved
through the line of pole-men opposite the door and
stood waiting, pressing against the outer tingle of the
smuglet's power. Then suddenly a high and dreadful
screaming burst from the inside of the building and
the tingling vanished.

Hector leaped to the door, unlocked it and flung it
wide.

The smuglet crawled from the opening, like some
great gray mouse, it dragged itself on crippled fore-
paws, its paralyzed hindquarters furrowing the dust
behind it. Ripped, torn, and streaked with blackish
blood, it pulled itself from them away from the predator that followed, tearing at it, leaping high in feline
play upon it. It shrank toward Hector and the humans, hoping, perhaps, for the blessing of a quick
death.

"*Ub. ubbu, ubu, bu. bu*—" it choked, rising again to
a shriek as the worrying shape that followed flung
itself after the smuglet. The scream was cut merci-
fully short by the snap of Hector's handgun.

Then the bushkiller was away. Moving like a tawny
streak of light, it darted down the path that was
opened before it by the crowd. It had won clear and
was racing for the edge of the bush when Hector,
under the compulsion of a pity he had not believed

himself capable of feeling, lifted his gun and sent a thin yellow bolt racing after it.

The bushkiller crumpled in mid-leap, with half of its body burned away. Even so, it turned and came thrashing back before a second shot finished it. Silence again settled in the clearing and a great sigh went up from the watching people.

Hector, his face set in a still mask, reholstered his gun; and lifted the annunciator to his lips.

"All able-bodied men form a line," he said, "and we'll hand out weapons as long as they last."

It was two hours later. Inside the dome, the rifle crew were at their posts, tensely waiting. In front of the master control scanner and firing trips, Hector stood, Tica at his side.

She had not dared speak to him since he first came striding out of the bush. Now she put out a hand timidly to touch his arm.

"What?" he said, turning to look down at her.

"Do you—" she hesitated. "I'm sorry."

"Sorry?"

"For what I did," she answered. "Thinking you'd run off. Calling those men together. Breaking into the ultra-wave station." He shrugged, somewhat embarrassed.

"I don't blame you," he said. "You couldn't know what I didn't tell you. I suppose you had a right to expect the worst."

"But why?" she demanded. "Why didn't you tell me? Didn't you trust me?" He sighed; for the truth in this matter was something that it was very hard for him to admit.

"I thought you'd be safer if you didn't know," he said in a low voice. "I thought that you'd sleep through until this morning and by that time—it doesn't make sense, does it?"

She wondered at him.

"No," she said, truthfully. "It doesn't seem like you. Why should my safety concern you?"

He made a gesture of impatience with his big hands.

"You don't belong here," he said half angrily. "You don't know what you let yourself in for. I do." He checked himself, suddenly. "That's not quite straight. The truth is—hunting up the bushkiller in the hope that it could do what we couldn't, was a gamble. A gamble with the odds on our side, but still a gamble. Several things could have gone wrong, such as not being able to find a bushkiller in time, or the beast's killing itself on the poles, instead of letting itself be forced into the ventilator. It was the sort of thing that would have given your committee a Roman holiday if it hadn't succeeded. I couldn't risk that."

"You were against me," she murmured.

"What?" he said.

"Nothing." She lifted her face to him, shaking her hair back over her shoulders. "What would you have done if the bushkiller idea hadn't worked?" He smiled wryly.

"Shoved a homemade time bomb in through the ventilator," he said. "And hoped there'd be enough handguns left in working order to fight it out on the ground." She shivered. Before she could say anything further, one of the gun crew spoke up, looking over from the scanner in front of him.

"Enemy at two-thirty-four; culmination arc, one sixteen. Six ships."

Hector's big hands moved swiftly and easily over the controls in front of him and the outlines of six pencil-shaped objects swam into the master screen before him.

"Check," he said. He spoke over his shoulder to Tica. "Stay inside the dome. And don't get in the way."

"All right." Her answer was barely pitched above a whisper, but Hector was not listening, wholly absorbed now by the controls in front of him.

"Range two by two by eight," he said.

"Range two by two by eight—check," the answer came from across the room.

"Check all stations."

"Check"—"Check"—"Check"—"Check"—the word ran around the interior of the dome as the crew spoke up from their several posts.

Tica turned away from him and moved over to the screen that showed the area outside the station. The clearing was deserted and the brush hid the armed men. The sky above looked peaceful, empty.

"Correction two by two by seven." Hector's voice went on behind her, the crew voices answering.

"Correction, two by two, by seven—check."

"On target."

"Fire."

There was no sound, no vibration in the big dome, no indication of the destroying beam that for a moment reached out thousands of miles into space. The quiet voices went on around her with the calm emotionlessness of bookkeepers checking accounts.

"Hit one."

"Target—check."

"Dispersal tactics, two thirty-three, by north eight-seven. Check two."

"Two-check."

"Fire."

"Correction—"

The voices went on, steadily, monotonously. The hours slipped by. In the dome, Tica, and in the bush, the colonists, waited.

The bright sun of Lamia passed its zenith and sank westward. At the screen, listening to the voices behind her, Tica was vaguely aware that the titanic, silent duel between the station and the alien had accounted for two ships. Abruptly there was a cessation of the action in the dome. She turned, surprised, to Hector.

"What happened?" she said. "Did you get them all?"

He looked at her wearily. She remembered suddenly that this man had not slept or eaten since they had landed on the planet some twenty-four hours before.

"They've ducked behind the planet to hide," he said. Hope rose in her.

"Maybe they're going away."

He shook his head.

"No," he said. "They'll be back. Two will cover from the air and two will land crews to see if they can't take the station by hand-to-hand attack." He lifted his voice to the rifle crew. "Take it easy, but watch both hemispheres."

He turned stiffly from the master screen and snapped on a pickup that connected with the men in the bush.

"Get me J. J." he said.

"Right here, Commander." The bearded slim figure took form on the pickup's screen.

"Get your men on their toes," ordered Hector. "There'll be a landing within the next thirty minutes. Remember, you fight these aliens by moving. Each man by himself. Shoot and run. A spindle-shipper is stronger than a human at close grips; but they don't understand knives, so your bushrunners may have a chance that way. If they do come close enough for knife-work, strike for the bottom of the trunk. The breathing sac is down there and once you puncture that, it paralyzes them."

"Right," answered J. J. laconically. "We'll be ready. Anything else?"

"That's all," said Hector, and broke the connection.

VII

With startling abruptness, the enemy was upon them.

The office-silence of the rifle dome was disrupted by the horrifying bedlam of war, as two ships, having crept up behind the low overcast, went roaring through the air above the station, belching names. The riven air screamed before them and the dome rocked under the impact of their weapons, rocked on the pounded soil like a child's boat rocks on a rippled pool. Tica felt herself flung back into the chair that faced the outside screen. She clung there, frightened and desperate, while before her eyes giant hands dealt out carnage. The ground around the station was one raging red inferno. Behind her the shouted commands of Hector rang against the bedlam as he traded blow for blow with the covering ships and fenced off the horizon-hopping pair that would have landed.

"Twenty-three—six—oh! Release! Fire! Release! Fire!" The master control trips jumped in his hands as he switched suddenly from the computed aiming of the crew at the high ships to the point-blank range of the hedge-hopping pair. He tasted blood from his upper lip, split when the first concussion had hurled him against his control panel. A savage joy filled him as he fired.

The high ships were dropping as they blasted. Outside the dome glowed, and the tough stubborn metal softened and ran in reluctant drops as its outer shell melted before the direct touch of the alien beams. Inside the refrigerating unit shrieked at full capacity as its heat pump channeled the outside temperatures deep into the earth where the anchoring rock fused and bubbled under the abnormal temperatures forced upon them. Recklessly, Hector ignored the overhead attack, fighting back the would-be landing party and luring the top attackers down until suddenly he caught them in line, one behind the other. Then suddenly abandoning all his ground defense, he threw full power on the lead ship.

It glowed, shone, and suddenly, like a black mouth

opening, a dark hole melted in its armor. Unchecked, the sudden beam raved through it; and like a crippled crazy thing, it flung itself floundering backward and its own weapons broke a path for the rifle beam through the defenses of its sister ship. For a second they hung like two flaring comets in Hector's screen, then swung together. The heavens vanished in a sudden, silent wash of white and brilliant light.

These two space craft were gone. But the other two had landed.

Hector turned and flung himself at the pickup. But it was dead. He turned again, thrusting Tica roughly from the outside screen and looked through it.

The bush no longer hid the city from the dome. Now one large cinderous area surrounded the rifle, wide enough to leave the dome in plain sight. In the tangled area beyond, the two remaining ships were hidden and even now the barrel-bodied, stumpy-armed alien would be pouring out of them for their march to take the dome and thus disarm the city.

Hector jiggled once more with the pickup, then, discarding it, threw the switches that broke free and opened the half-melted dome door. It swung back, and, motioning the rifle crew to stay where they were, he hurdled the blistering sill and ran for the bush, his side-arm held loosely in one big hand.

Behind him a wave of heat from the half-cooked metal of the outer shell washed back into the dome and the rifle crew hurriedly closed the door and took their posts for the last defense of the dome that might come if Hector and J. J., with the riflemen, could not stop the alien fighters. And in front of the outside screen, Tica waited, and watched.

Hector ran easily, at a loping dog-trot. The only haste was his urge to reach J. J., as soon as possible. For speed was no defense. If any of the alien had already managed to reach the fringe of bush on the edge of the burnt area, Hector was a sitting duck. He could only hope that the humans had held them.

But no guns winked, and no alien beams whispered their pale yellow death at him. He reached the bush in safety.

Now his tactics changed. He went warily forward, his handgun at the ready, slipping from one piece of cover to the other, for to come suddenly on his own men might be easily as bad as coming so upon the alien.

He moved like a shadow through the bush, in the general direction of where he knew J. J.'s men should be. And as he went a murmur rose on the soft air, a murmur that as he approached, grew in volume until the separate sounds that made it up could be faintly distinguished. From a long distance they came and he knew them well. The sounds of the fighting mad, the wounded and the dying.

He came to where J. J.'s command post should have been. But the trampled clearing was empty, except for one dead man, his head half burnt away. The corpse lay beside the pickup that should have answered Hector's call from the dome. Battle had been joined not far from here, it seemed, and then swung westward. Hector leaned down, took the dead man's knife and pushed on toward the sound.

The first encounter came without warning, a slight breath of air, the hint of a color half-seen for a flash with the corner of an eye, and the swish and fall of one of the purple trees beam-cut through at his side.

He dropped; and rolled. A second later the pale yellow beam sliced the earth where he had lain. Grimly, his gun before him, he wriggled a circuitous route toward its source.

When he had reached a point of safety, he raised his head cautiously behind the screen of a bush's many narrow leaves and looked. For a moment he saw nothing. Then there was a slight stir among the foliage twenty yards away and a spindle-shipper stepped into view. He stopped, and stood there, a heavy gun cradled in his short round arm, his stocky body upright and stolid-looking except for the erectile flaps of his sense-organs that waved gently to all quarters of the compass. Hector lifted his gun, sighted and squeezed. The alien went down, thrashing, half burnt in two, but still alive with the astounding vitality of his race.

Hector turned and ran. The sound of the dying alien would draw others of his own race to him. Since the spindle-shippers were between him and the humans, this might create a gap in their line through which he could reach J. J. and his men.

He ran, shouting his name to warn the humans to hold their fire. For a long moment he had no answer; and he had time to think that possibly he had made a mistake and that the humans were not where he thought they might be. Then a shrill whoop answered him and he stumbled over a small bushy hillock to sprawl panting among a roughly-dressed group of bushrunners.

He rolled over on his back and struggled for breath. A dry chuckle made him turn his head and discover J. J. The bearded bushrunner was squatting not ten feet from him, one eye cocked in the direction that Hector had come, a gun in his hands.

"You sure sounded like your pants were on fire, Commander," he said. "I—" He interrupted himself suddenly, whipped the gun to his shoulder and fired. "Got him," he continued calmly. "I figured there'd be at least one following you up."

He rose and strolled over to stand looking down at Hector, who, somewhat recovered, pushed himself up to a sitting position.

"I couldn't get you on the pickup," he said. "The man on your end's killed. What's the situation here?" J. J. frowned.

"So Cary's dead," he said. "He always was kind of careless. Well, I'll tell you, Commander. We aren't holding them. Not by a damn sight. You want to know why?"

"Of course," answered Hector. J. J. grinned without humor.

"Those city-sheep have been plain ungrateful," he said. "They just didn't appreciate those shiny new guns you handed out at all. Just about all of them have sneaked off and cut for the hills."

"Didn't you stop them?" demanded Hector sharply.

"The boys have been kind of busy with these here walking barrels," he said, dryly, "if you've noticed."

In silence Hector accepted the rebuke. The bush-runners were his only ground force, and he needed them.

"How do things stand now?" he asked. J. J., hunkered down beside him and, picking up a stick, began to draw in the soft loose earth with it.

"The ships are here and here," he said, diagramming. "When they first landed, we tried to surround them, but they broke through right off and started to spread toward the rifle dome. I figured they might head straight for the city, but—"

"They won't," interrupted Hector. "It won't be safe for them to take off as long as the rifle is operating. They'll have to destroy it first before they try any looting."

J. J. nodded.

"Anyway," he went on, "they pushed us back. Now this circle here is the open space around the rifle. This is their line at right angles to it, and this is ours. They keep trying to swing us in against it and we keep fading away in front of them, so the whole fight is sort of spiraling in on it. In half—maybe three quarters of an hour—we're going to be up on the edge, both them and us. What happens then, I don't know."

"I do," said Hector. "I've fought them before. They'll try to rush the dome under covering fire, and hold position there long enough to mine it. They don't worry about loss of life. Once at the dome, they'll try to hold half the edge of the clearing. Then we won't be able to fire into them from the opposite side. It'll end up as a hand-to-hand around the dome. Have you got some good men for that?"

"Commander," drawled the bushrunner, "they're all good men for that."

"All right," said Hector. "Let's get going."

They fell back, firing as they went.

In the rifle dome, Tica waited.

It was deathly still in there. The rifle crew had dogged down the sealing door over the ventilator and they were running on compressed air from the storage tanks. The anchor beams that held them solid to the great field of igneous rock two miles beneath the surface of the earth, were locked in place and the main door was fused tight. There was nothing left but the waiting.

Seated in front of the outside scanner, Tica watched. It was as if she sat, disembodied, on the high muzzle of the rifle itself and looked out over the wasted area and the brush beyond. Of the fight proper, nothing was visible to her. Only occasionally she caught the momentary shimmer of beams like cloud-trapped rays of sudden sunshine in a room; and the audio brought the hoarse murmur of the battle sounds distantly to her ear.

But that was enough. Little by little, by these signs and tokens, she could see the battle drawing steadily closer to the blasted clearing and the dome. She watched in helpless fascination as this approached until, at last, both sides were there, the aliens in one rough half-circle hidden in the brush to the north. The humans in an identical half-circle to the south.

Then the yellow beams began to play across the four-mile distance of open ground. The dome, caught in the crossfire, glowed momentarily red where a beam would hit, then faded quickly back to the massy gray of its normal color. For several long minutes the gun battle went on. Then suddenly, from the alien side of the clearing, a horde of the stumpy creatures burst, charging on the dome.

They were not fast—not nearly so fast as men might be—but their advance had a pounding inexorability about it. They moved within a screen of their own living flesh, an outer ring tight-packed about those in the center to catch the impact of the beams from the human side of the natural arena. An inner group fired over the lumpy shoulders of the others, and moved swiftly to take the place of those in the outer ring that fell.

They left their dead behind them to mark their path, gray writhing bodies or still corpses, against the cindered black, like the flaky shedding of some monster snake. But they came on.

Now the firing redoubled on the human side. Soon from the tattered bush there sprung a loose wave of humans—smaller, more scattered, but swifter than the alien. Scattered, not bunched, they raced across the blasted ground toward the dome and the gray approaching horde, their shrill yells echoing on the afternoon air.

Dodging, shifting, leaping, like leaves in an autumn wind, they ran. And like leaves they fell to the alien guns beaming from the far side of the clearing. But speed was with them and the open pattern of their charging. They had started later than the alien group, but they were gaining. They had gained. By the time they were three quarters of the way to the dome, the lost ground had been made up.

Now they were close. Now the dome shielded nearly all of them from opposing fire. Now they had reached it, just as the alien came up from the other side and the area around the silent muzzle of the space rifle became a straining, struggling mass of white and gray bodies.

So the end came. Neither side could now fire into the stabbing, close locked bodies around the dome. The time for guns was over. The time for hand to hand combat was here. From both sides, the embattled groups streamed forth onto the field and dust rose as they closed together. Beneath it, man to alien, alien to man, in single combat they locked and swayed.

Above, like an invisible spirit, Tica twisted the controls of the scanner, searching through the dust and haze for the tall figure of Hector. As if she had been a silent ghost drifting through the carnage, the combat unreeled before her, from the close-packed dogfight around the dome to the scattered battle farther out. Faces, bodies, half-glimpsed, came and went—a bushrunner with his left arm torn away, sinking the knife held in his right hand to its handle in the enemy who had dismembered him. A boy of Bonny's age, his mouth stretched open in a scream as the thick arms of an alien bent him back until his spine cracked and he dangled like a broken doll. Then at last she found Hector.

He was one of a group with J. J., and some others who were grimly hacking their way toward the dome. He towered, berserk, taller than the aliens, taller than the humans that surrounded him. The long bushrunner's knife in his hand flashed as he sliced his way through the pack of gray bodies to the dome. Like furious, leaping rats they flung themselves upon him. He shook them off, his knifeblade slick with the sheen of the oily oozings from the alien gashed bodies. Savagely he fought his way to the dome, to the dome's very door. And then the press of combat cut him off from the men behind him and he went down beneath a wave of aliens, that rolled over him and hid him at last from view.

He did not rise again.

VIII

Chilled and weak with a strange, numb sickness, Tica turned from the screen and walked unsteadily across to a dark corner of the dome. The upcurving metal wall stopped her and she put her hands against it, leaning her hot forehead against the smooth metal. She did not cry. She did not faint. She merely stood there, at last beyond all feeling. And the dome, the crew, the battle passed away from her like a forgotten dream, so that she walked alone in the hell that she had made herself and lay in the grave that she herself had dug. For a long time she suffered silently, until she was aware of a voice speaking from a great distance and a hand on her shoulder. Whose she did not know.

Slowly, she came back to the world of the living. The voice was the voice of one of the gun crew. It was his hand on her shoulder, gently insistent.

"Miss," he was saying, "Miss, it's all over."

Dumbly, she nodded and turned from the wall. The heavy door was once more broken open and stood wide. Fresh dusty air eddied in through the wide opening and the clearing beyond was silent. She walked toward it.

She stepped over the sill and onto the ground. From bush line to ragged, blackened line of bush, the bodies lay, in groups, in pairs and singly. For a long moment she looked, and then, as if driven by a terrible compulsion, she turned toward the mound of bodies where she had seen Hector fall. She walked toward them. Reaching down, she felt for the first time the touch of alien flesh as her small hands closed about a thick gray arm, and she tugged.

Slowly the body came loose and tumbled from the pile. Straining, she seized the next and was aware of hands helping her. The crewman had followed her out and was pulling with her.

Together they lifted the bodies off until there were no more to lift. They stood, looking down at Hector.

"I'm sorry, Miss," said the crewman, awkwardly.

She knelt, and with the corner of her tunic, wiped the dust gently from the silent face.

And the lips moved. A whisper of breath husked from the dry throat.

"He's alive!" cried the crewman.

"Alive?" she echoed stupidly. The words had no meaning for her. "Alive?"

"He's alive!" repeated the crewman. He straightened suddenly, turning swiftly to the two great silver ships with their Frontier Guard insignia blazing in the sun halfway on the open space now between dome and city. I'll go get help."

He ran off, Tica continued to kneel by Hector, without understanding.

The crewman came back with four men in black Guard uniforms and a power litter. She watched them load Hector carefully on it and saw it shoot swiftly into the air on its way to the spaceship. But still she felt nothing. The spaceships, the litter, nothing was real. Reality had stopped for her with the sight of Hector going down under the smother of gray bodies.

She turned away.

"Better stop her," the voice of one of the uniformed men came dimly to her ears. "She's in a bad state of shock."

But no one had time. There were too many wounded to be attended.

She wandered among the dead, not understanding. Something heavy and cold within her drove her on. Twilight was darkening the field when she came at last to J. J., squatted beside a figure on the ground.

The bearded bushrunner looked up at her for the first time with no mockery in his eyes.

"You and me both," he said simply; and pointed down. "Look."

                              *   *   *

The still figure was Bonny. Tica knelt on the other side of him. The boy was breathing shallowly, but his eyes were closed and there was a trickle of blood from one corner of his mouth. Tica reached down automatically to wipe it away.

"Leave be," said J. J., holding her hand back. "It's no use. He's been crushed." She took her hand back and he looked at her with sad bitterness.

"You didn't know, did you?" he said. "He's my kid." His eyes lifted and strayed around the field.

"Him—and these others," he said. "All were good boys I knew. All gone. And down there's the city, not even touched. And back there in the hills are those shopkeeping cowards—all safe and whole."

"Distantly across the field came a shout.

"J. J.! Come here. We need you!"

The bushrunner rose to his feet, looking down.

"I guess I got to go," he said. "Stick with him, will you? It won't be for long."

But he lingered still for a moment, looking down at the dying boy, and the woman kneeling beside him.

"Tell me," he said, with sudden abrupt bitterness. "What good are cities?"

"J. J.!" cried the voice again, imperatively. He turned and went.

Tica stayed.

The boy's breathing continued shallowly. Numbly, Tica knelt, watching. Finally there was a slight choke in his throat. A new little trickle of blood flowed out, and Bonny opened his eyes. His eyes focused with effort on the face above him.

"Miss?" he whispered wonderingly. "Miss?"

"Sh-h," she answered automatically. "Don't talk." He made a feeble effort to raise his head, but could not.

"They kind of got me, Miss," he said.

"No," she said. "No." But the lie stuck in her throat. He shook his head feebly, a fraction of an inch.

"Yes," he said, huskily. "I can tell." There was a second's pause during which he fought for breath.

"Listen," he said, urgently. "I got a couple of things I'd like to tell you."

"You mustn't talk."

"Listen!" he said, and his voice was stronger now. "That's something you got to get over—this telling people what to do. I got to talk. And I'm short of time. I listened, and I heard about you from what the Commander and J. J. said. So I know. And I got something to pass on to you. My grandma used to say folks got to trust their feelings. Makes life a sight easier on them—and everybody else."

He stopped. His words echoed bleakly in her mind. Feel? How could she feel? The feeling part of her had died with the dead around her. She was cold and empty inside. She could not even feel glad that Hector was alive. She had not been able to summon up a tear when she had thought him dead. I have seen things to tell humanity about when I go back, she thought, things they should know. But I cannot speak because I have thought too long. I cannot feel.

"Miss?" the husky whisper brought her back to the boy in front of her.

"Yes?" she said.

"There was something else—"

"Go on," she said, dully. He hesitated, avoiding her eye.

"I—" his whisper was desperate, urgent, weakening. "Can I whisper it in your ear?"

For a second the cold emptiness inside her was touched.

"Of course," she said, and leaned her head down to his lips. Through the curtain of her hair the faint warmth of his breath touched her ear.

"I love you," he whispered.

Like the sweet warmth of the spring rain on the frozen ground, the words beat down on the icy cold within her, the dam crumbled and the floodtide of her emotions swept forth to bring her back once more to the world of the living. Her heart broke in a sudden wash of tears and she kissed him, hugging the bright tangled head close to her breast.

Beneath her, the boy choked suddenly and stiffened. A final rush of blood rushed from his mouth to stain her tunic, but she paid it no attention. For, when she looked down at his face, she saw that he was smiling. Still, even still in death, he was smiling.

In anguish, but without restraint, like someone who had bought back life at a great price, but counts the cost worth while, Tica went upon the cindered plain.

GORDON R. DICKSON

Winner of every award science fiction and fantasy to offer, Gordon Dickson is one of the major authors of this century. He creates heroes and enemies, not just characters in books; his stories celebrate bravery and virtue and the best in all of us. Collect some of the very best of Gordon Dickson's writing by ordering the books below.

POUL ANDERSON

Poul Anderson is one of the most honored authors of our time. He has won seven Hugo Awards, three Nebula Awards, and the Gandalf Award for Achievement in Fantasy, among others. His most popular series include the Polesotechnic League/Terran Empire tales and the Time Patrol series. Here are fine books by Poul Anderson available through Baen Books:

THE GAME OF EMPIRE

A *new* novel in Anderson's Polesotechnic League/Terran Empire series! Diana Crowfeather, daughter of Dominic Flandry, proves well capable of following in his adventurous footsteps.

FIRE TIME

Once every thousand years the Deathstar orbits close enough to burn the surface of the planet Ishtar. This is known as the Fire Time, and it is then that the barbarians flee the scorched lands, bringing havoc to the civilized South.

AFTER DOOMSDAY

Earth has been destroyed, and the handful of surviving humans must discover which of three alien races is guilty before it's too late.

THE BROKEN SWORD

It is a time when Christos is new to the land, and the Elder Gods and the Elven Folk still hold sway. In 11th-century Scandinavia Christianity is beginning to replace the old religion, but the Old Gods still have power, and men are still oppressed by the folk of the Faerie. "Pure gold!"—Anthony Boucher.

THE DEVIL'S GAME

Seven people gather on a remote island, each competing for a share in a tax-free fortune. The "contest" is ostensibly sponsored by an eccentric billionaire—but the rich man is in league with an alien masquerading as a demon . . . or is it the other way around?

THE ENEMY STARS
Includes for the first time the sequel to "The Enemy Stars": "The Ways of Love." Fast-paced adventure science fiction from a master.

SEVEN CONQUESTS
Seven brilliant tales examine the many ways human beings—most dangerous and violent of all species—react under the stress of conflict and high technology.

STRANGERS FROM EARTH
Classic Anderson: A stranded alien spends his life masquerading as a human, hoping to contact his own world. He succeeds, but the result is a bigger problem than before . . . What if our reality is a fiction? Nothing more than a book written by a very powerful Author? Two philosophers stumble on the truth and try to puzzle out the Ending . . .

You can order all of Poul Anderson's books listed above with this order form. Check your choices below and send the combined cover price/s to: Baen Books, Dept. BA, 260 Fifth Avenue, New York, New York 10001.*

THE GAME OF EMPIRE • 55959-1 • 288 pp. • $3.50 _____
FIRE TIME • 55900-1 • 288 pp. • $2.95 _____
AFTER DOOMSDAY • 65591-4 • 224 pp. • $2.95 _____
THE BROKEN SWORD • 65382-2 • 256 pp. • $2.95 _____
THE DEVIL'S GAME • 55995-8 • 256 pp. • $2.95 _____
THE ENEMY STARS • 65339-3 • 224 pp. • $2.95 _____
SEVEN CONQUESTS • 55914-1 • 288 pp. • $2.95 _____
STRANGERS FROM EARTH • 65627-9 • 224 pp. • $2.95 _____